# THE TWILIGHT
# OF THE GODS
# AND OTHER TALES

First Warbler Classics Edition 2025

An expanded edition of *The Twilight of the Gods* (1888) was first published in 1903 by John Lane and The Bodley Head, London, and by Dodd, Mead and Company, New York

T. E. Lawrence's introduction first published in a 1924 edition of *The Twilight of the Gods* published by John Lane and The Bodley Head, London, and by Dodd, Mead and Company, New York

Biographical Essay © 2025 Warbler Press

ISBN 978-1-965684-60-3 (paperback)
ISBN 978-1-965684-61-0 (e-book)

warblerpress.com

*Publisher's Note*
The first edition of these tales was published in 1888. This volume includes an additional twelve stories, which first appeared in the 1903 edition.

# THE TWILIGHT
# OF THE GODS
# AND OTHER TALES

## RICHARD GARNETT

INTRODUCTION BY T. E. LAWRENCE

warbler classics

To

Horace Howard Furness
and
Georg Brandes.

Dabo duobus testibus meis.

# CONTENTS

## INTRODUCTION
### by T. E. Lawrence

HOW KIND A nurse has the British Museum been, sometimes, to poets! In the Department of Fishes O'Shaughnessy sang of fountains, whole rivers of tears. Barbellion among the beasts found himself his richest subject for dissection; and this Dr. Garnett in the horrific dome (bald within and without like an empty ostrich-egg), which is the Reading Room, was used to chuckle over the *Twilight of the Gods.*

They seem to have been moved by contraries, these central-heated artists. Much poring over Japanese prints makes a Binyon re-create Arthurian legends. In the Assyrian Basement I have heard a keeper whose charge (if hardly his care) was Babylonian burst into modern song. Assur-nasir-Pal reminded him of an only girl. He was an ordinary man, incapable of literature even at his highest; but in him was working the spirit of contrariety, which has made the real artists blossom so strangely in their police-guarded halls. The Director, no doubt, could be moved only to Limericks, while Epic would be the choice of the man with red dress-cuffs and lapels, who takes your umbrella at the door. Incidentally this is the best place in London to lose an acquired or embarrassing umbrella. It costs no more than the pain of carrying off a brass disc; and that's not all loss, for there is one special pattern of slot machine in which these discs perform miracles.

Many other personal details of the Museum are curious; but Mr. Lane *did* promise to pay me twenty guineas for an introduction to the *Twilight;* and so unprecedented an event in my writing career demands and deserves more attention than it appears to be getting. So here is back again for Dr. Garnett....

The Reading Room, his province, is wise, rich, sober, warm, decent (even dingy), industrious; but it lacks humour, it lacks polish, and all that crackling display of surface virtue which comprehends smartness, and is much more. Consequently, because the Museum was hushed, Dr. Garnett would be—on paper—lively. Because the great ceiling coved so solemnly overhead, he would be flippant. Because his readers were so deadly serious, he would be sprightly.

Which is not to say that he too was not serious and bookish and sincere. The great national Museum may be a great necropolis for the public, a charnel-house wherein the mouldering bones of dead civilisations are somewhat indecently displayed. For the staff it is a Temple, and themselves the devotees. For them the world outside the windows is that which is indecent in display. They live with the best materials of the past, studying them, endeavouring by every context of literature and history to understand them more fully, to see them more remarkably in the round. For this select few on earth, Greece and Rome, Babylon and Egypt are not dead. These empires are in their department (or in old So-and-So's next door), things of vital importance, growing daily larger and clearer, their bread-and-butter, their ideal, their study, the business of their working hours and the chosen pastime of their leisure. Inestimable is this privilege of a twenty-four-hour-day preoccupation with the censored fittest of sixty centuries…and I am happy to remember how for some years the B.M. made me estimable in its employment.

Dr. Garnett's department, the Reading Room, is one which forces a sympathetic president to be somewhat universal. Rome and Greece, Chaldea and Egypt: those were real enough to him; but their reality was not exclusive, to him alone of the staff. His dealings throughout the open hours were with living people, inquirers all, whether they were great scholars with minds so deep in the well of learning that never could they be raised to the life of day, or simple souls who had perhaps not heard of Sanchoniathon or Vopiscus. People would sidle up to him at his desk to ask for the best book upon caterpillars, for a Keats manuscript, to know how many protons might be in a cubic foot of Bessemer steel. The Library is the ultimate reference book of the world, and its presiding genius the Index.

Courteously and unerringly Dr. Garnett would advise upon bee-keeping or bimetallism, while inwardly his mind was picturing Caucasus or Pandemonium and little themes of Albert of Aix or Hesychius were running through his head. Never did he abdicate from his chair of scholarship. In this book are his *obiter scripta*, reactions of his spirit against drudgery, and what a bouquet and flavour they have! Book-learned in the best sense, he was a worthy priest of the Museum, that last temple of the classical theogony.

I like to imagine the puzzled debate in the Greek sculpture halls, at night in the quiet moon-lit emptiness after the public had withdrawn, as the carved Gods on their marble pedestals heard his carpet slippers flipflapping softly where the nailed soles of P.C. 7872889 had made harsh day music. Dr. Garnett came through so shyly, carefully, among the ranked Gods, since perhaps he did not quite know if his faith was founded on print, or on Pentelic marble…and the Gods too remained aloof, shy and speechless, for they are as little used to worshippers as men are to Gods. The Die-hard section, Ares, Zeus himself, Hera, were for dismissing him: better, they said, no worshipper at all than one who had exposed their rents and patches to a mocking world. The beautiful Athene, the confused Apollo leaned by reason to this party: though their instincts lay with Esculapius, with Hermes, with Prometheus, the modernists, who stoutly pleaded that seas and centuries were consider-ations to be admitted in argument even by Gods, and that for a reformed Olympus there lay yet a hope in the constituencies. "Here," they said, "is one who has made our question again a living issue. He in Britain, Anatole over there in France, are rousing public interest. Pull yourselves together, provide copy, show yourselves, wear your plaster noses" (Demeter burst into tears), "become News; and from these Apostles will be born an army at whose head we will regain our provinces." Conservatism, of course, carried it. Gods are ever slow to overtake a reform movement. They slipped back again into the Elgin Room, and stood there mutilated but immobile on the dingily-labelled pedestals when the attendants came round with the feather brushes in the morning. Dr. Garnett was born an age too soon or too late.

Yet in these Gods he did virtually believe: his drawing of them is to the life, visualised, with that routine apology of the sensitive *dévot* who hides his beliefs and his beloved from the arrows of vulgar contempt by dressing them in motley, to evoke not anger but laughter from the crowd. Last and most slippery refuge of faith! but how tender must be the God who is small enough for the worshipper to fondle and protect, and play the shield to! Dr. Garnett's intimacy with his Gods betrays sincerity. Not the last, no doubt, but the latest of the Pagans confesses himself. The scholarship in these tales is beautiful: so deep, so unobtrusive, so easy and exact. The high-roads of the classic have been much trodden, so that they are become white, straight, dusty tracks. Scholarship which is sure of itself, and not ambitious to go far or fast, often takes more delight in by-ways. where there are winding paths, quaint resting-places, a luxuriance of overgrown foliage. Dr. Garnett was a very sure scholar, who had done the plain things and the big things and was tired of them. In this book lies his leisure, as much for our delight as his. It wants no learning to enjoy *The Twilight of the Gods;* but the more learning you have, the more odd corners and hidden delights you will find in it.

The Gods are the main element. Poisons, the science of toxins, are perhaps third element. Second place, I think, falls to black magic. Here again, so far as my competence extends, Dr. Garnett is serious. His spells are real, his sorcery accurate, according to the best dark-age models. His curious mind must have found another escape from the reading-desk in the attempts of our ancestors to see through the veil of flesh, downwards.

"It will be a tough business," observed the sorcerer. "It will require fumigations."

"Yes," said the bishop, "and suffumigations."

"Aloes and mastic," advised the sorcerer.

"Aye," assented the bishop, "and red sanders."

"We must call in Primeumaton," said the warlock.

"Clearly," said the bishop, "and Amioram."

"Triangles," said the sorcerer.

"Pentacles," said the bishop.

"In the hour of Methon," said the sorcerer.

"I should have thought Tafrac," suggested the bishop, "but I defer to your better judgment."

"I can have the blood of a goat?" queried the wizard.

"Yes," said the bishop, "and of a monkey also."

"Does your Lordship think that one might venture to go so far as a little unweaned child?"

"If absolutely necessary," said the bishop.

"I am delighted to find such liberality of sentiment on your Lordship's part," said the sorcerer. "Your Lordship is evidently of the profession."

It seems to me that the learned Doctor would have been in some danger, too, if the nineteenth century had been the ninth or the seventeenth.

On the point of scholarship let us give the book a first-class. Ditto in magic, in alchemy, in toxicology; ditto in wit and humour. Yet they say it never sold. As literature my experience (despite Mr. Lane's solitary swallow) is not professional enough to make my opinion of the book worth while. Swinburne loved it: my introduction to it came at second hand from him. Flecker, the inquiring poet, stole his first copy. Mr. Wells, a writer of very different texture, has praised it in print. Wilde's satisfaction is some testimony to the wit. *The Yellow Book* published some of it. Perhaps all these people borrowed or stole copies: apparently their satisfaction and their praise of it were not enough to exhaust the editions which the publisher offered. Now he is trying an illustrated edition. Such good wine can well endure to be bushed largely; and therefore, apart from that possible twenty guineas, I cannot refuse the opportunity to say clearly, and I hope infectiously, how very much I have enjoyed the book for nearly twenty years; and what a passport to the sympathy of many chance-met literary men my knowledge of it has been.

So please, purchasers-of-this-edition, don't lend your copies too freely. For one thing, you probably won't get them back. It's packed with a delicious callous cruelty, of the playful sort which thrills bookish men. There is an ever-springing irony which provokes smiling. Smiling is decorous in the Reading Room (always think of that), where an open laugh would shatter the air like a stone in a quiet pool. The readers sit all round the edge, like the frogs round the pool; and you know how a large stone floods the water into all their mouths and stops the croaking. This book will make you chuckle: nothing vulgar. There is a polish and perfection of incongruity, like goggles on an aged bust: a wit so fine that its point has reflections down a chain of three or four passages to which the original alludes: allusions recondite, and yet so broad and human that I've heard the chuckles spread from the reader across a barrack full of troops. There is finished care side by side with recklessness, mad gaiety over all the marvellous bundle of contradictions. What a brood for the old Reading Room to have hatched!

T. E. L.
*24th May, 1924.*

# THE TWILIGHT OF THE GODS

Truth fails not, but her outward forms that bear
The longest date do melt like frosty rime.

## I

THE FOURTH CHRISTIAN century was far past its meridian, when, high above the summit of the supreme peak of Caucasus, a magnificent eagle came sailing on broad fans into the blue, and his shadow skimmed the glittering snow as it had done day by day for thousands of years. A human figure—or it might be superhuman, for his mien seemed more than mortal—lifted from the crag, to which he hung suspended by massy gyves and rivets, eyes mournful with the presentiment of pain. The eagle's screech clanged on the wind, as with outstretched neck he stooped earthward in ever narrowing circles; his huge quills already creaked in his victim's ears, whose flesh crept and shrank, and involuntary convulsions agitated his hands and feet. Then happened what all these millenniums had never witnessed. No thunderbolt had blazed forth from that dome of cloudless blue; no marksman had approached the inaccessible spot; yet, without vestige of hurt, the eagle dropped lifeless, falling sheer down into the unfathomable abyss below. At the same moment the bonds of the captive snapped asunder, and, projected by an impetus which kept him clear of the perpendicular precipice, he alighted at an infinite depth on a sun-flecked greensward amid young ash and oak, where he long lay deprived of sense and motion.

The sun fell, dew gathered on the grass, moonshine glimpsed through the leaves, stars peeped timidly at the prostrate figure, which remained prostrate and unconscious still. But as sunlight was born anew in the East a thrill passed over the slumberer, and he became conscious, first of an indescribably delicious feeling of restful ease, then of a gnawing pang, acute as the beak of the eagle for which he at first mistook it. But his wrists, though still encumbered with bonds and trailing fetters, were otherwise at liberty, and eagle there was none. Marvelling at his inward and invisible foe, he struggled to his feet, and found himself contending with a faintness and dizziness heretofore utterly unknown to him. He dimly felt himself in the midst of things grown wonderful by estrangement and distance. No grass, no flower, no leaf had met his eye for thousands of years, nothing but the impenetrable azure, the transient cloud, sun, moon, and star, the lightning flash, the glittering peaks of ice, and the solitary eagle. There seemed more wonder in a blade of grass than in all these things, but all was blotted in a dizzy swoon, and it needed his utmost effort to understand that a light sound hard by, rapidly growing more distinct, was indeed a footfall. With a violent effort he steadied himself by grasping a tree, and had hardly accomplished so much when a tall dark maiden, straight as an arrow, slim as an antelope, wildly beautiful as a Dryad, but liker a Maenad with her aspect of mingled disdain and dismay, and step hasty as of one pursuing or pursued, suddenly checked her speed on perceiving him.

"Who art thou?" he exclaimed.

"Gods! Thou speakest Greek!"

"What else should I speak?"

"What else? From whom save thee, since I closed my father's eyes, have I heard the tongue of Homer and Plato?"

"Who is Homer? Who is Plato?"

The maiden regarded him with a look of the deepest astonishment.

"Surely," she said, "thy gift has been bestowed upon thee to little purpose. Say not, at least, that thou usest the speech of the Gods to blaspheme them. Thou art surely yet a votary of Zeus?"

"I a votary of Zeus!" exclaimed the stranger. "By these fetters, no!" And, weak as he was, the forest rang with his disdainful laughter.

"Farewell," said the maiden, as with dilating form and kindling eye she gathered up her robes. "I parley with thee no more. Thou art tenfold more detestable than the howling mob down yonder, intent on rapine and destruction. They know no better, and can no other. But thou, apt in speaking the sacred tongue yet brutally ignorant of its treasures, knowing the father of the Gods only to revile him! Let me pass."

The stranger, if willing to hinder her, seemed little able. His eyes closed, his limbs relaxed, and without a cry he sank senseless on the sward.

In an instant the maiden was kneeling by his side. Hastily undoing a basket she carried on her arm, she drew forth a leather flask, and, supporting the sunken head with one hand, poured a stream of wine through the lips with the other. As the gurgling purple coursed down his throat the sufferer opened his eyes, and thanked her silently with a smile of exquisite sweetness. Removing the large leaves which shaded the contents of the basket, she disclosed ripe figs and pomegranates, honeycomb and snow-white curd, lying close to each other in tempting array. The stranger took of each alternately, and the basket was well-nigh emptied ere his appetite seemed assuaged.

The observant maiden, meanwhile, felt her mood strangely altered.

"So have I imaged Ulysses to myself," she thought as she gazed on the stranger's goodly form, full of vigour, though not without traces of age, the massive brow, the kindly mouth, the expression of far-seeing wisdom. "Such a man ignorant of letters, and a contemner of Zeus!"

The stranger's eloquent thanks roused her from a reverie. The Greek tongue fell upon her ear like the sweetest music, and she grieved when its flow was interrupted by a question addressed directly to herself.

"Can a God feel hunger and thirst?"

"Surely no," she rejoined.

"I should have said the same yesterday," returned the stranger.

"Wherefore not to-day?"

"Dear maiden," responded he, with winning voice and manner, "we must know each other better ere my tale can gain credence with thee. Do thou rather unfold what thine own speech has left dark to me. Why the language of the Gods, as should seem, is here understood by thee and me alone; what foes Zeus has here other than myself; what is the profane crowd of which thou didst speak; and why, alone and defenceless, thou ascendest this mountain. Think of me, if thou wilt, as one fallen from the clouds."

"Strange man," returned the maiden, "who knowest Homer's speech and not Homer's self, who renouncest Zeus and resemblest him, hear my tale ere I require thine. Yesterday I should have called myself the last priestess of Apollo in this fallen land, to-day I have neither shrine nor altar. Moved by I know not what madness, my countrymen have long ago forsaken the worship of the Gods. The temples crumbled into ruin, prayer was no longer offered or sacrifice made as of old, the priestly revenues were plundered; the sacred vessels carried away; the voice of oracles became dumb; the divine tongue of Greece was forgotten,[1] its scrolls of wisdom mouldered unread, and the deluded people turned to human mechanics and fishermen. One faithful servant of Apollo remained, my father; but 'tis seven days since he closed his eyes for ever. It was time, for yesternoon the heralds proclaimed

---

1  *The divine tongue of Greece was forgotten,*—Hereby we may detect the error of those among the learned who have identified Caucasia with Armenia. "Hellenic letters," says Mr. Capes, writing of Armenia in the fourth century, "were welcomed with enthusiasm, and young men of the slenderest means crowded to the schools of Athens" ("University Life in Ancient Athens," p. 73).

by order of the King that Zeus and the Olympians should be named no more in Caucasia."

"Ha!" interrupted the stranger, "I see it all. Said I not so?" he shouted, gazing into the sky as if his eye could pierce and his voice reach beyond the drifting clouds. "But to thy own tale," he added, turning with a gesture of command to the astonished Elenko.

"It is soon told," she said. "I knew that it was death to serve the Gods any more, yet none the less in my little temple did fire burn upon Apollo's altar this morning. Scarcely was it kindled ere I became aware of a ruffianly mob thronging to sack and spoil. I was ready for death, but not at their hands. I caught up this basket, and escaped up the mountain. On its inaccessible summit, it is reported, hangs Prometheus, whom Zeus (let me bow in awe before his inscrutable counsels) doomed for his benevolence to mankind. To him, as Aeschylus sings, Io of old found her way, and from him received monition and knowledge of what should come to pass. I will try if courage and some favouring God will guide me to him; if not, I will die as near Heaven as I may attain. Tell me on thy part what thou wilt, and let me depart. If thou art indeed Zeus's enemy, thou wilt find enough on thy side down yonder."

"I have been Zeus's enemy," returned the stranger, mildly and gravely, "I am so no longer. Immortal hate befits not the mortal I feel myself to have become. Nor needest thou ascend the peak further. Maiden, I am Prometheus!"

## II

It is a prerogative of the Gods that, when they do speak sooth, mortals must needs believe them. Elenko hence felt no incredulity at the revelation of Prometheus, or sought other confirmation than the bonds and broken links of chain at his wrists and ankles.

"Now," he cried, or rather shouted, "is the prophecy fulfilled with which of old I admonished the Gods in the halls of Olympus. I told them that Zeus should beget a child mightier than himself, who should send him and them the way he had sent his father. I knew not that this child was already begotten, and that his name was Man. It has taken Man ages to assert himself, nor has he yet, as it would seem, done more than enthrone a new idol in the place of the old. But for the old, behold the last traces of its authority in these fetters, of which the first smith will rid me. Expect no thunderbolt, dear maiden; none will come: nor shall I regain the immortality of which I feel myself bereaved since yesterday."

"Is this no sorrow to thee?" asked Elenko.

"Has not my immortality been one of pain?" answered Prometheus. "Now I feel no pain, and dread one only."

"And that is?"

"The pain of missing a certain fellow-mortal," answered Prometheus, with a look so expressive that the hitherto unawed maiden cast her eyes to the ground. Hastening away from the conversation to which, nevertheless, she inly purposed to return.

"Is Man, then, the maker of Deity?" she asked.

"Can the source of his being originate in himself?" asked Prometheus. "To assert this were self-contradiction, and pride inflated to madness. But of the more exalted beings who have like him emanated from the common principle of all existence, Man, since his advent on the earth, though not the creator, is the preserver or the destroyer. He looks up to them, and they are; he out-grows them, and they are not. For the barbarian and Triballian gods there is no return; but the Olympians, if dead as deities, survive as impersonations of Man's highest conceptions of the beautiful. Languid and spectral indeed must be their existence in this barbarian age; but better days are in store for them."

"And for thee, Prometheus?"

"There is now no place," replied he, "for an impeacher of the Gods. My cause is won, my part is played. I am rewarded for my love of man by myself becoming human. When I shall have proved myself also mortal I may haply traverse realms which Zeus never knew, with, I would hope, Elenko by my side."

Elenko's countenance expressed her full readiness to accompany Prometheus as far beyond the limits of the phenomenal world as he might please to conduct her. A thought soon troubled her delicious reverie, and she inquired:

"Peradventure, then, the creed which I have execrated may be truer and better than that which I have professed?"

"If born in wiser brains and truer hearts, aye," answered Prometheus, "but of this I can have no knowledge. It seems from thy tale to have begun but ill. Yet Saturn mutilated his father, and his reign was the Golden Age."

While conversing, hand locked in hand, they had been strolling aimlessly down the mountain. Turning an abrupt bend in the path, they suddenly found themselves in presence of an assembly of early Christians.

These confessors were making the most of Elenko's dilapidated temple, whose smoking shell threw up a sable column in the background. The effigies of Apollo and the Muses had been dragged forth, and were being diligently broken up with mallets and hammers. Others of the sacrilegious throng were rending scrolls, or dividing vestments, or firing the grove of laurel that environed the shrine, or pelting the affrighted birds as they flew forth. The sacred vessels, however, at least those of gold and silver, appeared safe in the guardianship of an episcopal personage of shrewd and jovial aspect, under whose inspection they were being piled up by a troop of sturdy young ecclesiastics, the only weapon-bearers among the rabble. Elenko stood riveted to the ground. Prometheus, to her amazement, rushed forward to one of the groups with a loud "By all the Gods and Goddesses!" Following his movements, she saw that the object of his interest was an enormous dead eagle carried by one of the mob. The multitude, startled by his cry and his emotion, gazed eagerly at the strangers, and instantly a shout went up:

"The heathen woman!"

"With a heathen man!"

And clubs began to be brandished, and stones to be picked up from the ground.

Prometheus, to whom the shouts were unintelligible, looked wistfully at Elenko. As their eyes met, Elenko's countenance, which had hitherto been all disdain and defiance, assumed an expression of irresolution. A stone struck Prometheus on the temple, drawing blood; a hundred hands went up, each weighted with a missile.

"Do as I," cried Elenko to him, and crossed herself.

Prometheus imitated her, not unsuccessfully for a novice.

The uplifted arms were stayed, some even sank down.

By this time the Bishop had bustled to the front, and addressed a torrent of questions to Prometheus, who merely shook his head, and turned to inspect the eagle.

"Brethren," said the Bishop, "I smell a miracle!" And, turning to Elenko, he rapidly proceeded to cross-examine her.

"Thou wert the priestess of this temple?"

"I was."

"Thou didst leave it this morning a heathen?"

"I did."

"Thou returnest a Christian?"

Elenko blushed fire, her throat swelled, her heart beat violently. All her soul seemed concentrated in the gaze she fastened on the pale and bleeding Prometheus. She remained silent—but she crossed herself.

"Who then has persuaded thee to renounce Apollo?"

Elenko pointed to Prometheus.

"An enemy of Zeus, then?"

"Zeus has not such another enemy in the world."

"I knew it, I was sure of it," exclaimed the Bishop. "I can always tell a Christian when I see him. Wherefore speaks he not?"

"He is ancient, for all his vigorous mien. His martyrdom began ere our present speech was, nor could he learn this in his captivity."

"Martyrdom! Captivity!" exclaimed the prelate gleefully, "I thought we were coming thither. An early martyr, doubtless?"

"A very early martyr."

"Fettered and manacled?"

"Behold his wrists and ankles."

"Tortured, of course?"

"Incredibly."

"Miraculously kept alive to this day?"

"In an entirely supernatural manner."

"Now," said the Bishop, "I would wager my mitre and ring that his life was prolonged by the daily ministrations of yonder fowl that he caresses with such singular affection?"

"Never," replied Elenko, "for one day did that most punctual bird omit to visit him."

"Hurrah!" shouted the Bishop. "And now, its mission accomplished, the blessed creature, as I am informed, is found dead at the foot of the mountain. Saints and angels! this is glorious! On your knees, ye infidels!"

And down they all went, the Bishop setting the example. As their heads were bowed to the earth, Elenko made a sign to Prometheus, and when the multitude looked up, it beheld him in the act of imparting the episcopal blessing.

"Tell him that we are all his brethren," said the Bishop, which announcement became in Elenko's mouth, "Do as I do, and cleave to thy eagle."

A procession was formed. The new saint, his convert, and the eagle, rode in a car at the head of it. The Bishop, surrounded by his bodyguard, followed with the sacred vessels of Apollo, to which he had never ceased to direct a vigilant eye throughout the whole proceedings. The multitude swarmed along singing hymns, or contending for the stray feathers of the eagle. The representatives of seven monasteries put in their claims for the links of Prometheus's fetters, but the Bishop scouted them all. He found time to whisper to Elenko:

"You seem a sensible young person. Just hint to our friend that we don't want to hear anything about his theology, and the less he talks about the primitive Church the better. No doubt he is a most intelligent man, but he cannot possibly be up to all the recent improvements."

Elenko promised most fervently that Prometheus' theological sentiments should remain a mystery to the public. She then began to reflect very seriously on the subject of her own morals. "This day," she said to herself, "I have renounced all the Gods, and told lies enough to last me my life, and for no other reason than that I am in love. If this is a sufficient reason, lovers must have a different code of morality from the rest of the world, and indeed it would appear that they have. Will you die for me? Yes. Admirable. Will you lie for me? No. Then you don't love me. Βαλλ εισ κορακασ εισ Ταιναρον εισ Ὀγγ Κογγ."

<h2 style="text-align:center">III</h2>

ELENKO soon found that there was no pausing upon the path to which she had committed herself. As the sole medium of communication between Prometheus and the religious public, her time was half spent in instructing Prometheus in the creed in which he was supposed to have instructed her, and half in framing the edifying sentences which passed for the interpretation of discourses for the most part far more interesting to herself than if they had been what they professed to be. The rapt and impassioned attention which she was observed to bestow on his utterances on such occasions all but gained her the reputation of a saint, and was accepted as a sufficient set-off against the unhallowed affection which she could not help manifesting for the memory of her father. The judicious reluctance of the Caucasian ecclesiastics to inquire over-anxiously into the creeds and customs of the primitive Church was a great help to her; and another difficulty was removed by the Bishop, who, having no idea of encouraging a rival thaumaturgist, took an early opportunity of signifying that it was rather in the line of Desmotes (for by this name the new saint passed) to be the subject than the instrument of miracles, and that, at all events, no more were to be looked for from him at his time of life. The warmth with which Elenko espoused this view raised her greatly in his good opinion, and he was always ready to come to her aid when she became entangled in chronological or historical difficulties, or seasoned her versions of Desmotes' speeches with reminiscences of Plato or Marcus Aurelius, or when her invention failed altogether. On such occasions, if objectors grew troublesome, the Bishop would thunder, "Brethren, I smell a heresy!" and no more was said. One minor trouble both to Prometheus and Elenko was the affection they were naturally expected to manifest towards the carcase of the wretched eagle, which many identified with the eagle of the Evangelist John. Prometheus was of a forgiving disposition, but Elenko wished nothing more ardently than that the whole aquiline race might have but one neck, and that she might wring it. It somewhat comforted her to observe that the eagle's plumage was growing thin, while the eagle's custodian was growing fat.

But she had worse troubles to endure than any that eagles could occasion. The youth of those who resorted to her and Prometheus attracted remark from the graver members of the community. Young ladies found the precepts of the handsome and dignified saint indispensable to their spiritual health; young men were charmed with their purity as they came filtered through the lips of Elenko. Is man more conceited than woman, or more confiding? Elenko should certainly have been at ease; no temptress, however enterprising, could well be spreading her nets for an Antony three hundred years old. Prometheus, on the contrary, might have found cause for jealousy in many a noble youth's unconcealed admiration of Elenko. Yet he seemed magnificently unconscious of any cause for apprehension, while Elenko's heart swelled till it was like to burst. She had the further satisfaction of knowing herself the best hated woman in Caucasia, between the enmity of those of whose admirers she had made an involuntary conquest, and of those who found her standing between them and Prometheus. Her monopoly of Greek, she felt sure, was her only security. Two constant attendants at Prometheus's receptions particularly alarmed her, the Princess Miriam, niece of the Bishop, a handsome widow accustomed to have things as she wished them; and a tall veiled woman who seemed unknown to all, but whose unseen eyes, she instinctively knew, were never averted from the unconscious Prometheus.

It was therefore with some trepidation that she received a summons to the private apartment of the Princess Miriam.

"Dear friend," the Princess began, "thou knowest the singular affection which I have invariably entertained for thee."

"Right well do I know it," responded Elenko. ("The thirty-first lie to-day," she added wearily to herself.)

"It is this affection, dear friend," continued the Princess, "which induces me on the present occasion to transgress the limits of conventional propriety, and make a communication distressing to thee, but infinitely more so to myself."

Elenko implored the Princess to make no such sacrifice in the cause of friendship, but the great lady was resolute.

"People say," she continued—

"What say they?"

"That thy relation to Desmotes is indiscreet. That it is equivocal. That it is offensive. That it is sacrilegious. That, in a word, it is improper."

Elenko defended herself with as much energy as her candour would allow.

"Dear friend," said the Princess, "thou dost not imagine that I have part or lot in these odious imputations? Even could I deem them true, should I not think charitably of thee, but yesterday a heathen, and educated in impiety by a foul sorcerer? My poor lamb! But tongues must be stopped, and I have now to advise thee how this may be accomplished."

"Say on."

"People will always talk so long as thou art the sole medium of communication with the holy man. Some deem him less ignorant of our speech than he seems, but concerning this I inquire not: for, in society, what seems, is. Enough that thy colloquies expose thee to scandal. There is but one remedy. Thou must yield thy place to another. It is meet that thou forthwith instruct in that barbarous dialect some matron of unblemished repute and devout aspirations; no mere ignorant devotee, however, but a woman of the world, whose prudence and experience may preserve the holy man from the pitfalls set for him by the unprincipled. Manifestly she must be a married person, else nought were gained, yet must she not be chargeable with forsaking her duties towards her husband and children. It follows that she must be a widow. It were also well that she should be of kin to some influential personage, to whose counsel she might have recourse in times of difficulty, and whose authority might protect her against the slanderous and evil disposed. I have not been able to meet any one endowed with all these qualifications, excepting myself. I therefore propose to thee that thou shouldst instruct me in the speech of Desmotes, and when I am qualified to take thy place my uncle shall elevate thee to the dignity of Abbess, or bestow thee upon some young clergyman of extraordinary desert."

Elenko intimated, perhaps with more warmth than necessary, her aversion to both propositions, and the extreme improbability of the Princess ever acquiring any knowledge of Greek by her instrumentality.

"If this is the case," said the Princess, with perfect calmness, "I must have recourse to my other method, which is infallible."

Elenko inquired what it might be.

"I shall represent to my uncle, what indeed he very well knows, that a saint is, properly speaking, of no value till he is dead. Not until his decease are his relics available, or pilgrimages to his shrine feasible. It is solely in anticipation of this event that my uncle is keeping Desmotes at all; and the sooner it comes to pass, the sooner will my revered relative come by his own. Only think of the capital locked up in the new church, now so nearly completed, on the spot where they picked up the eagle! How shall it be dedicated to Desmotes in Desmotes' lifetime? Were it not a most blissful and appropriate coincidence if the day of the consecration were that of the saint's migration to a better world? I shall submit this view of the case to my uncle: he is accustomed to hear reason from me, of whom, between ourselves, he is not a little afraid. Thou mayest rely upon it that about the time of the consecration Desmotes will ascend to heaven; while thou, it is gravely to be feared, wilt proceed in the opposite direction. Would'st thou avert this unpleasantness, think well of my first proposal. I give thee credit for loving Desmotes, and suppose, therefore, that thou wilt make some sacrifice for his sake. I am a Kettle, thou art a Pot. Take heed how thou knockest against me!"

Elenko sped back to bear tidings of the threatened collision to Prometheus. As she approached his chamber she heard with astonishment two voices in eager conversation, and discovered with still greater amazement that their dialogue was carried on in Greek. The second speaker, moreover, was evidently a female. A jealous pang shot through Elenko's breast; she looked cautiously in, and discerned the same mysterious veiled woman whose demeanour had already been an enigma to her. But the veil was thrown back, and the countenance went far to allay Elenko's disquiet. It bore indeed traces of past beauty, but was altogether that of one who had known better days; worn and faded, weary and repining. Elenko's jealousy vanished, though her surprise redoubled, when she heard Prometheus address the stranger as "Sister."

"A pretty brother I have got," rejoined the lady, in high sharp tones: "to leave me in want! Never once to inquire after me!"

"Nay, sister, or sister-in-law," responded Prometheus, "if it comes to that, where were you while I was on Caucasus? The Oceanides ministered to me, Hermes came now and then, even Hercules left a card; but I never saw Pandora."

"How could I compromise Epimetheus, Prometheus?" demanded Pandora. "Besides, my attendant Hope was always telling me that all would come right, without any meddling of mine."

"Let her tell you so now," retorted Prometheus.

"Tell me now! Do you pretend not to know that the hussey forsook Olympus ten years ago, and has turned Christian?"

"I am sure I am very sorry to hear it. Somehow, she never forsook *me*. I can't imagine how you Gods get on without her."

"Get on! We are getting off. Except Eros and Plutus, who seem as usual, and the old Fates, who go on spinning as if nothing had happened, none of us expects to last for another ten years. The sacrifices have dwindled down to nothing. Zeus has put down his eagle. Hera has eaten her peacocks. Apollo's lyre is never heard—pawned, no doubt. Bacchus drinks water, and Venus— well, you can imagine how she gets on without him and Ceres. And here you are, sleek and comfortable, and never troubling yourself about your family. But you had better, or I swear I will tell Zeus; and we shall see whether these Christians will keep you with your ante-chamber full of starving gods. Take a day to think of what I have been saying!"

And away she flounced, not noticing Elenko. Long and earnestly did the pair discuss the perils that menaced them, and at the end of their deliberations Elenko sought the Bishop, and briefly imparted the Princess Miriam's ultimatum.

"It is painful to a spiritual man," replied the prelate, "to be accessory to a murder. It is also repugnant to his feelings to deny a beloved niece anything on which she has set her heart. To avoid such grievous dilemma, I judge it well that ye both ascend to heaven without further ceremony."

That night the ascent of Prometheus and Elenko was witnessed by divers credible persons. The new church was consecrated shortly afterwards. It was amply stored with relics from the wardrobe of Prometheus and what remained of the eagle. The damsels of the capital regained their admirers, and those who had become enamoured of Prometheus mostly transferred their affections to the Bishop. Everybody was satisfied except the Princess Miriam, who never ceased to deplore her indulgence in giving Elenko the chance of first speech with her uncle.

"If I had been five minutes beforehand with the minx!" she said.

## IV

THE heaven to which Prometheus and Elenko had ascended was situated in a sequestered valley of Laconia. A single winding path led into the glen, which was inhabited only by a few hunters and shepherds, who still observed the rites of the ancient faith; and sometimes, deeming but to show kindness to a mortal, refreshed or sheltered a forlorn and hungry Deity. Saving at the entrance the vale was walled round by steep cliffs, for the most part waving with trees, but here and there revealing the naked crag. It was traversed by a silvery stream, in its windings enclosing Prometheus's and Elenko's cottage, almost as in an island. The cot, buried in laurel and myrtle, had a garden where fig and mulberry, grape and almond, ripened in their season. A few goats browsed on the long grass, and yielded their milk to the household. Bread and wine, and flesh when needed, were easily procured from the

neighbours. Beyond necessary furniture, the cottage contained little but precious scrolls, obtained by Elenko from Athens and the newly founded city of
Constantine. In these, under her guidance, Prometheus read of matters that
never, while he dwelt on Olympus, entered the imagination of any God.

It is a chief happiness of lovers that each possesses treasures wholly their
own, which they may yet make fully the possession of the other. These treasures are of divers kinds, beauty, affection, memory, hope. But never were
such treasures of knowledge shared between lovers as between Prometheus
and Elenko. Each possessed immeasurable stores, hitherto inaccessible to the
other. How trifling seemed the mythical lore which Elenko had gleaned as
the minister of Phœbus to that now imparted by Prometheus! The Titan had
seen all, and been a part of all that he had seen. He had bowed beneath the
sceptre of Uranus, he had witnessed his fall, and marked the ocean crimson
with his blood. He remembered hoary Saturn a brisk active Deity, pushing
his way to the throne of Heaven, and devouring in a trice the stone that now
resists his fangs for millenniums. He had heard the shields of the Corybantes
clash around the infant Zeus; he described to Elenko how one day the sea
had frothed and boiled, and undraped Aphrodite had ascended from it in
the presence of the gazing and applauding amphitheatre of cloud-cushioned
gods. He could depict the personal appearance of Cybele, and sketch the
character of Enceladus. He had instructed Zeus, as Chiron had instructed
Achilles; he remembered Poseidon afraid of the water, and Pluto of the dark.
He called to mind and expounded ancient oracles heretofore unintelligible:
he had himself been told, and had disbelieved, that the happiest day of his
own life would be that on which he should feel himself divested of immortality. Of the younger gods and their doings he knew but little; he inquired with
interest whether Bacchus had returned in safety from his Indian expedition,
and whether Proserpine had a family of divine imps.

Much more, nevertheless, had Elenko to teach Prometheus than she could
learn from him. How trivial seemed the history of the gods to what he now
heard of the history of men! Were these indeed the beings he had known "like
ants in the sunless recesses of caves, dwelling deep-burrowing in the earth,
ignorant of the signs of the seasons," to whom he had given fire and whom
he had taught memory and number, for whom he had "brought the horse
under the chariot, and invented the sea-beaten, flaxen-winged chariot of the
sailor?" And now, how poorly showed the gods beside this once wretched
brood! What Deity could die for Olympus, as Leonidas had for Greece?
Which of them could, like Iphigenia, dwell for years beside the melancholy
sea, keeping a true heart for an absent brother? Which of them could raise

his fellows nearer to the source of all Deity, as Socrates and Plato had raised men? Who could portray himself as Phidias had portrayed Athene? Could the Muses speak with their own voices as they had spoken by Sappho's? He was especially pleased to see his own moral superiority to Zeus so eloquently enforced by Æschylus, and delighted in criticising the sentiments which the other poets had put into the mouths of the gods. Homer, he thought, must have been in Olympus often, and Aristophanes not seldom. When he read in the Cyclops of Euripides, "Stranger, I laugh to scorn Zeus's thunderbolts," he grew for a moment thoughtful. "Am I," he questioned, "ending where Polyphemus began?" But when he read a little further on:

> The wise man's only Jupiter is this,
> To eat and drink during his little day,
> And give himself no care—

"No," he said, "the Zeus that nailed me to the rock is better than this Zeus. But well for man to be rid of both, if he does not put another in their place; or, in dropping his idolatry, has not flung away his religion. Heaven has not departed with Zeus." And, taking his lyre, he sang:

> What floods of lavish splendour
>   The lofty sun doth pour!
> What else can Heaven render?
>   What room hath she for more?
>
> Yet shall his course be shortly done,
>   And after his declining
> The skies that held a single Sun
>   With thousands shall be shining.

## V

It was not long ere the gods began to find their way to Prometheus's earthly paradise, and who came once came again. The first was Epimetheus, who had probably suffered least of all from the general upset, having in truth little to lose since his ill-starred union with Pandora. He had indeed reason for thankfulness in his practical divorce from his spouse, who had settled in Caucasia, and gave Greek lessons to the Princess Miriam. Would Prometheus lend him half a talent? a quarter? a tenth? a hundredth? Thanks, thanks. Prometheus might rely upon it that his residence should not be divulged on any account.

Notwithstanding which assurance, the cottage was visited next day by eleven gods and demigods, mostly Titans. Elenko found it trying, and was really alarmed when by and by the Furies, having made over their functions to the Devil, strolled up to take the air, and dropped in for a chat, bringing Cerberus. But they behaved exceedingly well, and took back a message from Elenko to Eurydice. Ere long she was on most intimate terms with all the dethroned divinities, celestial, infernal, and marine.

Beautiful and blessed beyond most things is youthful enthusiasm, looking up to something it feels or deems above itself. Beautiful, too, as autumn sunshine is maturity looking down with gentleness on the ideal it has surpassed, and reverencing it still for old ideas and associations. The thought of beholding a Deity would once have thrilled Elenko with rapture, if this had not been checked by awe at her own presumption. The idea that a Deity, other than some disgraced offender like Prometheus, could be the object of her compassion, would never have entered her mind. And now she pitied the whole Olympian cohort most sincerely, not so much for having fallen as for having deserved to fall. She could not conceal from herself how grievously they were one and all behind the age. It was impossible to make Zeus comprehend how an idea could be a match for a thunderbolt. Apollo spoke handsomely of Homer, yet evidently esteemed the Iliad and Odyssey but lightly in comparison with the blind bard's hymn to himself. Ceres candidly admitted that her mind was a complete blank on the subject of the Eleusinian mysteries. Aphrodite's dress was admirable for summer, but in winter seemed obstinate conservatism; and why should Pallas make herself a fright with her Gorgon helmet, now that it no longer frightened anybody? Where Elenko would fain have adored she found herself tolerating, excusing, condescending. How many Elenkos are even now tenderly nursing ancient creeds, whose main virtue is the virtue of their professors!

One autumn night all the principal gods were assembled under Prometheus's roof, doing justice to the figs and mulberries, and wine cooled with Taygetan snow. The guests were more than usually despondent. Prometheus was moody and abstracted, his breast seemed labouring with thought. "So looked my Pythoness," whispered Apollo to his neighbour, "when about to deliver an oracle."

And the oracle came—in lyric verse, not to infringe any patent of Apollo's—

> When o'er the towers of Constantine
> An Orient Moon begins to shine,
> Waning nor waxing aught, and bright

> In daytide as in deep of night:
> Then, though the fane be brought
>   To wreck, the God shall find,
> Enthroned in human thought,
>   A temple in the mind.

"And what becomes of us while this prodigious moonshine is concocting?" demanded Zeus, who had become the most sceptical of any of the gods.

"Go to Elysium," suggested Prometheus.

"There's an idea!" cried Zeus and Pallas together.

"To Elysium! to Elysium!" exclaimed the other gods, and all rose tumultuously, saving two.

"I go not," said Eros, "for where Love is, there is Elysium. And yonder rising moon tells me that my hour is come." And he flitted forth.

"Neither go I," said an old blind god, "for where Plutus is, Elysium is not. Moreover, mankind would follow after me. But I too must away. Strange that I should have abode so long under the roof of a pair of perfect virtue." And he tottered out.

But the other gods swept forth into the moonlight, and were seen no more. And Prometheus picked up the forsaken sandals of Hermes, and bound them on his own feet, and grasped Elenko, and they rose up by a dizzy flight to empty heaven. All was silent in those immense courts, vacant of everything save here and there some rusty thunderbolt or mouldering crumb of ambrosia. Above, around, below, beyond sight, beyond thought, stretched the still deeps of æther, blazing with innumerable worlds. Eye could rove nowhither without beholding a star, nor could star be beheld from which the Gods' hall, with all its vastness, would not have been utterly invisible. Elenko leaned over the battlements, and watched the racing meteors. Prometheus stood by her, and pointed out in the immeasurable distance the little speck of shining dust from which they had flown.

"There? or here?" he asked.

"There!" said Elenko.

# THE POTION OF LAO-TSZE

And there the body lay, age after age,
  Mute, breathing, beating, warm, and undecaying,
Like one asleep in a green hermitage,
  With gentle sleep about its eyelids playing,
And living in its dreams beyond the rage
  Of death or life; while they were still arraying
In liveries ever new the rapid, blind,
And fleeting generations of mankind.

IN THE DAYS of the Tang dynasty China was long happy under the sceptre of a good Emperor, named Sin-Woo. He had overcome the enemies of the land, confirmed the friendship of its allies, augmented the wealth of the rich, and mitigated the wretchedness of the poor. But most especially was he admired and beloved for his persecution of the impious sect of Lao-tsze, which he had well-nigh exterminated.

It was but natural that such an Emperor should congratulate himself upon his goodness and worth; yet, as no human bliss is perfect, sorrow could not fail to enter his mind.

"It is grievous to reflect," said he to his courtiers, "that if, as ye all affirm, there hath not been any Emperor of equal merit with myself before my time, neither will any such arise after me, my subjects must inevitably be sufferers by my death."

To which the courtiers unanimously responded, "O Emperor, live for ever!"

"Happy thought!" exclaimed the Emperor; "but wherewithal shall it be executed?"

The Prime Minister looked at the Chancellor, the Chancellor looked at the Treasurer, the Treasurer looked at the Chamberlain, the Chamberlain looked at the Principal Bonze, the Principal Bonze looked at the Second Bonze, who, to his great surprise, looked at him in return.

"When the turn comes to me," murmured the inferior functionary, "I would say somewhat."

"Speak!" commanded the Emperor.

"O Uncle of the stars," said the Bonze, "there are those in your Majesty's dominions who possess the power of lengthening life, who have, in fact, discovered the Elixir of Immortality."[1]

"Let them be immediately brought hither," commanded the Emperor.

"Unhappily," returned the Bonze, "these persons, without exception, belong to the abominable sect of Lao-tsze, whose members your Majesty long ago commanded to cease from existence, with which august order they have for the most part complied. In my own diocese, where for some years after your Majesty's happy accession we were accustomed to impale twenty thousand annually, it is now difficult to find twenty, with the utmost diligence on the part of the executioners."

"It has of late sometimes appeared to me," said the Emperor, "that there may be more good in that sect than I have been led to believe by my counsellors."

"I have always thought," said the Prime Minister, "that they were rather misguided than wilfully wicked."

"They are a kind of harmless lunatics," said the Chancellor; "they should, I think, be made wards in Chancery."

"Their money does not appear different from other men's," said the Treasurer.

"I," said the Chamberlain, "have known an old woman who had known another old woman who belonged to this sect, and who assured her that she had been very good when she was a little girl."

"If," said the Emperor, "it appears that his Grace the Principal Bonze hath in any respect misled us, his property will necessarily be confiscated to the Imperial Treasury, and the Second Bonze will succeed to his office. It is needful, however, to ascertain before all things whether this sect does really possess the Elixir of Immortality, for on that the entire question of its deserts obviously depends. Our Counsellor the Second Bonze having, next to myself, the greatest interest in the matter, I desire him to make due inquiries and report to us at the next council, when I shall be prepared to state what fine will be imposed upon him, should he not have succeeded."

That night all the members of the Lao-tsze sect inhabiting prisons under

---

1    *Who have discovered the Elixir of Immortality.*—The belief in this elixir was general in China about the seventh century, A.D., and many emperors used great exertions to discover it. This fact forms the groundwork of Leopold Schefer's novel, "Der Unsterblichkeitstrank," which has furnished the conception, though not the incidents, of "The Potion of Lao-Tsze."

the jurisdiction of the Principal Bonze were decapitated, and the P.B. laid his own head upon his pillow with some approach to peace of mind, trusting that the knowledge of the Elixir of Immortality had perished with them.

The Second Bonze, having a different object to attain, proceeded in a different manner. He sent for his captives, and discoursed to them touching the evil arts of unprincipled courtiers, and the facility with which they mislead even the best intentioned princes. For years had he, the Second Bonze, pleaded the cause of toleration at court; and had at length succeeded in enlightening his Majesty to such an extent that there was every prospect of an edict of indulgence being shortly promulgated, provided always that the Elixir of Life was previously forthcoming.

The unfortunate heretics would have been only too thankful to prolong the Emperor's life indefinitely in consideration of securing peace for their own, but they could only inform the Bonze of the general tradition of their sect. This was that the knowledge of Lao-tsze's secret was confined to certain adepts, most of whom were plunged into so deep a trance that any communication with them was impossible. For the administration of the miraculous draught, it appeared, was attended with this inconvenience, that it threw the partaker into a deep sleep, lasting any time between ten years and eternity, according to the depth of his potation. During its continuance the ordinary operations of nature were suspended, and the patient awoke with precisely the same bodily constitution, old or young, as he had possessed on falling into his lethargy; and though still liable to wounds and accidents, he or she continued to enjoy undiminished health and vigour for a period equal to the duration of the trance, after which he sank back into the ranks of mortality, unless he could repeat the potion. All the adepts who had come to life under his present Majesty's most clement reign had immediately emigrated: the only persons, therefore, capable of giving information were now buried in slumber, and of course would only speak when they should awake. They were mostly concealed in the recesses of caverns, those inhabited by wild beasts being usually preferred for the sake of better security, as no tiger or bear would harm a follower of Lao-tsze. The witnesses, therefore, advised the Bonze to ascertain the residences of the most ferocious tigers in his diocese, and to wait upon them personally, in the hope of thus discovering what he sought.

This suggestion was exceedingly unpalatable to the Bonze, who felt almost equally unwilling to venture himself into a wild beast's den or to give any other person the chance of making the discovery. While he hesitated in unspeakable perplexity he was informed that an old man, about to expire at the age of an hundred and twenty years, desired to have speech with him. Thinking so venerable a personage likely to have at least a glimmering of the great secret, the Bonze hurried to his bedside.

"Our master, Lao-tsze," began the old man, "forbids us to leave this world with anything undisclosed which may contribute to the advantage of our fellow-creatures. Whether he deemed the knowledge of the cup of immortality conducive to this end I cannot say, but the question doth not arise, for I do not possess it. Hear my tale, nevertheless. Ninety years ago, being a hunter, it was my hap to fall into the jaws of an enormous tiger, who bore me off to his cavern. I there found myself in the presence of two ladies, one youthful and of surpassing loveliness, the other haggard and wrinkled. The younger lady expostulated with the tiger, and he forthwith released me. My gratitude won the women's confidence, and I learned that they were disciples of Lao-tsze who had repaired to the cavern to partake of the miraculous draught, which they were just about to do. They were, it appeared, mother and daughter, and I distinctly remember that the composition of the beverage was known to the daughter only. This impressed me, for I should naturally have expected the contrary. The tiger escorted me home. I forswore hunting, and became, and have secretly continued, a disciple of Lao-tsze. I will now indicate the position of the cavern to thee: whether the ladies will still be found in it is beyond my power to say."

And having pointed out the direction of the cavern, he expired.

The thing had to be done. The Bonze dressed himself up as much like a votary of Lao-tsze as possible, provided himself with a body-guard of *bona fide* disciples, and, accompanied by a small army of huntsmen and warriors as well, marched in quest of the den of the tiger. It was discovered about nightfall, and having tethered a small boy near the entrance, that his screams when being devoured might give notice of the tiger's issue from or return to his habitation, the Bonze and his myrmidons took up a flank position and awaited the dawn. The distant howls of roaming beasts of prey entirely deprived the holy man of his rest, but nothing worse befell him, and when in the morning the small boy, instead of providing the tiger with a breakfast, was heard crying for his own, the besiegers mustered up courage to enter the cavern. The glare of their torches revealed no tiger: but, to the Bonze's inexpressible delight, two females lay on the floor of the cave, corresponding in all respects to the description of the old man. Their costume was that of the preceding century. One was wrinkled and hoary; the inexpressible loveliness of the other, who might have seen seventeen or eighteen summers, extorted a universal cry of admiration, followed by a hush of enraptured silence. Warm, flexible, fresh in colour, breathing naturally as in slumber, the figures lay, the younger woman's arm underneath the elder woman's neck, and her chin nestling on the other's shoulder. The countenance of each seemed to indicate happy dreams.

"Can this indeed be but a trance?" simultaneously questioned several of the Bonze's followers.

"*Fiat experimentum in corpore vili!*" exclaimed the Bonze; and he thrust his long hunting spear into the elder woman's bosom. Blood poured forth freely, but there was no change in the expression of the countenance. No struggle announced dissolution; not until the body grew chill and the limbs stiff could they be sure the old woman was indeed dead.

"Carry the young woman like porcelain," ordered the priest, and like the most fragile porcelain the exquisite young beauty was borne from the cavern smiling in her trance and utterly unconscious, while the corpse of her aged companion was abandoned to the hyænas. So often did the bearers pause to look on her beauty that it was found necessary to drape the countenance entirely, until reaching the closed sedan in which, vigilantly watched by the Bonze, she was transported to the Imperial palace.

And so she was brought to the Emperor, and he worshipped her. She was laid on a couch of cloth of gold in the Imperial apartments. Wonderful was the contrast between her youthful beauty, so still in its repose, and the old haggard Emperor, fevered with the lust of beauty and love of life.

"O Majesty," said his wisest counsellor, "is there any sect in thy dominions that possesses the secret of perpetual youth?"

And the Emperor made proclamation, but no such sect could be found. And he mourned exceedingly, and caused strong perfumes to be burned around the sleeper, and conches to be blown and gongs beaten in her ears, hoping that she would awake ere he was dead or wholly decrepit. But she stirred not. And he shut himself up with her and passed his time praying to Fo for her awakening.

But one day the door of the chamber was beaten down, and his old wife came in passionately upbraiding him.

"Sin-Woo," she cried, "thou hast not the heart of a man! Thou wouldest be deathless, leaving me to die! I shall be laid in the grave, and thou wilt reign with another! Wherefore have I been true to thee, if not that our ashes might mingle at the last? Thou hoary sensualist!"

"Su-Ti," said the Emperor, with feeling, "thou dost grievously misjudge me. I am no heartless sensualist, no butterfly sipper at the lips of beauty. Is not my soul entirely possessed by this divine creature, whom I love with an affection infinitely exceeding that which I have entertained for thee at any period? And how knowest thou," added he, striving to soothe her, "that I will not give thee to drink of the miraculous potion?"

"And keep my grey hairs and wrinkles through all time! Nay, Sin-Woo, I am no fool like thee, and were I so, I am not in love with any youth. And know I not that even if I would accept the boon, thou would'st never give it?"

And she rushed away in fury and hanged herself by her Imperial girdle. Whereupon all the other wives and concubines of the Emperor did likewise, as custom and reason prescribe. All the palace was filled with lamentation and funerals. But the Emperor lamented not, nor turned his gaze from the sleeper, nor did the sleeper awaken.

And his son came to him angry with exceeding wrath.

"Thou hast murdered my mother. Thou would'st rob me of the crown that is rightfully mine. I, born to be an Emperor, shall die a subject! Nay, but I will save thee from thyself. I will pierce thy leman with the sword, or burn her with fire."

And the Emperor, fearing he would do as he threatened, commanded him to be slain, as also his brothers and sisters. And he paid no heed to the affairs of State, but gave all into the hand of the Second, now the Principal Bonze. And the laws ceased to be observed, and rebellions broke out in the provinces, and enemies invaded the country, and there was famine in the land.

And now the Emperor was well-nigh ten years nearer to the gates of death than when the Sleeping Beauty had been brought to his court. The love of beauty was nearly quenched in him, but the longing for life grew more intense. He became angry with the sleeper, that she awakened not, and with his little remaining strength smote her fiercely on the cheeks, but she gave no sign of reviving. Remembering that if he gained the potion of immortality he would himself be plunged into a trance, he made all preparations for the interregnum. He decreed that he was to be seated erect on his throne, with all his imperial insignia, and it was to be death to any one who should presume to remove any of them. His slumbering figure was to preside at all councils, and to be consulted in every act of state, and all ministers and officers were to do homage daily. The revived Sleeping Beauty was to partake of the draught anew, at the same time and in the same manner as himself, that she might awake with him, and that he might find her charms unimpaired. All the ministers swore solemnly to observe these regulations; firmly purposing to burn the sleeper, if sleep he ever did, at the very first opportunity, and scatter his ashes to the winds. Then they would fight for the Empire among themselves; each, meanwhile, was mainly occupied in striving to gain the rebels over to his interest, insomuch that the people grew more miserable day by day.

And as the aged Emperor waxed more and more feeble, he began to see visions. Legions of little black imps surrounded him crying, "We are thy sins, and would be punished—would'st thou by living for ever deprive us of our due?" And fair female forms came veiled with drooping heads, and murmured, "We are thy virtues, and would be rewarded—would'st thou cheat us?" And other figures came, dark but lovely, and whispered, "We are thy dead friends who have long waited for thee—would'st thou take to thyself new friends, and forget us?" And others said, "We are thy memories—wilt thou live on till we are all withered in thy heart?" And others said, "We are thy strength and thy beauty, thy memory and thy wit—canst thou live, knowing thou wilt never see us more?" And at last came two warders, officers of the King of Death, and one of them was laughing. And the other asked why he laughed, and he replied:

"I laugh at the Emperor, who thinks to escape our master, not knowing that the moment of his decease was engraved with a pen of iron upon a rock of adamant a million million years or ever this world was."

"And when comes it?" asked the other.

"In ten minutes," said the first.

When the Emperor heard this he was wild with terror, and tottered to the couch on which the Sleeping Beauty lay. "Oh, awake!" he cried, "awake and save me ere it is too late!" And, oh wonder! the sleeper stirred, and opened her eyes.

If she had been so beautiful while sleeping, what was she when awake! But the love of life had overcome the love of beauty in the Emperor's bosom, and he saw not the eyes like stars, and the bloom as of peaches and lilies, or the aspect grand and smiling as daybreak. He could only cry, "Give me the potion, lest I die, give me the potion!"

"That cannot I," she said. "The secret was known only to my daughter."

"Who is thy daughter?"

"The hoary woman, she who slept with me in the cavern."

"That aged crone thy daughter, daughter to thee so youthful and so fresh?"

"Even so," she said, "I bore her at sixteen, and slumbered for seventy years. When I awoke she was withered and decrepit: I youthful as when I closed my eyes. But she had learned the secret, which I never knew."

"The Bonze shall be crucified!" yelled the Emperor.

"It is too late," said she; "he is torn in pieces already."

"By whom?"

"By the multitude that are now coming to do the like unto thee."

And as she spoke the doors were burst open, and in rushed the people, headed by the most pious Bonze in the Empire (after the late Principal Bonze), who plunged a sword into the Emperor's breast, exclaiming:

"He who despises this life in comparison with another deserves to lose the life which he has." Words, saith the historian Li, which have been thought worthy to be inscribed in letters of gold in the Hall of Confucius.

And the people were crying, "Kill the sorceress!" But she looked upon them, and they cried, "Be our Empress!"

"Remember," said she, "that ye will have to bear with me for a hundred years!"

"Would," said they, "that it might be a hundred thousand!"

So she took the sceptre, and reigned gloriously.[2] Among her good acts is enumerated her toleration of the followers of Lao-tsze. Since, however, they have ceased to be persecuted by man, it is observed that wild beasts have lost their ancient respect for them, and devour them with no less appetite than the members of other sects and denominations.

---

2  P. 38. *So she took the sceptre, and reigned gloriously.*—In A.D. 683, the Dowager-Empress Woo How, upon her husband's death, caused her son to be set aside, and ruled prosperously until her decease in 703. In our day we have seen China virtually governed by female sovereigns.

# ABDALLAH THE ADITE

AN AGED HERMIT named Sergius dwelt in the wilds of Arabia, addicting himself to the pursuit of religion and alchemy. Of his creed it could only be said that it was so much better than that of his neighbours as to cause him to be commonly esteemed a Yezidi, or devil worshipper. But the better informed deemed him a Nestorian monk, who had retired into the wilderness on account of differences with his brethren, who sought to poison him.

The imputation of Yezidism against Sergius was the cause that a certain inquisitive young man resorted to him, trusting to obtain light concerning the nature of demons. But he found that Sergius could give him no information on that subject, but, on the contrary, discoursed so wisely and beautifully on holy things, that his pupil's intellect was enlightened, and his enthusiasm was inflamed, and he longed to go forth and instruct the ignorant people around him; the Saracens, and the Sabaeans, and the Zoroastrians, and the Carmathians, and the Baphometites, and the Paulicians, who are a remnant of the ancient Manichees.

"Nay, good youth," said Sergius, "I have renounced the sending forth of missionaries, having made ample trial with my spiritual son, the Prophet Abdallah."

"What!" exclaimed the youth, "was Abdallah the Adite thy disciple?"

"Even so," said Sergius. "Hearken to his history.

"Never have I instructed so promising a pupil as Abdallah, nor when he was first my disciple do I deem that he was other than the most simple-minded and well-intentioned of youths. I always called him son, a title I have never bestowed on another. Like thee, he had compassion on the darkness around him, and craved my leave to go forth and dispel it.

"'My son,' said I, 'I will not restrain thee: thou art no longer a child. Thou hast heard me discourse on the subject of persecution, and knowest that poison was administered to me personally on account of my inability to perceive the supernatural light emanating from the navel of Brother Gregory. Thou art aware that thou wilt be beaten with rods and pricked with goads, chained and starved in a dungeon, very probably blinded, very possibly burned with fire?'

"'All these things I am prepared to undergo,' said Abdallah; and he embraced me and bid me farewell.

"After certain moons he returned covered with weals and scars, and his bones protruded through his skin.

"'Whence are these weals and scars?' asked I, 'and what signifies this protrusion of thy bones?'

"'The weals and the scars,' answered he, 'proceed from the floggings inflicted upon me by command of the Caliph; and my bones protrude by reason of the omission of his officers to furnish me with either food or drink in the dungeon wherein I was imprisoned by his orders.'

"'O my son,' exclaimed I, 'in the eyes of faith and right reason these scars are lovelier than the moles of beauty, and the sight of thy bones is like the beholding of hidden treasure!'

"And Abdallah strove to look as though he believed me; nor did he entirely fail therein. And I took him, and fed him, and healed him, and sent him forth a second time into the world.

"And after a space he returned, covered as before with wounds and bruises, but comely and somewhat fat.

"'Whence this sleekness of body, my son?' I asked.

"'Through the charity of the Caliph's wives,' he answered, 'who have fed me secretly, I having assured them that in remembrance of this good work each of them in the world to come would have seven husbands.'

"'How knewest thou this, my son?' I inquired.

"'In truth, father,' he said, 'I did not know it; but I thought it probable.'

"'O my son! my son!' exclaimed I, 'thou art on a dangerous road. To win over weak ignorant people by promises of what they shall receive in a future life, whereof thou knowest no more than they do! Knowest thou not that the inestimable blessings of religion are of an inward and spiritual nature? Did I ever promise any disciple any recompense for his enlightenment and good deeds, save flogging, starvation, and burning?'

"'Never, father,' said he, 'and therefore thou hast had no follower of thy law save one, and he hath broken it.'

"He left me after a shorter stay than before, and again went forth to preach. After a long time he returned in good condition of body, yet manifestly having something upon his mind.

"'Father,' he said, 'thy son hath preached with faithfulness and acceptance, and turned thousands unto righteousness. But a sorcerer hath arisen, saying,

"Why follow ye Abdallah, seeing that he breathes not fire out of his mouth and nostrils?" And the people give ear unto the words that come from this man's lips, when they behold the flame that cometh from his nose. And unless thou teachest me to do as he doth I shall assuredly perish.'

"And I told Abdallah that it was better to perish for the truth's sake than to prolong life by lies and deceit. But he wept and lamented exceeding sore, and in the end he prevailed with me; and I taught him to breathe flame and smoke out of a hollow nut filled with combustible powder. And I took a certain substance called soap, but little known in this country, and anointed his feet therewith. And when he and the sorcerer met, both breathing flame, the people knew not which to follow; but when Abdallah walked over nine hot ploughshares, and the sorcerer could not touch one of them, they beat his brains out, and became Abdallah's disciples.

"A long time afterward Abdallah came to me again, this time with a joyful, and yet with somewhat of a troubled look, carrying a camel-hair blanket, which he undid, and lo! it was full of bones.

"'O father,' he said, 'I bring thee happy tidings. We have found the bones of the camel of the prophet Ad, upon which his revelation was engraved by him.'

"'If this be so,' said I, 'thou art acquainted with the precepts of the prophet, and hast no need of mine.'

"'Nay, but father,' said he, 'although the revelation was without question originally engraved by the prophet on these very bones, it hath come to pass by the injury of time that not one letter of his writing can be distinguished. I have therefore come to ask thee to write it over again.'

"'What!' I exclaimed, 'I forge a revelation in the name of the prophet Ad! Get thee behind me!'

"'Thou knowest, father,' he rejoined, 'that if we had the original words of the prophet Ad here they would profit us nought, as by reason of their antiquity none would understand them. Seeing therefore that I myself cannot write, it is meet that thou shouldst set down in his name those things which he would have desired to deliver had he been now among us; but if thou wilt not, I shall ask Brother Gregory.'

"And when I heard him speak of having recourse to that cheat and impostor my spirit was grieved within me, and I wrote the Book of Ad myself. And I was heedful to put in none but wholesome and profitable precepts, and more especially did I forbid polygamy, having perceived a certain inclination thereunto in my disciple.

"After many days he came again, and this time he was in violent terror and agitation, and hair was wanting to the lower part of his countenance.

"'O Abdallah,' I inquired, 'where is thy beard?'

"'In the hands of my ninth wife,' said he.

"'Apostate!' I exclaimed, 'hast thou dared to espouse more wives than one? Rememberest thou not what is written in the Book of the prophet Ad?'

"'O father,' he said, 'the revelation of Ad being, as thou knowest, so exceedingly ancient, doth of necessity require a commentary. This hath been supplied by one of my disciples, a young Syrian and natural son of Gregory, as I opine. This young man can not only write, but write to my dictation, an accomplishment in which thou hast been found lacking, O Sergius. In this gloss it is set forth how, since woman hath the ninth part of the soul of man, the prophet, in enjoining us Adites (as we now call ourselves) to take but one wife, doth instruct us to take nine; to espouse a tenth would, I grant, be damnable. It ensues, therefore, that having become enamoured of a most charming young virgin, I am constrained to repudiate one of the wives whom I have taken already. To this, each thinking that it may be her turn speedily, if not now, they will in no wise consent, and have maltreated me as thou seest, and the dens of wild beasts are at this moment abodes of peace, compared to my seraglio. What is even worse, they threaten to disclose to the people the fact, of which they have unhappily become aware, that the revelation of the blessed Ad is not written upon the bones of a camel at all, but of a cow, and will therefore be accounted spurious, inasmuch as the prophet is not recorded to have ridden upon this quadruped. And seeing that thou didst inscribe the characters, O father, I cannot but fear that the fury of the people will extend unto thee, and that thou wilt be even in danger of thy life from them.'

"This argument of Abdallah's had much weight with me, and I the more readily consented to his request as he did not on this occasion require any imposture at my hands, but merely the restitution of his domestic peace. And I went with him to his wives, and discoursed with them, and they agreed to abide by my sentence. And, willing to please him, I directed that he should marry the beautiful virgin, and put away one of his wives who was old and ugly, and endowed with the dispositions of Sheitan.

"'O father,' said Abdallah, 'thou hast brought me from death unto life! And thou, Zarah,' he continued, 'wilt lose nought, but gain exceedingly, in becoming the spouse of the wise and virtuous Sergius.'

"'I marry Zarah!' I exclaimed, 'I! a monk!'

"'Surely,' said he, 'thou would'st not take away her husband without giving her another in his stead?'

"'If he does I will throttle him,' cried Zarah.

"And I wept sore, and made great intercession. And it was agreed that there should be a delay of forty days, in which space if any one else would marry Zarah, I should be free of her. And I promised all my substance to any one who would do this, and no one was found. And she was offered to thirteen criminals doomed to suffer death, and they all chose death. And at the last I was constrained to marry her. And truly I have now the comfort of thinking that if I have offended by encouraging Abdallah's deceits, or otherwise, the debt is paid, and Eternal Justice hath now nothing against me; for verily I was an inmate of Gehenna until it came to pass that she was herself translated thither. And respecting the manner of her translation, inquire not thou too curiously. It was doubtless a token of the displeasure of Heaven at her enormities that the water of the well of Kefayat, which had been known as the Diamond of the Desert, became about this time undrinkable, and pernicious to man and beast.

"As I sat in my dwelling administering to the estate of my deceased wife, which consisted principally of wines and strong liquors, Abdallah again appeared before me.

"'Hast thou come,' said I, 'to solicit me to abet thee in any new imposture? Know, once for all, that I will not.'

"'On the contrary,' said he, 'I am come to set thee at ease by proving to thee that I shall not again require thy assistance. Follow me.'

"And I followed him to a great plain, where was a host of armed horsemen and footmen, more than I could number. And they bore banners on which the name of Abdallah was embroidered in letters of gold. And in the midst was an ark of gold, with the bones of Ad's camel, or cow. And by this was a great pile of the heads of men, and warriors were continually casting more and more upon the heap.

"'How many?' asked Abdallah.

"'Twelve thousand, O Apostle of God,' answered they, 'but there are more to come.'

"'Thou monster!' said I to Abdallah.

"'Nay, father,' said he, 'there will not be more than sixteen thousand in all, and these men were unbelievers. Moreover we have spared such of their women as were young and handsome, and have taken them for our concubines, as is ordained in the eleventh supplement to the Book of Ad, just promulgated by my authority. But come, I have other things to manifest unto thee.'

"And he led me where a stake was driven into the earth, and a man was chained unto it, and fuel was heaped all around him, and many stood by with lighted torches in their hands.

"'O Abdallah,' I exclaimed, 'wherefore this atrocity?'

"'This man,' he replied, 'is a blasphemer, who hath said that the Book of Ad is written on the bones of a cow.'

"'But it *is* written on the bones of a cow!' I cried.

"'Even so,' said he, 'and therefore is his heresy the more damnable, and his punishment the more exemplary. Had it been indeed written on the bones of a camel, he might have affirmed what pleased him.'

"And I shook off the dust from my feet, and hastened to my dwelling. The rest of Abdallah's acts thou knowest, and how he fell warring with the Carmathians. And now I ask thee, art thou yet minded to go forth as a missionary of the truth?"

"O Sergius," said the young man, "I perceive that the temptations are greater, and the difficulties far surpassing what I had thought. Yet will I go, and I trust by Heaven's grace not to fail utterly."

"Then go," said Sergius, "and Heaven's blessing go with thee! Come back in ten years, should I be living, and if thou canst declare that thou hast forged no scriptures, and worked no miracles, and persecuted no unbelievers, and flattered no potentate, and bribed no one with the promise of aught in heaven or earth, I will give thee the philosopher's stone."

# ANANDA THE MIRACLE WORKER[1]

THE HOLY BUDDHA, Sakhya Muni, on dispatching his apostles to proclaim his religion throughout the peninsula of India, failed not to provide them with salutary precepts for their guidance. He exhorted them to meekness, to compassion, to abstemiousness, to zeal in the promulgation of his doctrine, and added an injunction never before or since prescribed by the founder of any religion—namely, on no account to perform any miracle.

It is further related, that whereas the apostles experienced considerable difficulty in complying with the other instructions of their master, and sometimes actually failed therein, the prohibition to work miracles was never once transgressed by any of them, save only the pious Ananda, the history of whose first year's apostolate is recorded as follows.

Ananda repaired to the kingdom of Magadha, and instructed the inhabitants diligently in the law of Buddha. His doctrine being acceptable, and his speech persuasive, the people hearkened to him willingly, and began to forsake the Brahmins whom they had previously revered as spiritual guides. Perceiving this, Ananda became elated in spirit, and one day he exclaimed:

"How blessed is the apostle who propagates truth by the efficacy of reason and virtuous example, combined with eloquence, rather than error by imposture and devil-mongering, like those miserable Brahmins!"

As he uttered this vainglorious speech, the mountain of his merits was diminished by sixteen yojanas, and virtue and efficacy departed from him, insomuch that when he next addressed the multitude they first mocked, then hooted, and finally pelted him.

When matters had reached this pass, Ananda lifted his eyes and discerned a number of Brahmins of the lower sort, busy about a boy who lay in a fit upon the ground. They had long been applying exorcisms and other

---

1  *Ananda the Miracle Worker.*—This story was originally published in *Fraser's Magazine* for August, 1872. A French translation appeared in the *Revue Britannique* for November, 1872. Buddha's prohibition to work miracles rests, so far as the present writer's knowledge extends, on the authority of Professor Max Müller ("Lectures on the Science of Religion"). It should be needless to observe that Ananda, "the St. John of the Buddhist group," is not recorded to have contravened this or any other of his master's precepts.

approved methods with scant success, when the most sagacious among them suggested:

"Let us render the body of this patient an uncomfortable residence for the demon; peradventure he will then cease to abide therein."

They were accordingly engaged in branding the sufferer with hot irons, filling his nostrils with smoke, and otherwise to the best of their ability disquieting the intrusive devil. Ananda's first thought was, "The lad is in a fit;" the second, "It were a pious deed to deliver him from his tormentors;" the third, "By good management this may extricate me from my present uncomfortable predicament, and redound to the glory of the most holy Buddha."

Yielding to this temptation, he strode forward, chased away the Brahmins with an air of authority, and, uplifting his countenance to heaven, recited the appellations of seven devils. No effect ensuing, he repeated seven more, and so continued until, the fit having passed off in the course of nature, the patient's paroxysms ceased, he opened his eyes, and Ananda restored him to his relatives. But the people cried loudly, "A miracle! a miracle!" and when Ananda resumed his instructions, they gave heed to him, and numbers embraced the religion of Buddha. Whereupon Ananda exulted, and applauded himself for his dexterity and presence of mind, and said to himself:

"Surely the end sanctifies the means,"

As he propounded this heresy, the eminence of his merits was reduced to the dimensions of a mole-hill, and he ceased to be of account in the eyes of any of the saints, save only of Buddha, whose compassion is inexhaustible.

The fame of his achievement, nevertheless, was bruited about the whole country, and soon reached the ears of the king, who sent for him, and inquired if he had actually expelled the demon.

Ananda replied in the affirmative.

"I am indeed rejoiced," returned the king, "as thou now wilt without doubt proceed to heal *my* son, who has lain in a trance for twenty-nine days."

"Alas! dread sovereign," modestly returned Ananda, "how should the merits which barely suffice to effect the cure of a miserable Pariah avail to restore the offspring of an Elephant among Kings?"

"By what process are these merits acquired?" demanded the monarch.

"By the exercise of penance," responded Ananda, "in virtue of which the austere devotee quells the winds, allays the waters, expostulates convincingly with tigers, carries the moon in his sleeve, and otherwise performs all acts and deeds appropriate to the character of a peripatetic thaumaturgist."

"This being so," answered the king, "thy inability to heal my son manifestly arises from defect of merit, and defect of merit from defect of penance. I will therefore consign thee to the charge of my Brahmins, that they may aid thee to fill up the measure of that which is lacking."

Ananda vainly strove to explain that the austerities to which he had referred were entirely of a spiritual and contemplative character. The Brahmins, enchanted to get a heretic into their clutches, immediately seized upon him, and conveyed him to one of their temples. They stripped him, and perceived with astonishment that not one single weal or scar was visible anywhere on his person. "Horror!" they exclaimed; "here is a man who expects to go to heaven in a whole skin!" To obviate this breach of etiquette, they laid him upon his face, and flagellated him until the obnoxious soundness of cuticle was entirely removed. They then departed, promising to return next day and operate in a corresponding manner upon the anterior part of his person, after which, they jeeringly assured him, his merits would be in no respect less than those of the saintly Bhagiratha, or of the regal Viswamitra himself.

Ananda lay half dead upon the floor of the temple, when the sanctuary was illuminated by the apparition of a resplendent Glendoveer, who thus addressed him:

"Well, backsliding disciple, art thou yet convinced of thy folly?"

Ananda relished neither the imputation on his orthodoxy nor that on his wisdom. He replied, notwithstanding, with all meekness:

"Heaven forbid that I should repine at any variety of martyrdom that tends to the propagation of my master's faith."

"Wilt thou then first be healed, and moreover become the instrument of converting the entire realm of Magadha?"

"How shall this be accomplished?" demanded Ananda.

"By perseverance in the path of deceit and disobedience," returned the Glendoveer.

Ananda winced, but maintained silence in the expectation of more explicit directions.

"Know," pursued the spirit, "that the king's son will revive from his trance at the expiration of the thirtieth day, which takes place at noon to-morrow. Thou hast but to proceed at the fitting period to the couch whereon he is deposited, and, placing thy hand upon his heart, to command him to rise forthwith. His recovery will be ascribed to thy supernatural powers, and the establishment of Buddha's religion will result. Before this it will be needful that I should perform an actual cure upon thy back, which is within the compass of my capacity. I only request thee to take notice, that thou wilt on this occasion be transgressing the precepts of thy master with thine eyes open. It is also meet to apprise thee that thy temporary extrication from thy present difficulties will only involve thee in others still more formidable."

"An incorporeal Glendoveer is no judge of the feelings of a flayed apostle," thought Ananda. "Heal me," he replied, "if thou canst, and reserve thy admonitions for a more convenient opportunity."

"So be it," returned the Glendoveer; and as he extended his hand over Ananda, the latter's back was clothed anew with skin, and his previous smart simultaneously allayed. The Glendoveer vanished at the same moment, saying, "When thou hast need of me, pronounce but the incantation, *Gnooh Imdap Inam Mua*,[2] and I will immediately be by thy side."

The anger and amazement of the Brahmins may be conceived when, on returning equipped with fresh implements of flagellation, they discovered the salubrious condition of their victim. Their scourges would probably have undergone conversion into halters, had they not been accompanied by a royal officer, who took the really triumphant martyr under his protection, and carried him off to the palace. He was speedily conducted to the young prince's couch, whither a vast crowd attended him. The hour of noon not having yet arrived, Ananda discreetly protracted the time by a seasonable discourse on the impossibility of miracles, those only excepted which should be wrought by the professors of the faith of Buddha. He then descended from his pulpit, and precisely as the sun attained the zenith laid his hand upon the bosom of the young prince, who instantly revived, and completed a sentence touching the game of dice which had been interrupted by his catalepsy.

The people shouted, the courtiers went into ecstasies, the countenances of the Brahmins assumed an exceedingly sheepish expression. Even the king seemed impressed, and craved to be more particularly instructed in the law of Buddha. In complying with this request, Ananda, who had made marvellous progress in worldly wisdom during the last twenty-four hours, deemed it needless to dilate on the cardinal doctrines of his master, the misery of existence, the need of redemption, the path to felicity, the prohibition to shed blood. He simply stated that the priests of Buddha were bound to perpetual poverty, and that under the new dispensation all ecclesiastical property would accrue to the temporal authorities.

"By the holy cow!" exclaimed the monarch, "this is something like a religion!"

The words were scarcely out of the royal lips ere the courtiers professed themselves converts. The multitude followed their example. The Brahminical church was promptly disestablished and disendowed, and more injustice was

---

2   The mystic formula of the Buddhists, read backwards.

committed in the name of the new and purified religion in one day than the old corrupt one had occasioned in a hundred years.

Ananda had the satisfaction of feeling able to forgive his adversaries, and of valuing himself accordingly; and to complete his felicity, he was received in the palace, and entrusted with the education of the king's son, which he strove to conduct agreeably to the precepts of Buddha. This was a task of some delicacy, as it involved interference with the princely youth's favourite amusement, which had previously consisted in torturing small reptiles.

After a short interval Ananda was again summoned to the monarch's presence. He found his majesty in the company of two most ferocious ruffians, one of whom bore a huge axe, and the other an enormous pair of pincers.

"My chief executioner and my chief tormentor," said the king.

Ananda expressed his gratification at becoming acquainted with such exalted functionaries.

"Thou must know, most holy man," resumed the king, "that need has again arisen for the exercise of fortitude and self-denial on thy part. A powerful enemy has invaded my dominions, and has impiously presumed to discomfit my troops. Well might I feel dismayed, were it not for the consolations of religion; but my trust is in thee, O spiritual father! It is urgent that thou shouldst accumulate the largest amount of merit with the least delay possible. I am unable to invoke the ministrations of thy old friends the Brahmins to this end, they being, as thou knowest, in disgrace, but I have summoned these trusty and experienced counsellors in their room. I find them not wholly in accord. My chief tormentor, being a man of mild temper and humane disposition, considers that it might at first suffice to employ gentle measures, such, for example, as suspending thee head downwards in the smoke of a wood fire, and filling thy nostrils with red pepper. My chief executioner, taking, peradventure, a too professional view of the subject, deems it best to resort at once to crucifixion or impalement. I would gladly know thy thoughts on the matter."

Ananda expressed, as well as his terror would suffer him, his entire disapproval of both the courses recommended by the royal advisers.

"Well," said the king, with an air of resignation, "if we cannot agree upon either, it follows that we must try both. We will meet for that purpose to-morrow morning at the second hour. Go in peace!"

Ananda went, but not in peace. His alarm would have well-nigh deprived him of his faculties if he had not remembered the promise made him by his former deliverer. On reaching a secluded spot he pronounced the mystic formula, and immediately became aware of the presence, not of a radiant

Glendoveer, but of a holy man, whose head was strewn with ashes, and his body anointed with cow-dung.

"Thy occasion," said the Fakir, "brooks no delay. Thou must immediately accompany me, and assume the garb of a Jogi."

Ananda rebelled excessively in his heart, for he had imbibed from the mild and sage Buddha a befitting contempt for these grotesque and cadaverous fanatics. The emergency, however, left him no resource, and he followed his guide to a charnel house, which the latter had selected as his domicile. There, with many lamentations over the smoothness of his hair and the brevity of his nails, the Jogi besprinkled and besmeared Ananda agreeably to his own pattern, and scored him with chalk and ochre until the peaceful apostle of the gentlest of creeds resembled a Bengal tiger. He then hung a chaplet of infants' skulls about his neck, placed the skull of a malefactor in one of his hands and the thigh-bone of a necromancer in the other, and at nightfall conducted him into the adjacent cemetery, where, seating him on the ashes of a recent funeral pile, he bade him drum upon the skull with the thigh-bone, and repeat after himself the incantations which he began to scream out towards the western part of the firmament. These charms were apparently possessed of singular efficacy, for scarcely were they commenced ere a hideous tempest arose, rain descended in torrents, phosphoric flashes darted across the sky, wolves and hyænas thronged howling from their dens, and gigantic goblins, arising from the earth, extended their fleshless arms towards Ananda, and strove to drag him from his seat. Urged by frantic terror, and the example and exhortations of his companion, he battered, banged, and vociferated, until on the very verge of exhaustion; when, as if by enchantment, the tempest ceased, the spectres disappeared, and joyous shouts and a burst of music announced the occurrence of something auspicious in the adjoining city.

"The hostile king is dead," said the Jogi; "and his army has dispersed. This will be attributed to thy incantations. They are coming in quest of thee even now. Farewell until thou again hast need of me."

The Jogi disappeared, the tramp of a procession became audible, and soon torches glared feebly through the damp, cheerless dawn. The monarch descended from his state elephant, and, prostrating himself before Ananda, exclaimed:

"Inestimable man! why didst thou not disclose that thou wert a Jogi? Never more shall I feel the least apprehension of any of my enemies, so long as thou continuest an inmate of this cemetery."

A family of jackals were unceremoniously dislodged from a disused sepulchre, which was allotted to Ananda for his future residence. The king permitted no alteration in his costume, and took care that the food doled out to him should have no tendency to impair his sanctity, which speedily gave promise of attaining a very high pitch. His hair had already become as matted and his nails as long as the Jogi could have desired, when he received a visit from another royal messenger. The Rajah, so ran the regal missive, had been suddenly and mysteriously attacked by a dangerous malady, but confidently anticipated relief from Ananda's merits and incantations.

Ananda resumed his thigh-bone and his skull, and ruefully began to thump the latter with the former, in dismal expectation of the things that were to come. But the spell seemed to have lost its potency. Nothing more unearthly than a bat presented itself, and Ananda was beginning to think that he might as well desist when his reflections were diverted by the apparition of a tall and grave personage, wearing a sad-coloured robe, and carrying a long wand, who stood by his side as suddenly as though just risen from the earth.

"The caldron is ready," said the stranger.

"What caldron?" demanded Ananda.

"That wherein thou art about to be immersed."

"I immersed in a caldron! wherefore?"

"Thy spells," returned his interlocutor, "having hitherto failed to afford his majesty the slightest relief, and his experience of their efficacy on a former occasion forbidding him to suppose that they can be inoperative, he is naturally led to ascribe to their pernicious influence that aggravation of pain of which he has for some time past unfortunately been sensible. I have confirmed him in this conjecture, esteeming it for the interest of science that his anger should fall upon an impudent impostor like thee rather than on a discreet and learned physician like myself. He has consequently directed the principal caldron to be kept boiling all night, intending to immerse thee therein at daybreak, unless he should in the meantime derive some benefit from thy conjurations."

"Heavens!" exclaimed Ananda, "whither shall I fly?"

"Nowhere beyond this cemetery," returned the physician, "inasmuch as it is entirely surrounded by the royal forces."

"Wherein, then," demanded the agonized apostle, "doth the path of safety lie?"

"In this phial," answered the physician. "It contains a subtle poison. Demand to be led before the king. Affirm that thou hast received a sovereign medicine from the hands of benignant spirits. He will drink it and perish, and thou wilt be richly rewarded by his successor."

"Ayaunt, tempter!" cried Ananda, hurling the phial indignantly away. "I defy thee! and will have recourse to my old deliverer—*Gnooh Imdap Inam Mua!*"

But the charm appeared to fail of its effect. No figure was visible to his gaze, save that of the physician, who seemed to regard him with an expression of pity as he gathered up his robes and melted rather than glided into the encompassing darkness.

Ananda remained, contending with himself. Countless times was he on the point of calling after the physician and imploring him to return with a potion of like properties to the one rejected, but something seemed always to rise in his throat and impede his utterance, until, worn out by agitation, he fell asleep and dreamed this dream.

He thought he stood at the vast and gloomy entrance of Patala.[3] The lugubrious spot wore a holiday appearance; everything seemed to denote a diabolical gala. Swarms of demons of all shapes and sizes beset the portal, contemplating what appeared to be preparations for an illumination. Strings of coloured lamps were in course of disposition in wreaths and festoons by legions of frolicsome imps, chattering, laughing, and swinging by their tails like so many monkeys. The operation was directed from below by superior fiends of great apparent gravity and respectability. These bore wands of office, tipped with yellow flames, wherewith they singed the tails of the imps when such discipline appeared to them to be requisite. Ananda could not refrain from asking the reason of these festive preparations.

"They are in honour," responded the demon interrogated, "of the pious Ananda, one of the apostles of the Lord Buddha, whose advent is hourly expected among us with much eagerness and satisfaction."

The horrified Ananda with much difficulty mustered resolution to inquire on what account the apostle in question was necessitated to take up his abode in the infernal regions.

"On account of poisoning," returned the fiend laconically.

Ananda was about to seek further explanations, when his attention was arrested by a violent altercation between two of the supervising demons.

"Kammuragha, evidently," croaked one.

"Damburanana, of course," snarled the other.

"May I," inquired Ananda of the fiend he had before addressed, "presume to ask the signification of Kammuragha and Damburanana?"

"They are two hells," replied the demon. "In Kammuragha the occupant

---

3    The Hindoo Pandemonium.

is plunged into melted pitch and fed with melted lead. In Damburanana he is plunged into melted lead and fed with melted pitch. My colleagues are debating which is the more appropriate to the demerits of our guest Ananda."

Ere Ananda had had time to digest this announcement a youthful imp descended from above with agility, and, making a profound reverence, presented himself before the disputants.

"Venerable demons," interposed he, "might my insignificance venture to suggest that we cannot well testify too much honour for our visitor Ananda, seeing that he is the only apostle of Buddha with whose company we are likely ever to be indulged? Wherefore I would propose that neither Kammuragha nor Damburanana be assigned for his residence, but that the amenities of all the two hundred and forty-four thousand hells be combined in a new one, constructed especially for his reception."

The imp having thus spoken, the senior demons were amazed at his precocity, and performed a *pradakshina*, exclaiming, "Truly thou art a highly superior young devil!" They then departed to prepare the new infernal chamber, agreeably to his recipe.

Ananda awoke, shuddering with terror.

"Why," he exclaimed, "why was I ever an apostle? O Buddha! Buddha! how hard are the paths of saintliness! How prone to error are the well-meaning! How huge is the absurdity of spiritual pride!"

"Thou hast discovered that, my son?" said a gentle voice in his vicinity.

He turned and beheld the divine Buddha, radiant with a mild and benignant light. A cloud seemed rolled away from his vision, and he recognised in his master the Glendoveer, the Jogi, and the Physician.

"O holy teacher!" exclaimed he in extreme perturbation, "whither shall I turn? My sin forbids me to approach thee."

"Not on account of thy sin art thou forbidden, my son," returned Buddha, "but on account of the ridiculous and unsavoury plight to which thy knavery and disobedience have reduced thee. I have now appeared to remind thee that this day all my apostles meet on Mount Vindhya to render an account of their mission, and to inquire whether I am to deliver thine in thy stead, or whether thou art minded to proclaim it thyself."

"I will render it with my own lips," resolutely exclaimed Ananda. "It is meet that I should bear the humiliation of acknowledging my folly."

"Thou hast said well, my son," replied Buddha, "and in return I will permit thee to discard the attire, if such it may be termed, of a Jogi, and to appear in our assembly wearing the yellow robe as beseems my disciple. Nay, I will even infringe my own rule on thy behalf, and perform a not inconsiderable miracle by immediately transporting thee to the summit of Vindhya, where the faithful are already beginning to assemble. Thou wouldst otherwise incur much risk of being torn to pieces by the multitude, who, as the shouts now approaching may instruct thee, are beginning to extirpate my religion at the instigation of the new king, thy hopeful pupil. The old king is dead, poisoned by the Brahmins."

"O master! master!" exclaimed Ananda, weeping bitterly, "and is all the work undone, and all by my fault and folly?"

"That which is built on fraud and imposture can by no means endure," returned Buddha, "be it the very truth of Heaven. Be comforted; thou shalt proclaim my doctrine to better purpose in other lands. Thou hast this time but a sorry account to render of thy stewardship; yet thou mayest truly declare that thou hast obeyed my precept in the letter, if not in the spirit, since none can assert that thou hast ever wrought any miracle."

# THE CITY OF PHILOSOPHERS[1]

## I

NATURE IS MANIFOLD, not infinite, though the extent of the resources of which she can dispose almost enables her to pass for such. Her cards are so multitudinous that the pairs are easily shuffled into ages so far asunder that their resemblance escapes remark. But sometimes her mischievous daughter Fortune manages to thrust these duplicates into such conspicuous places that their similarity cannot pass unobserved, and Nature is caught plagiarising from herself. She is thus detected dealing a king—or knave—a second time in the person of a king who has already fallen from her pack as an emperor. Brilliant, careless, selfish, yet good-natured *vau-riens*, the Roman Emperor Gallienus and our Charles the Second excelled in every art save the art of reigning, and might have excelled in that also if they would have taken the trouble. The circumstances of their reigns were in many respects as similar as their characters. Both were the sons of grave and strict fathers, each of whom had met with terrible misfortunes: one deprived of his liberty by his enemies, the other of his head by his own subjects. Each of the sons had been grievously vexed by rebels, but Charles's troubles from this quarter had mostly ended where those of Gallienus began. Each saw his dominions ravaged by pestilence in a manner beyond all former experience. The Goths destroyed the temple of the Ephesian Diana, and the Dutch burned the English fleet at Chatham. Charles shut up the Exchequer, and Gallienus debased the coinage. Charles accepted a pension from Louis XIV., and Gallienus devolved the burden of his Eastern provinces on a Syrian Emir. Their tastes and pursuits were as similar as their histories. Charles excelled as a wit and a critic; Gallienus as a poet and a gastronomer. Charles was curious about chemistry, and founded the Royal Society. In the third century the conception of the systematic investigation of nature did not exist. Gallienus, therefore, could not patronise exact science; and the great literary light of the age, Longinus, irradiated the court of Palmyra. But the Emperor

---

1  *The City of Philosophers.*—This story has been translated into French by M. Sarrazin.

bestowed his favour in ample measure on the chief contemporary philosopher, Plotinus, who strove to unite the characters of Plato and Pythagoras, of
sage and seer. Like Schelling in time to come, he maintained the necessity of
a special organ for the apprehension of philosophy, without perceiving that
he thereby proclaimed philosophy bankrupt, and placed himself on the level
of the Oriental hierophants, with whose sublime quackeries the modest sage
could not hope to contend. So extreme was his humility, that he would not
claim to have been consciously united to the Divinity more than four times
in his life; without condemning magic and thaumaturgy, he left their practice to more adventurous spirits, and contented himself with the occasional
visits of a familiar demon in the shape of a serpent. He experienced, however,
frequent visitations of trance or ecstasy, sometimes lasting for a long period;
and it may have been in one of these that he was inspired by the idea of asking
the Emperor for a decayed city in Campania, there to establish a philosophic
commonwealth[2] as nearly upon the model of Plato's Republic as the degeneracy of the times would allow.

"I cannot," said Gallienus, when the project had been explained to him,
"object in principle to aught so festive and jocose. The age is turned upside
down; its comedians are lamentable, and its sages ludicrous. It must moreover, I apprehend, be sated with the earthquakes, famines, pestilences, and
barbarian invasions with which it hath been exclusively regaled for so long,
and must crave something enlivening, of the nature of thy proposition. But
whether, when we arrive at the consideration of ways and means, I shall find
my interview with my treasurer enlivening, is gravely to be questioned. I have
heard homilies enough on my prodigality, which merely means that I prefer
spending my treasures on myself to saving them for my successor, whose title
will probably have been acquired by cutting my throat."

"I know," said Plotinus, "that the expenses of administering an empire
must necessarily be prodigious. I am aware that the principal generals are
only kept to their allegiance by enormous bribes. I well understand that the
Empress must have pearls, and that the Roman populace must have panthers;
and that, since Egypt has revolted, the hippopotamus is worth his weight in
gold. I am further aware that the proposed colossal statue of your Majesty
in the same metal, including a staircase, with room in the head for a child,
like another Pallas in the brain of Zeus, must alone involve very considerable

---

2   *There to establish a philosophic commonwealth.*—The petition was actually preferred, and
would have been granted but for the disordered condition of the empire. Gallienus, though not
the man to save a sinking state, possessed the accomplishments which would have adorned an
age of peace and culture.

outlay. But I am encouraged by your Majesty's wise and statesmanlike measure of debasing the currency; since, money having become devoid of value, there can be no difficulty in devoting any amount of it to any purpose required."

"Plotinus," said Gallienus, "in this age the devil is taking the hindmost, and we are the hindmost. There are tidings to-day of a new earthquake in Bithynia, and three days' darkness, also of outbreaks of pestilence, and incursions of the barbarians, too numerous as well as too disagreeable to mention. At this moment some revolted legion is probably forcing the purple upon some reluctant general; and the Persian king, a great equestrian, is doubtless mounting his horse by the aid of my father's back. If I had been an old Roman, I should by this time have avenged my father, but I am a man of my age. Take the money for thy city, and see that it yields me some amusement at any rate. I assume, of course, that thou wilt exercise severe economy, and that cresses and spring water will be the diet of thy philosophers. Farewell, I go to Gaul to encounter Postumus. Willingly would I leave him in peace in Gaul if he would leave me in peace in Italy; but I foresee that if I do not attack him there he will attack me here. As if the Empire were not large enough for us all! What an ass the fellow must be!"

And so Gallienus changed his silk for steel, and departed for his Gallic campaign, where he bore himself more stoutly than his light talk would have led those who judged him by it to expect. Plotinus, provided with an Imperial rescript, undertook the regulation of his philosophical commonwealth in Campania, where a brief experience of architects and sophists threw him into an ecstasy, not of joy, which endured an unusually long time.

## II

On awakening from his long trance, Plotinus's first sensation was one of bodily hunger, the second of an even keener appetite for news of his philosophical Republic. In both respects it promised well to perceive that his chamber was occupied by his most eminent scholar, Porphyry, though he was less gratified to observe his disciple busied, instead of with the scrolls of the sages, with an enormous roll of accounts, which appeared to be occasioning him much perplexity.

"Porphyry!" cried the master, and the faithful disciple was by his couch in a moment.

We pass over the mutual joy, the greetings, the administration of restoratives and creature comforts, the eager interrogations of Porphyry respecting the things his master had heard and seen in his trance, which proved to be unspeakable.

"And now," said Plotinus, who with all his mysticism was so good a man of business that, as his biographers acquaint us, he was in special request as a trustee, "and now, concerning this roll of thine. Is it possible that the accounts connected with the installation of a few abstemious lovers of wisdom can have swollen to such a prodigous bulk? But indeed, why few? Peradventure all the philosophers of the earth have flocked to my city."

"It has, indeed," said Porphyry evasively, "been found necessary to incur certain expenses not originally foreseen."

"For a library, perhaps?" inquired Plotinus. "I remember thinking, just before my ecstasy, that the scrolls of the divine Plato, many of them autographic, might require some special housing."

"I rejoice to state," rejoined Porphyry, "that it is not these volumes that have involved us in our present difficulties with the superintendent of the Imperial treasury, nor can they indeed, seeing that they are now impignorated with him."

"Plato's manuscripts pawned!" exclaimed Plotinus, aghast. "Wherefore?"

"As part collateral security for expenses incurred on behalf of objects deemed of more importance by the majority of the philosophers."

"For example?"

"Repairing bath and completing amphitheatre."

"Bath! Amphitheatre!" gasped Plotinus.

"O dear master," remonstrated Porphyry, "thou didst not deem that philosophers could be induced to settle in a spot devoid of these necessaries? Not a single one would have stayed if I had not yielded to their demands, which, as regarded the bath, involved the addition of exedrae and of a sphaeristerium."

"And what can they want with an amphitheatre?" groaned Plotinus.

"They *say* it is for lectures," replied Porphyry;

"I trust there is no truth in the rumour that the head of the Stoics is three parts owner of a lion of singular ferocity."

"I must see to this as soon as I can get about," said Plotinus, turning to the accounts. "What's this? To couch and litter for head of Peripatetic school!"

"Who is so enormously fat," explained Porphyry, "that these conveniences are really indispensable to him. The Peripatetic school is positively at a standstill."

"And no great matter," said Plotinus; "its master Aristotle was at best a rationalist, without perception of the supersensual. What's this? To Maximus, for the invocation of demons."

"That," said Porphyry, "is our own Platonic dirty linen, and I heartily wish we were washing it elsewhere. Thou must know, dear master, that during thy trance the theurgic movement has attained a singular development, and that thou art regarded with disdain by thy younger disciples as one wholly behind the age, unacquainted with the higher magic, and who can produce no other outward and visible token of the Divine favour than the occasional companionship of a serpent."

"I would not assert that theurgy may not be lawfully undertaken," replied Plotinus, "provided that the adept shall have purified himself by a fast of forty months."

"It may be from neglect of this precaution," said Porphyry, "that our Maximus finds it so much easier to evoke the shades of Commodus and Caracalla than those of Socrates and Marcus Aurelius; and that these good spirits, when they do come, have no more recondite information to convey than that virtue differs from vice, and that one's grandmother is a fitting object of reverence."

"I fear this must expose Platonic truth to the derision of Epicurean scoffers," remarked Plotinus.

"O master, speak not of Epicureans, still less of Stoics! Wait till thou hast regained thy full strength, and then take counsel of some oracle."

"What meanest thou?" exclaimed Plotinus, "I insist upon knowing."

Porphyry was saved from replying by the hasty entrance of a bustling portly personage of loud voice and imperious manner, in whom Plotinus recognised Theocles, the chief of the Stoics.

"I rejoice, Plotinus," he began, "that thou hast at length emerged from that condition of torpor, so unworthy of a philosopher, which I might well designate as charlatanism were I not so firmly determined to speak no word which can offend any man. Thou wilt now be able to reprehend the malice or obtuseness of thy deputy, and to do me right in my contention with these impure dogs."

"Which be they?" asked Plotinus.

"Do I not sufficiently indicate the followers of Epicurus?" demanded the Stoic.

"O master," explained Porphyry, "in allotting and fitting up apartments designed for the respective sects of philosophers I naturally gave heed to what I understood to be the principles of each. To the Epicureans, as lovers of pleasure and luxury, I assigned the most commodious quarters, furnished the same with soft cushions and costly hangings, and provided a liberal table. I should have deemed it insulting to have offered any of these things to the frugal followers of Zeno, and nothing can surpass my astonishment at the manner in which the austere Theocles has incessantly persecuted me for choice food and wine, stately rooms and soft couches."

"O Plotinus," replied Theocles, "let me make the grounds of my conduct clear to thee. In the first place, the honour of my school is in my keeping. What will the vulgar think when they see the sty of Epicurus sumptuously adorned, and the porch of Zeno shabby and bare? Will they not deem that the Epicureans are highly respected and the Stoics made of little account? Furthermore, how can I and my disciples manifest our contempt for gold, dainties, wine, fine linen, and all the other instruments of luxury, unless we have them to despise? Shall we not appear like foxes, vilipending the grapes that we cannot reach? Not so; offer me delicacies that I may reject them, wine that I may pour it into the kennel, Tyrian purple that I may trample upon it, gold that I may fling it away; if it break an Epicurean's head, so much the better."

"Plotinus," said Hermon, the chief of the Epicureans, who had meanwhile entered the apartment, "let this hypocrite have what he wants, and send him away. I and my followers are perfectly willing to remove at once into the inferior apartments, and leave ours for his occupation with all their furniture, and the reversion of our bill of fare. Thou should'st know that the imputations of the vulgar against our sect are the grossest calumnies. The Epicurean places happiness in tranquil enjoyment, not in luxury or sensual pleasures. There is not a thing I possess which I am not perfectly willing to resign, except the society of my female disciple."

"Thy female disciple!" exclaimed the horrified Plotinus. "Thou art worse than the Stoic!"

"Plotinus," said the Epicurean, "consider well ere, as is the manner of Platonists, thou committest thyself to a proposition of a transparently foolish nature. Thou desirest to gather all sorts of philosophers around thee, but to what end, if they are restrained from manifesting their characteristic tenets? Thou mightest as well seek to illustrate the habits of animals by establishing a menagerie in which panthers should eat grass, and antelopes be dieted on rabbits. An Epicurean without his female companion, unless by his own choice, is no more an Epicurean than a Cynic is a Cynic without his rags and his impudence. Wilt thou take from me my Pannychis, an object pleasing to the eye, and leave yonder fellow his tatters and his vermin?"

The apartment had gradually filled with philosophers, and Hermon was pointing to a follower of Diogenes whose robe so fully bespoke his obedience to his master's precepts that his skin seemed almost clean in comparison.

"Consider also," continued the Epicurean, "that thou art thyself by no means exempt from scandal."

"What does the man mean?" demanded Plotinus, turning to Porphyry.

"Get them away," whispered the disciple, "and I will tell thee."

Plotinus hastily conceded the point raised with reference to the interesting Pannychis, and the philosophers went off to effect their exchange of quarters. As soon as the room was clear, he repeated:

"What *does* the man mean?"

"I suppose he is thinking of Leaena," said Porphyry.

"The most notorious character in Rome, who, finding her charms on the wane, has lately betaken herself to philosophy?"

"The same."

"What of her?"

"She has followed thee here. She affects the greatest devotion to thee. She vows that nothing shall make her budge until thou hast recovered from thy ecstasy, and admitted her as thy disciple. She has rejected numerous overtures from the philosopher Theocles; entirely for thy sake, she affirms. She comes three times a day to inquire respecting thy condition, and I fear it must be acknowledged that she has once or twice managed to get into thy chamber."

"O ye immortal Gods!" groaned Plotinus.

"Here she is!" exclaimed Porphyry, as a woman of masculine stature and bearing, with the remains of beauty not unskilfully patched, forced an entrance into the room.

"Plotinus," she exclaimed, "behold the most impassioned of thy disciples. Let us celebrate the mystic nuptials of Wisdom and Beauty. Let the claims of my sex to philosophic distinction be vindicated in my person."

"The question of the admission of women to share the studies and society of men," rejoined Plotinus, "is one by no means exempt from difficulty."

"How so? I deemed it had been determined long ago in favour of Aspasia?"

"Aspasia," said Plotinus, "was a very exceptional woman."

"And am not I?"

"I hope, that is, I conceive so," said Plotinus. "But one may be an exceptional woman without being an Aspasia."

"How so? Am I inferior to Aspasia in beauty?"

"I should hope not," said Plotinus ambiguously.

"Or in the irregularity of my deportment?"

"I should think not," said Plotinus, with more confidence.

"Then why does the Plato of our age hesitate to welcome his Diotima?"

"Because," said Plotinus, "you are not Diotima, and I am not Plato."

"I am sure I am as much like Diotima as you are like Plato," retorted the lady. "But let us come to our own time. Do I not hear that that creature Pannychis has obtained the freedom of the philosophers' city, and the right to study therein?"

"She takes private lessons from Hermon, who is responsible for her."

"The very thing!" exclaimed Leaena triumphantly. "I take private lessons from thee, and thou art responsible for me. Venus! what's that?"

The exclamation was prompted by the sudden appearance of an enormous serpent, which, emerging from a chink in the wall, glided swiftly towards the couch of Plotinus. He reached forward to greet it, uttering a cry of pleasure.

"My guardian, my tutelary dæmon," he exclaimed, "visible manifestation of Æsculapius! Then I am not forsaken by the immortal gods."

"Take away the monster," cried Leaena, in violent agitation, "the nasty thing! Plotinus, how can you? Oh, I shall faint! I shall die! Take it away, I say. You must choose between it and me."

"Then, Madam," said Plotinus, civilly but firmly, "I choose *it*."

"Thank Æsculapius we are rid of her," he added, as Leaena vanished from the apartment.

"I wish I knew that," said Porphyry.

And indeed after no long time a note came up from Theocles, who was sure that Plotinus would not refuse him that privilege of instructing a female disciple which had been already, with such manifest advantage to philosophical research, accorded to his colleague Hermon. No objection could well be made, especially as Plotinus did not foresee how many chambermaids, and pages, and cooks, and perfumers, and tiring women and bath attendants would be required, ere Leaena could feel herself moderately comfortable. How unlike the modest Pannychis! who wanted but half a bed, which need not be stuffed with the down of hares or the feathers of partridges, without which sleep refused to visit Leaena's eyelids.

It was natural that Plotinus should appeal to Gallienus, now returned from the Gallic expedition, but he could extract nothing save mysterious intimations that the Emperor had his eye upon the philosophers, and that they might find him among them when they least expected it. Plotinus's spirits drooped, and Porphyry was almost glad when he again relapsed into an ecstasy.

### III

WHEN Plotinus's eyes were at length opened, they fell not this time upon the faithful Porphyry, but upon two youthful followers of Plato who were beguiling the tedium of their vigil at his bedside by a game of dice, which prevented their observing his resuscitation. After a moment's hesitation Plotinus resolved to lie quiet in the hopes of hearing something that might indicate what influences were in the ascendant in the philosophical republic. He had not long to wait.

"Dice is dull work for long," said one of the young men, indolently throwing himself back, and letting his caster fall upon the floor. "To think how much better one might be employed, but for having to watch this old fool here! I've a great mind to call up a slave."

"All the slaves are sure to have gone to the show, unless any of them should be Christians. Besides, Porphyry would hear you, he's only in a cat's sleep," returned his companion.

"Well, I mean to say it's a shame. All the town will be in the theatre by this time."

"How many gladiators, said you?"

"Forty pairs, the best show Campania has seen time out of mind."

"How has it all come about?"

"Oh, news comes of the death of Postumus, killed by his own soldiers, and this passes as a great victory for want of a better, 'We must have a day of thanksgiving,' says Theocles. 'Right,' says Leaena, 'I am dying to see an exhibition of gladiators.' Theocles demurs at first, expecting to have to find the money—but Leaena tugs at his beard, and he gives in. Just at the nick of time the right sort of fellow pops up nobody knows whence, a lanista with hair like curling helichryse, as Theocritus has it, and a small army of gladiators, whom, out of devotion to the Emperor, he offers to exhibit for nothing. Who so pleased as Theocles now? He takes the chair as archon with Leaena by his side, and off goes every soul in the place, except Pannychis, who cannot bear the sight of blood, and Porphyry, who is an outrageous humanitarian, and us poor devils left in charge of this old dreamer."

"Couldn't we leave him to mind himself? He isn't likely to awake yet."

"Try him with your cloak-pin." The student detached the implement in question, which was about the size of a small stiletto. Feeling uncertain what part of his person was to be the subject of experiment, Plotinus judged it advisable to manifest his recovery in an unmistakable fashion.

"O dear Master, what joy!" cried both the students in a breath. "Porphyry! Porphyry!"

The trusty scholar appeared immediately, and under pretence of fetching food, the two neophytes eloped to the amphitheatre.

"What means all this, Porphyry?" demanded Plotinus sternly. "The City of

Philosophers polluted by human blood! The lovers of wisdom mingling with the dregs of the rabble!"

Porphyry's account, which Plotinus could only extract by consenting to eat while his disciple talked, corresponded in all essential particulars with that of the two young men.

"And I see not," added he, "what we can do in the matter. This abomination is supposed to be in honour of the Emperor's victories. If we interfere with it we shall be executed as rebels, supposing that we are not first torn to pieces as rioters."

"Porphyry," replied Plotinus, "I should esteem this disgrace to philosophy a disgrace to myself if I did not my utmost to avert it. Remain thou here, and perform my funeral rites if it be necessary."

But to this Porphyry would by no means consent, and the two philosophers proceeded to the amphitheatre together. It was so crowded that there was no room on the seats for another person. Theocles was enthroned in the chair of honour, his beard manifesting evident traces of the depilatories administered by Leaena, who nevertheless sat by his side, her voluptuous face gloating over the anticipated banquet of agony. The philosophic part of the spectators were ranged all around, the remaining seats were occupied by a miscellaneous public. The master of the gladiators, a man of distinguished appearance, whose yellow locks gave him the aspect of a barbarian prince, stood in the arena surrounded by his myrmidons. The entry of Plotinus and Porphyry attracted his attention: he motioned to his followers, and in an instant the philosophers were seized, bound, and gagged without the excited assembly being in the least conscious of their presence.

Two men stepped out into the arena, both fine and attractive figures. The athletic limbs, the fair complexion, the curling yellow hair of one proclaimed the Goth; he lightly swung his huge sword in his right hand, and looked as if his sole arm would easily put to flight the crowd of effeminate spectators. The other's beauty was of another sort; young, slender, pensive, spiritual, he looked like anything rather than a gladiator, and held his downward pointed sword with a negligent grasp.

"Guard thyself!" cried the Goth, placing himself in an attitude of offence.

"I spill not the blood of a fellow-creature," answered the other, casting his sword away from him.

"Coward!" yelled well-nigh every voice in the amphitheatre.

"No," answered the youth with a grave smile, "Christian."

His shield and helmet followed his sword, he stood entirely defenceless before his adversary.

"Throw him to my lion," cried Theocles.

"Or thy lioness," suggested Hermon.

This allusion to Leaena provoked a burst of laughter. Suddenly the Goth aimed a mighty blow at the head of the unresisting man. A shorn curl fell to the ground, the consummate skill of the swordsman averted all further contact between his blade and the Christian, who remained erect and smiling, without having moved a muscle or an eyelash.

"Master," said the Goth, addressing the lanista, "I had rather fight ten armed men than this unarmed one."

"Good," returned his lord, with a gesture of approval. "Retire both of you."

A roar of disapprobation broke out from the spectators, which seemed not to produce the slightest effect on the lanista.

"Turn out the next pair," they cried.

"I shall not," said he.

"Wherefore?"

"Because I do not choose."

"Rogue! Cheat! Swindler! Cast him into prison! Throw him to the lion!" Such epithets and recommendations rained from the spectators' seats, accompanied by a pelting of more substantial missiles. In an instant the yellow hair and common dress lay on the ground, and those who knew him not by the features could by the Imperial ornaments recognise the Emperor Gallienus. With no less celerity his followers, the Goth and the Christian excepted, disencumbered themselves of their exterior vesture, and stood forward in the character of Roman soldiers.

"Friends," cried Gallienus, turning to the plebeian multitude, "I am not about to balk you of your sport."

At a sign from him the legionaries ascended to the seats allotted to the philosophic portion of the audience, and a torrent of wisdom in their persons, including that of Leaena, flung forth with the energy of a catapult, descended abruptly and violently to the earth. They were instantly seized and dragged into an erect attitude by the remainder of the soldiery, who, amid the most tempestuous peals of laughter and applause from the delighted public, thrust swords into their hands, ranged them in opposite ranks, and summoned them to begin the fight and quit themselves like men. It was equally ludicrous and pitiable to see the bald, mostly grey-bearded men, their garments torn in their expulsion and their persons bruised by the fall, confronting each other with quaking limbs, helplessly brandishing their weapons or feebly calling their adversaries to come on, while the soldiers prodded them from behind with spears, and urged them into the close quarters they so anxiously desired to avoid. Plotinus, helpless with his bonds and gag, looked on in impotent horror. Gallienus was often cruel, but could he intend such a revolting massacre? There must be something behind.

The honour of developing the Emperor's purpose was reserved for Theocles, who, with admirable presence of mind, had ever since he found he must fight been engaged in trying to select the weakest antagonist. After hesitating between the unwieldy chief of the Peripatetics and the feminine Leaena he fixed on the latter, partly moved, perhaps, by the hope of avenging his beard. With a martial cry he sprang towards her, and upraised his weapon for a swashing blow. But he had sadly miscalculated. Leaena was hardly less versed in the combats of Mars than in those of Venus, having, in fact, commenced her distinguished career as a camp-follower of the Emperor Gordian. A tremendous stroke caught him on the hand; his blade dropped to the earth; why did not the fingers follow? Leaena elucidated the problem by a still more violent blow on his face; torrents of blood gushed forth indeed, but only from the nose. The sword doubled up; it had neither point nor edge.[3] Encouraged by this opportune discovery the philosophers attacked each other with infinite spirit and valour. Infuriated by the blows given and received, by the pokings and proddings of the military, and the hilarious derision of the public, they cast away the shivered blades and resorted to the weapons of Nature. They kicked, they cuffed, they scratched, they tore the garments from each other's shoulders, they foamed and rolled gasping in the yellow sand of the arena. At a signal from the Emperor the portal of the amphitheatre was thrown open, and the whole mass of clawing and cuffing philosophy was bundled ignominiously into the street.

By this time Gallienus was seated on his tribunal, and Plotinus, released from his bonds, was standing by his side.

"O Emperor," he murmured, deeply abashed, "what can I urge? Thou wilt surely demolish my city!"

"No, Plotinus," replied Gallienus, pointing to the Goth and the Christian, "there are the men who will destroy the City of Philosophers. Would that were all they will destroy!"

---

3   *The sword doubled up; it had neither point nor edge.*—Gallienus was fond of such practical jocularity. "Quum quidam gemmas vitreas pro veris vendiderat ejus uxori, atque illa, re prodita, vindicari vellet, surripi quasi ad leonem venditorem jussit. Deinde e cavea caponem emittit, mirantibusque cunctis rem tam ridiculam, per curionem dici jussit, 'Imposturam fecit et passus est': deinde negotiatorem dimisit" (Trebellius in Gallieno, cap. xii.).

# THE DEMON POPE

"So you won't sell me your soul?" said the devil.

"Thank you," replied the student, "I had rather keep it myself, if it's all the same to you."

"But it's not all the same to me. I want it very particularly. Come, I'll be liberal. I said twenty years. You can have thirty."

The student shook his head.

"Forty!"

Another shake.

"Fifty!"

As before.

"Now," said the devil, "I know I'm going to do a foolish thing, but I cannot bear to see a clever, spirited young man throw himself away. I'll make you another kind of offer. We won't have any bargain at present, but I will push you on in the world for the next forty years. This day forty years I come back and ask you for a boon; not your soul, mind, or anything not perfectly in your power to grant. If you give it, we are quits; if not, I fly away with you. What say you to this?"

The student reflected for some minutes. "Agreed," he said at last.

Scarcely had the devil disappeared, which he did instantaneously, ere a messenger reined in his smoking steed at the gate of the University of Cordova (the judicious reader will already have remarked that Lucifer could never have been allowed inside a Christian seat of learning), and, inquiring for the student Gerbert, presented him with the Emperor Otho's nomination to the Abbacy of Bobbio, in consideration, said the document, of his virtue and learning, well-nigh miraculous in one so young. Such messengers were frequent visitors during Gerbert's prosperous career. Abbot, bishop, archbishop, cardinal, he was ultimately enthroned Pope on April 2, 999, and assumed the appellation of Silvester the Second. It was then a general belief that the world would come to an end in the following year, a catastrophe which to many seemed the more imminent from the election of a chief pastor whose celebrity as a theologian, though not inconsiderable, by no means equalled his reputation as a necromancer.

The world, notwithstanding, revolved scatheless through the dreaded twelvemonth, and early in the first year of the eleventh century Gerbert was sitting peacefully in his study, perusing a book of magic. Volumes of algebra, astrology, alchemy, Aristotelian philosophy, and other such light reading filled his bookcase; and on a table stood an improved clock of his invention, next to his introduction of the Arabic numerals his chief legacy to posterity. Suddenly a sound of wings was heard, and Lucifer stood by his side.

"It is a long time," said the fiend, "since I have had the pleasure of seeing you. I have now called to remind you of our little contract, concluded this day forty years."

"You remember," said Silvester, "that you are not to ask anything exceeding my power to perform."

"I have no such intention," said Lucifer. "On the contrary, I am about to solicit a favour which can be bestowed by you alone. You are Pope, I desire that you would make me a Cardinal.

"In the expectation, I presume," returned Gerbert, "of becoming Pope on the next vacancy."

"An expectation," replied Lucifer, "which I may most reasonably entertain, considering my enormous wealth, my proficiency in intrigue, and the present condition of the Sacred College."

"You would doubtless," said Gerbert, "endeavour to subvert the foundations of the Faith, and, by a course of profligacy and licentiousness, render the Holy See odious and contemptible."

"On the contrary," said the fiend, "I would extirpate heresy, and all learning and knowledge as inevitably tending thereunto. I would suffer no man to read but the priest, and confine his reading to his breviary. I would burn your books together with your bones on the first convenient opportunity. I would observe an austere propriety of conduct, and be especially careful not to loosen one rivet in the tremendous yoke I was forging for the minds and consciences of mankind."

"If it be so," said Gerbert, "let's be off!"

"What!" exclaimed Lucifer, "you are willing to accompany me to the infernal regions!"

"Assuredly, rather than be accessory to the burning of Plato and Aristotle, and give place to the darkness against which I have been contending all my life."

"Gerbert," replied the demon, "this is arrant trifling. Know you not that no good man can enter my dominions? that, were such a thing possible, my empire would become intolerable to me, and I should be compelled to abdicate?"

"I do know it," said Gerbert, "and hence I have been able to receive your visit with composure."

"Gerbert," said the devil, with tears in his eyes, "I put it to you—is this fair, is this honest? I undertake to promote your interests in the world; I fulfil my promise abundantly. You obtain through my instrumentality a position to which you could never otherwise have aspired. Often have I had a hand in the election of a Pope, but never before have I contributed to confer the tiara on one eminent for virtue and learning. You profit by my assistance to the full, and now take advantage of an adventitious circumstance to deprive me of my reasonable guerdon. It is my constant experience that the good people are much more slippery than the sinners, and drive much harder bargains."

"Lucifer," answered Gerbert, "I have always sought to treat you as a gentleman, hoping that you would approve yourself such in return. I will not inquire whether it was entirely in harmony with this character to seek to intimidate me into compliance with your demand by threatening me with a penalty which you well knew could not be enforced. I will overlook this little irregularity, and concede even more than you have requested. You have asked to be a Cardinal. I will make you Pope—"

"Ha!" exclaimed Lucifer, and an internal glow suffused his sooty hide, as the light of a fading ember is revived by breathing upon it.

"For twelve hours," continued Gerbert. "At the expiration of that time we will consider the matter further; and if, as I anticipate, you are more anxious to divest yourself of the Papal dignity than you were to assume it, I promise to bestow upon you any boon you may ask within my power to grant, and not plainly inconsistent with religion or morals."

"Done!" cried the demon. Gerbert uttered some cabalistic words, and in a moment the apartment held two Pope Silvesters, entirely indistinguishable save by their attire, and the fact that one limped slightly with the left foot.

"You will find the Pontifical apparel in this cupboard," said Gerbert, and, taking his book of magic with him, he retreated through a masked door to a secret chamber. As the door closed behind him he chuckled, and muttered to himself, "Poor old Lucifer! Sold again!"

If Lucifer was sold he did not seem to know it. He approached a large slab of silver which did duty as a mirror, and contemplated his personal appearance with some dissatisfaction.

"I certainly don't look half so well without my horns," he soliloquised, "and I am sure I shall miss my tail most grievously."

A tiara and a train, however, made fair amends for the deficient append-
ages, and Lucifer now looked every inch a Pope. He was about to call the
master of the ceremonies, and summon a consistory, when the door was
burst open, and seven cardinals, brandishing poniards, rushed into the room.

"Down with the sorcerer!" they cried, as they seized and gagged him.

"Death to the Saracen!"

"Practises algebra, and other devilish arts!"

"Knows Greek!"

"Talks Arabic!"

"Reads Hebrew!"

"Burn him!"

"Smother him!"

"Let him be deposed by a general council," said a young and inexperienced
Cardinal.

"Heaven forbid!" said an old and wary one, *sotto voce*.

Lucifer struggled frantically, but the feeble frame he was doomed to
inhabit for the next eleven hours was speedily exhausted. Bound and helpless, he swooned away.

"Brethren," said one of the senior cardinals, "it hath been delivered by the
exorcists that a sorcerer or other individual in league with the demon doth
usually bear upon his person some visible token of his infernal compact. I
propose that we forthwith institute a search for this stigma, the discovery of
which may contribute to justify our proceedings in the eyes of the world."

"I heartily approve of our brother Anno's proposition," said another, "the
rather as we cannot possibly fail to discover such a mark, if, indeed, we desire
to find it."

The search was accordingly instituted, and had not proceeded far ere a
simultaneous yell from all the seven cardinals indicated that their investigation had brought more to light than they had ventured to expect.

The Holy Father had a cloven foot!

For the next five minutes the Cardinals remained utterly stunned, silent,
and stupefied with amazement. As they gradually recovered their faculties it
would have become manifest to a nice observer that the Pope had risen very
considerably in their good opinion.

"This is an affair requiring very mature deliberation," said one.

"I always feared that we might be proceeding too precipitately," said
another.

"It is written, 'the devils believe,'" said a third: "the Holy Father, therefore,
is not a heretic at any rate."

"Brethren," said Anno, "this affair, as our brother Benno well remarks, doth indeed call for mature deliberation. I therefore propose that, instead of smothering his Holiness with cushions, as originally contemplated, we immure him for the present in the dungeon adjoining hereunto, and, after spending the night in meditation and prayer, resume the consideration of the business tomorrow morning."

"Informing the officials of the palace," said Benno, "that his Holiness has retired for his devotions, and desires on no account to be disturbed."

"A pious fraud," said Anno, "which not one of the Fathers would for a moment have scrupled to commit."

The Cardinals accordingly lifted the still insensible Lucifer, and bore him carefully, almost tenderly, to the apartment appointed for his detention. Each would fain have lingered in hopes of his recovery, but each felt that the eyes of his six brethren were upon him: and all, therefore, retired simultaneously, each taking a key of the cell.

Lucifer regained consciousness almost immediately afterwards. He had the most confused idea of the circumstances which had involved him in his present scrape, and could only say to himself that if they were the usual concomitants of the Papal dignity, these were by no means to his taste, and he wished he had been made acquainted with them sooner. The dungeon was not only perfectly dark, but horribly cold, and the poor devil in his present form had no latent store of infernal heat to draw upon. His teeth chattered, he shivered in every limb, and felt devoured with hunger and thirst. There is much probability in the assertion of some of his biographers that it was on this occasion that he invented ardent spirits; but, even if he did, the mere conception of a glass of brandy could only increase his sufferings. So the long January night wore wearily on, and Lucifer seemed likely to expire from inanition, when a key turned in the lock, and Cardinal Anno cautiously glided in, bearing a lamp, a loaf, half a cold roast kid, and a bottle of wine.

"I trust," he said, bowing courteously, "that I may be excused any slight breach of etiquette of which I may render myself culpable from the difficulty under which I labour of determining whether, under present circumstances, 'Your Holiness,' or 'Your Infernal Majesty' be the form of address most befitting me to employ."

"Bub-ub-bub-boo," went Lucifer, who still had the gag in his mouth.

"Heavens!" exclaimed the Cardinal, "I crave your Infernal Holiness's forgiveness. What a lamentable oversight!"

And, relieving Lucifer from his gag and bonds, he set out the refection, upon which the demon fell voraciously.

"Why the devil, if I may so express myself," pursued Anno, "did not your Holiness inform us that you *were* the devil? Not a hand would then have been raised against you. I have myself been seeking all my life for the audience now happily vouchsafed me. Whence this mistrust of your faithful Anno, who has served you so loyally and zealously these many years?"

Lucifer pointed significantly to the gag and fetters.

"I shall never forgive myself," protested the Cardinal, "for the part I have borne in this unfortunate transaction. Next to ministering to your Majesty's bodily necessities, there is nothing I have so much at heart as to express my penitence. But I entreat your Majesty to remember that I believed myself to be acting in your Majesty's interest by overthrowing a magician who was accustomed to send your Majesty upon errands, and who might at any time enclose you in a box, and cast you into the sea. It is deplorable that your Majesty's most devoted servants should have been thus misled."

"Reasons of State," suggested Lucifer.

"I trust that they no longer operate," said the Cardinal. "However, the Sacred College is now fully possessed of the whole matter: it is therefore unnecessary to pursue this department of the subject further. I would now humbly crave leave to confer with your Majesty, or rather, perhaps, your Holiness, since I am about to speak of spiritual things, on the important and delicate point of your Holiness's successor. I am ignorant how long your Holiness proposes to occupy the Apostolic chair; but of course you are aware that public opinion will not suffer you to hold it for a term exceeding that of the pontificate of Peter. A vacancy, therefore, must one day occur; and I am humbly to represent that the office could not be filled by one more congenial than myself to the present incumbent, or on whom he could more fully rely to carry out in every respect his views and intentions."

And the Cardinal proceeded to detail various circumstances of his past life, which certainly seemed to corroborate his assertion. He had not, however, proceeded far ere he was disturbed by the grating of another key in the lock, and had just time to whisper impressively, "Beware of Benno," ere he dived under a table.

Benno was also provided with a lamp, wine, and cold viands. Warned by the other lamp and the remains of Lucifer's repast that some colleague had been beforehand with him, and not knowing how many more might be in the field, he came briefly to the point as regarded the Papacy, and preferred his claim in much the same manner as Anno. While he was earnestly cautioning Lucifer against this Cardinal as one who could and would cheat the very Devil himself, another key turned in the lock, and Benno escaped under the table, where Anno immediately inserted his finger into his right eye. The little squeal consequent upon this occurrence Lucifer successfully smothered by a fit of coughing.

Cardinal No. 3, a Frenchman, bore a Bayonne ham, and exhibited the same disgust as Benno on seeing himself forestalled. So far as his requests transpired they were moderate, but no one knows where he would have stopped if he had not been scared by the advent of Cardinal No. 4. Up to this time he had only asked for an inexhaustible purse, power to call up the Devil *ad libitum*, and a ring of invisibility to allow him free access to his mistress, who was unfortunately a married woman.

Cardinal No. 4 chiefly wanted to be put into the way of poisoning Cardinal No. 5; and Cardinal No. 5 preferred the same petition as respected Cardinal No. 4.

Cardinal No. 6, an Englishman, demanded the reversion of the Archbishoprics of Canterbury and York, with the faculty of holding them together, and of unlimited non-residence. In the course of his harangue he made use of the phrase *non obstantibus*, of which Lucifer immediately took a note.

What the seventh Cardinal would have solicited is not known, for he had hardly opened his mouth when the twelfth hour expired, and Lucifer, regaining his vigour with his shape, sent the Prince of the Church spinning to the other end of the room, and split the marble table with a single stroke of his tail. The six crouched and huddling Cardinals cowered revealed to one another, and at the same time enjoyed the spectacle of his Holiness darting through the stone ceiling, which yielded like a film to his passage, and closed up afterwards as if nothing had happened. After the first shock of dismay they unanimously rushed to the door, but found it bolted on the outside. There was no other exit, and no means of giving an alarm. In this emergency the demeanour of the Italian Cardinals set a bright example to their ultra-montane colleagues. "*Bisogna pazienzia,*" they said, as they shrugged their shoulders. Nothing could exceed the mutual politeness of Cardinals Anno and Benno, unless that of the two who had sought to poison each other. The Frenchman was held to have gravely derogated from good manners by alluding to this circumstance, which had reached his ears while he was under the table: and the Englishman swore so outrageously at the plight in which he found himself that the Italians then and there silently registered a vow that none of his nation should ever be Pope, a maxim which, with one exception, has been observed to this day.

Lucifer, meanwhile, had repaired to Silvester, whom he found arrayed in all the insignia of his dignity; of which, as he remarked, he thought his visitor had probably had enough.

"I should think so indeed," replied Lucifer. "But at the same time I feel myself fully repaid for all I have undergone by the assurance of the loyalty of my friends and admirers, and the conviction that it is needless for me to devote any considerable amount of personal attention to ecclesiastical affairs. I now claim the promised boon, which it will be in no way inconsistent with thy functions to grant, seeing that it is a work of mercy. I demand that the Cardinals be released, and that their conspiracy against thee, by which I alone suffered, be buried in oblivion."

"I hoped you would carry them all off," said Gerbert, with an expression of disappointment.

"Thank you," said the Devil. "It is more to my interest to leave them where they are."

So the dungeon-door was unbolted, and the Cardinals came forth, sheepish and crestfallen. If, after all, they did less mischief than Lucifer had expected from them, the cause was their entire bewilderment by what had passed, and their utter inability to penetrate the policy of Gerbert, who henceforth devoted himself even with ostentation to good works. They could never quite satisfy themselves whether they were speaking to the Pope or to the Devil, and when under the latter impression habitually emitted propositions which Gerbert justly stigmatised as rash, temerarious, and scandalous. They plagued him with allusions to certain matters mentioned in their interviews with Lucifer, with which they naturally but erroneously supposed him to be conversant, and worried him by continual nods and titterings as they glanced at his nether extremities. To abolish this nuisance, and at the same time silence sundry unpleasant rumours which had somehow got abroad, Gerbert devised the ceremony of kissing the Pope's feet, which, in a grievously mutilated form, endures to this day. The stupefaction of the Cardinals on discovering that the Holy Father had lost his hoof surpasses all description, and they went to their graves without having obtained the least insight into the mystery.

# THE CUPBEARER

THE MINISTER PHOTINIUS had fallen, to the joy of Constantinople. He had taken sanctuary in the immense monastery adjoining the Golden Gate in the twelfth region of the city, founded for a thousand monks by the patrician Studius, in the year 463. There he occupied himself with the concoction of poisons, the resource of fallen statesmen. When a defeated minister of our own day is indisposed to accept his discomfiture, he applies himself to poison the public mind, inciting the lower orders against the higher, and blowing up every smouldering ember of sedition he can discover, trusting that the conflagration thus kindled, though it consume the edifice of the State, will not fail to roast his own egg. Photinius's conceptions of mischief were less refined; he perfected his toxicological knowledge in the medical laboratory of the monastery, and sought eagerly for an opportunity of employing it; whether in an experiment upon the Emperor, or on his own successor, or on some other personage, circumstances must determine.

The sanctity of Studius's convent, and the strength of its monastic garrison, rendered it a safe refuge for disgraced courtiers, and in this thirtieth year of the Emperor Basil the Second (reckoning from his nominal accession) it harboured a legion of ex-prime ministers, patriarchs, archbishops, chief secretaries, hypati, anthypati, silentiarii, protospatharii, and even spatharo-candidati.[1] And this small army was nothing to the host that, maimed or blinded or tonsured or all three, dragged out their lives in monasteries or in dungeons or on rocky islets; and these again were few in comparison with the spirits of the traitors or the betrayed who wailed nightly amid the planes and cypresses of the Aretae, or stalked through the palatial apartments of verdantique and porphyry. But of those comparatively at liberty, but whose

---

1  *Hypati, anthypati, &c.*—*Hypati* and *anthypati* denote consuls and proconsuls, dignities of course merely titular at the court of Constantinople. *Silentiarii* were properly officers charged with maintaining order at court; but this duty, which was perhaps performed by deputy, seems to have been generally entrusted to persons of distinction. The *protospatharius* was the chief of the Imperial body-guard, of which the *spatharocandidati* constituted the *élite*.

liberty was circumscribed by the hallowed precincts of Studius, every soul was plotting. And never, perhaps, in the corrupt Byzantine Court, where true friendship had been unknown since Theodora quarrelled with Antonia, had so near an approach to it existed as in this asylum of villains. A sort of freemasonry came to prevail in the sanctuary: every one longed to know how his neighbour's plot throve, and grudged not to buy the knowledge by disclosing a little corner of his own. Thus rendered communicative, their colloquies would travel back into the past, and as the veterans of intrigue fought their battles over again, the most experienced would learn things that made them open their eyes with amazement. "Ah!" they would hear, "that is just where you were mistaken. You had bought Eromenus, but so had I, and old Nicephorus had outbid us both." "You deemed the dancer Anthusa a sure card, and knew not of her secret infirmity, of which I had been apprised by her waiting woman." "Did you really know nothing of that sliding panel? And were you ignorant that whatever one says in the blue chamber is heard in the green?" "Yes, I thought so too, and I spent a mint of money before finding out that the dog whose slaver that brazen impostor Panurgiades pretended to sell me was no more mad than he was." After such rehearsals of future dialogues by the banks of Styx, the fallen statesmen were observed to appear exceedingly dejected, but the stimulus had become necessary to their existence. None gossiped so freely or disclosed so much as Photinius and his predecessor Eustathius, whom he had himself displaced—probably because Eustathius, believing in nothing in heaven or earth but gold, and labouring under an absolute privation of that metal, was regarded even by himself as an extinct volcano.

"Well," observed he one day, when discoursing with Photinius is an unusually confidential mood, "I am free to say that for my own part I don't think over much of poison. It has its advantages, to be sure, but to my mind the disadvantages are even more conspicuous."

"For example?" inquired Photinius, who had the best reason for confiding in the efficacy of a drug administered with dexterity and discretion.

"Two people must be in the secret at least, if not three," replied Eustathius, "and cooks, as a rule, are a class of persons entirely unfit to be employed in affairs of State."

"The Court physician," suggested Photinius.

"Is only available," answered Eustathius, "in case his Majesty should send for him, which is most improbable. If he ever did, poison, praised be the Lord! would be totally unnecessary and entirely superfluous."

"My dear friend," said Photinius, venturing at this favourable moment on a question he had been dying to ask ever since he had been an inmate of the convent, "would you mind telling me in confidence, did you ever administer any potion of a deleterious nature to his Sacred Majesty?"

"Never!" protested Eustathius, with fervour. "I tried once, to be sure, but it was no use."

"What was the impediment?"

"The perverse opposition of the cupbearer. It is idle attempting anything of the kind as long as she is about the Emperor."

"*She!*" exclaimed Photinius.

"Don't you know *that*?" responded Eustathius, with an air and manner that plainly said, "You don't know much."

Humbled and ashamed, Photinius nevertheless wisely stooped to avow his nescience, and flattering his rival on his superior penetration, led him to divulge the State secret that the handsome cupbearer Helladius was but the disguise of the lovely Helladia, the object of Basil's tenderest affection, and whose romantic attachment to his person had already frustrated more conspiracies than the aged plotter could reckon up.

This intelligence made Photinius for a season exceedingly thoughtful. He had not deemed Basil of an amorous complexion. At length he sent for his daughter, the beautiful and virtuous Euprepia, who from time to time visited him in the monastery.

"Daughter," he said, "it appears to me that the time has now arrived when thou mayest with propriety present a petition to the Emperor on behalf of thy unfortunate father. Here is the document. It is, I flatter myself, composed with no ordinary address; nevertheless I will not conceal from thee that I place my hopes rather on thy beauty of person than on my beauty of style. Shake down thy hair and dishevel it, so!—that is excellent. Remember to tear thy robe some little in the poignancy of thy woe, and to lose a sandal. Tears and sobs of course thou hast always at command, but let not the frenzy of thy grief render thee wholly inarticulate. Here is a slight memorandum of what is most fitting for thee to say: thy old nurse's instructions will do the rest. Light a candle for St. Sergius, and watch for a favourable opportunity."

Euprepia was upright, candid, and loyal; but the best of women has something of the actress in her nature; and her histrionic talent was stimulated by her filial affection. Basil was for a moment fairly carried away by the consummate fact of her performance and the genuine feeling to her appeal; but he was himself again by the time he had finished perusing his late minister's long-winded and mendacious memorial.

"What manner of woman was thy mother?" he inquired kindly

Euprepia was eloquent in praise of her deceased parent's perfections of mind and person.

"Then I can believe thee Photinius's daughter, which I might otherwise have doubted," returned Basil. "As concerns him, I can only say, if he feels himself innocent, let him come out of sanctuary, and stand his trial. But I will give thee a place at Court."

This was about all that Photinius hoped to obtain, and he joyfully consented to his daughter's entering the Imperial court, exulting at having got in the thin end of the wedge. She was attached to the person of the Emperor's sister-in-law, the "Slayer of the Bulgarians" himself being a most determined bachelor.

Time wore on. Euprepia's opportunities of visiting her father were less frequent than formerly. At last she came, looking thoroughly miserable, distracted, and forlorn.

"What ails thee, child?" he inquired anxiously.

"Oh, father, in what a frightful position do I find myself!"

"Speak," he said, "and rely on my counsel."

"When I entered the Court," she proceeded, "I found at first but one human creature I could love or trust, and he—let me so call him—seemed to make up for the deficiencies of all the rest. It was the cupbearer Helladius."

"I hope he is still thy friend," interrupted Photinius. "The good graces of an Imperial cupbearer are always important, and I would have bought those of Helladius with a myriad of bezants."

"They were not to be thus obtained, father," said she. "The purest disinterestedness, the noblest integrity, the most unselfish devotion, were the distinction of my friend. And such beauty! I cannot, I must not conceal that my heart was soon entirely his. But—most strange it seemed to me then—it was long impossible for me to tell whether Helladius loved me or loved me not. The most perfect sympathy existed between us: we seemed one heart and one soul: and yet, and yet, Helladius never gave the slightest indication of the sentiments which a young man might be supposed to entertain for a young girl. Vainly did I try every innocent wile that a modest maiden may permit herself: he was ever the friend, never the lover. At length, after long pining between despairing fondness and wounded pride, I myself turned away, and listened to one who left me in no doubt of the sincerity of his passion."

"Who?"

"The Emperor! And, to shorten the story of my shame, I became his mistress."

"The saints be praised!" shouted Photinius. "O my incomparable daughter!"

"Father!" cried Euprepia, blushing and indignant. "But let me hurry on with my wretched tale. In proportion as the Emperor's affection became more marked, Helladius, hitherto so buoyant and serene, became a visible prey to despondency. Some scornful beauty, I deemed, was inflicting on him the tortures he had previously inflicted upon me, and, cured of my unhappy attachment, and entirely devoted to my Imperial lover, I did all in my power to encourage him. He received my comfort with gratitude, nor did it, as I had feared might happen, seem to excite the least lover-like feeling towards me on his own part."

"Euprepia," he said only two days ago, "never in this Court have I met one like thee. Thou art the soul of honour and generosity. I can safely trust thee with a secret which my bursting heart can no longer retain, but which I dread to breathe even to myself. Know first I am not what I seem, I am a woman!" And opening his vest—"

"We know all about that already," interrupted Photinius. "Get on!"

"If thou knowest this already, father," said the astonished Euprepia, "thou wilt spare me the pain of entering further into Helladia's affection for Basil. Suffice that it was impassioned beyond description, and vied with whatever history or romance records. In her male costume she had accompanied the conqueror of the Bulgarians in his campaigns, she had fought in his battles; a gigantic foe, in act to strike him from behind, had fallen by her arrow; she had warded the poison-cup from his lips, and the assassin's dagger from his heart; she had rejected enormous wealth offered as a bribe for treachery, and lived only for the Emperor. 'And now,' she cried, 'his love for me is cold, and he deserts me for another. Who she is I cannot find, else on her it were, not on him, that my vengeance should alight. Oh, Euprepia, I would tear her eyes from her head, were they beautiful as thine! But vengeance I must have. Basil must die. On the third day he expires by my hand, poisoned by the cup which I alone am trusted to offer him at the Imperial banquet where thou wilt be present. Thou shalt see his agonies and my triumph, and rejoice that thy friend has known how to avenge herself.'

"Thou seest now, father, in how frightful a difficulty I am placed. All my entreaties and remonstrances have been in vain: at my threats Helladia merely laughs. I love Basil with my whole heart. Shall I look on and see him murdered? Shall I, having first unwittingly done my friend the most grievous injury, proceed further to betray her, and doom her to a cruel death? I might anticipate her fell purpose by slaying her, but for that I have neither strength nor courage. Many a time have I felt on the point of revealing everything to her, and offering myself as her victim, but for this also I lack fortitude. I might convey a warning to Basil, but Helladia's vengeance is unsleeping, and nothing but her death or mine will screen him. Oh, father, father! what am I to do?"

"Nothing romantic or sentimental, I trust, dear child," replied Photinius.

"Torture me not, father. I came to thee for counsel."

"And counsel shalt thou have, but it must be the issue of mature deliberation. Thou mayest observe," continued he with the air of a good man contending with adversity, "how weak and miserable is man's estate even in the day of good fortune, how hard it is for purblind mortals to discern the right path, especially when two alluring routes are simultaneously presented for their decision! The most obvious and natural course, the one I should have adopted without hesitation half-an-hour ago, would be simply to let Helladia alone. Should she succeed—and Heaven forbid else!—the knot is loosed in the simplest manner. Basil dies—"

"Father!"

"I am a favourite with his sister-in-law," continued Photinius, entirely unconscious of his daughter's horror and agitation, "who will govern in the name of her weak husband, and is moreover thy mistress. She recalls me to Court, and all is peace and joy. But then, Helladia may fail. In that case, when she has been executed—"

"Father, father!"

"We are exactly where we were, save for the hold thou hast established over the Emperor, which is of course invaluable. I cannot but feel that Heaven is good when I reflect how easily thou mightest have thrown thyself away upon a courtier. Now there is a much bolder game to play, which, relying on the protection of Providence, I feel half disposed to attempt. Thou mightest betray Helladia."

"Deliver my friend to the tormentors!"

"Then," pursued Photinius, without hearing her, "thy claim on the Emperor's gratitude is boundless, and if he has any sense of what is seemly— and he is what they call chivalrous—he will make thee his lawful consort. I father-in-law of an Emperor! My brain reels to think of it. I must be cool. I must not suffer myself to be dazzled or hurried away. Let me consider. Thus acting, thou puttest all to the hazard of the die. For if Helladia should deny everything, as of course she would, and the Emperor should foolishly scruple to put her to the rack, she might probably persuade him of her innocence, and where wouldst thou be then? It might almost be better to be beforehand, and poison Helladia herself, but I fear there is no time now. Thou hast no evidence but her threats, I suppose? Thou hast not caught her tampering with poisons? There can of course be nothing in writing. I daresay I could find something, if I had but time. Canst thou counterfeit her signature?"

But long ere this Euprepia, dissolved in tears, her bosom torn by convulsive sobs, had become as inattentive to her parent's discourse as he had been to her interjections. Photinius at last remarked her distress: he was by no means a bad father.

"Poor child," he said, "thy nerves are unstrung, and no wonder. It is a terrible risk to run. Even if thou saidest nothing, and Helladia under the torture accused thee of having been privy to her design, it might have a bad effect on the Emperor's mind. If he put thee to the torture too—but no! that's impossible. I feel faint and giddy, dear child, and unable to decide a point of such importance. Come to me at daybreak to-morrow."

But Euprepia did not reappear, and Photinius spent the day in an agony of expectation, fearing that she had compromised herself by some imprudence. He gazed on the setting sun with uncontrollable impatience, knowing that it would shine on the Imperial banquet, where so much was to happen. Basil was in fact at that very moment seating himself among a brilliant assemblage. By his side stood a choir of musicians, among them Euprepia. Soon the cup was called for, and Helladia, in her masculine dress, stepped forward, darting a glance of sinister triumph at her friend. Silently, almost imperceptibly to the bulk of the company, Euprepia glided forward, and hissed rather than whispered in Helladia's ear, ere she could retire from the Emperor's side.

"Didst thou not say that if thou couldst discover her who had wronged thee, thou wouldst wreak thy vengeance on her, and molest Basil no further?"

"I did, and I meant it."

"See that thou keepest thy word. I am she!" And snatching the cup from the table, she quaffed it to the last drop, and instantly expired in convulsions.

We pass over the dismay of the banqueters, the arrest and confession of Helladia, the general amazement at the revelation of her sex, the frantic grief of the Emperor.

Basil's sorrow was sincere and durable. On an early occasion he thus addressed his courtiers:

"I cannot determine which of these two women loved me best: she who gave her life for me, or she who would have taken mine. The first made the greater sacrifice; the second did most violence to her feelings. What say ye?"

The courtiers hesitated, feeling themselves incompetent judges in problems of this nature. At length the youngest exclaimed:

"O Emperor, how can we tell thee, unless we know what thou thinkest thyself?"

"What!" exclaimed Basil, "an honest man in the Court of Byzantium! Let his mouth be filled with gold immediately!"

This operation having been performed, and the precious metal distributed in fees among the proper officers, Basil thus addressed the object of his favour:

"Manuel, thy name shall henceforth be Chrysostomus, in memory of what has just taken place. In further token of my approbation of thy honesty, I will confer upon thee the hand of the only other respectable person about the Court, namely, of Helladia. Take her, my son, and raise up a race of heroes! She shall be amply dowered out of what remains of the property of Photinius."

"Gennadius," whispered a cynical courtier to his neighbour, "I hope thou admirest the magnanimity of our sovereign, who deems he is performing a most generous action in presenting Manuel with his cast-off mistress, who has tried to poison him, and with whom he has been at his wits' end what to do, and in dowering her at the expense of another."

The snarl was just; but it is just also to acknowledge that Basil, as a prince born in the purple, had not the least idea that he was laying himself open to any such criticism. He actually did feel the manly glow of self-approbation which accompanies the performance of a good action: an emotion which no one else present, except Chrysostomus, was so much as able to conceive. It is further to be remarked that the old courtier who sneered at Chrysostomus was devoured by envy of his good fortune, and would have given his right eye to have been in his place.

"Chrysostomus," pursued Basil, "we must now think of the hapless Photinius. That unfortunate father is doubtless in an agony of grief which renders the forfeiture of the remains of his possessions indifferent to him. Thou, his successor therein, mayest be regarded as in some sort his son-in-law. Go, therefore, and comfort him, and report to me upon his condition."

Chrysostomus accordingly proceeded to the monastery, where he was informed that Photinius had retired with his spiritual adviser, and could on no account be disturbed.

"It is on my head to see the Emperor's orders obeyed," returned Chrysostomus, and forced the door. The bereaved parent was busily engaged in sticking pins into a wax effigy of Basil, under the direction of Panurgiades, already honourably mentioned in this history.

"Wretched old man!" exclaimed Chrysostomus, "is this thy grief for thy daughter?"

"My grief is great," answered Photinius, "but my time is small. If I turn not every moment to account, I shall never be prime minister again. But all is over now. Thou wilt denounce me, of course. I will give thee a counsel. Say that thou didst arrive just as we were about to place the effigy of Basil before a slow fire, and melt it into a caldron of bubbling poison."

"I shall report what I have seen," replied Chrysostomus, "neither more nor less. But I think I can assure thee that none will suffer for this mummery except Panurgiades, and that he will at most be whipped."

"Chrysostomus," said Basil, on receiving the report, "lust of power, a fever in youth, is a leprosy in age. The hoary statesman out of place would sell his daughter, his country, his soul, to regain it: yea, he would part with his skin and his senses, were it possible to hold office without them. I commiserate Photinius, whose faculties are clearly on the decline; the day has been when he would not have wasted his time sticking pins into a waxen figure. I will give him some shadow of authority to amuse his old days and keep him out of mischief. The Abbot of Catangion is just dead. Photinius shall succeed him."

So Photinius received the tonsure and the dignity, and made a very tolerable Abbot. It is even recorded to his honour that he bestowed a handsome funeral on his old enemy Eustathius.

Helladia made Chrysostomus an excellent wife, a little over-prudish, some thought. When, nearly two centuries afterwards, the Courts of Love came to be established in Provence, the question at issue between her and Euprepia was referred to those tribunals, which, finding the decision difficult, adjourned it for seven hundred years. That period having now expired, it is submitted to the British public.

# THE WISDOM OF THE INDIANS[1]

EVERYBODY KNOWS THAT in the reign of the Emperor Elagabalus Rome was visited by an embassy from India; whose members, on their way from the East, had held that memorable interview with the illustrious (though heretical) Christian philosopher Bardesanes which enabled him to formulate his doctrine of Fate, borrowed from the Indian theory of Karma, and therefore, until lately, grievously misunderstood by his commentators.

It may not, however, be equally notorious that the ambassadors returned by sea as far as Berytus, and upon landing there were hospitably entertained by the sage Euphronius, the head of the philosophical faculty of that University.

Euphronius naturally inquired what circumstance in Rome had appeared to his visitors most worthy of remark.

"The extreme evil of the Emperor's Karma," said they.

Euphronius requested further explanation.

"What have ye found so exceedingly reprehensible in the Emperor's conduct?" demanded Euphronius.

"To speak only," said the Indians, "of such of his doings as may fitly be recited to modest ears, we find him declaring war against Nature, and delighting in nothing that is not the contrary of what Heaven meant it to be. We see him bathing in perfumes, sailing ships in wine, feeding horses on grapes and lions on parrots, peppering fish with pearls, wearing gems on the soles of his feet, strewing his floor with gold-dust, paving the public streets with precious marbles, driving teams of stags, scorning to eat fish by the seaside, deploring his lot that he has never yet been able to dine on a phoenix. Enormous must have been the folly and wickedness which has incarnated itself in such a sovereign, and should his reign be prolonged, discouraging is the prospect for the morals of the next generation.

"According to you, then," said Euphronius, "the fates of men are not spun for them by Clotho, Lachesis, and Atropos, but by their predecessors?"

---

1 *The Wisdom of the Indians.*—Appeared in 1890 in *The Universal Review.* The idea was suggested by an incident in Dr. Bastian's travels in Burma.

"So it is," said they, "always remembering that man can rid himself of his Karma by philosophic meditation, combined with religious austerities, and that if all walked in this path, existence with all its evils would come to an end. Insomuch that the most bloodthirsty conqueror that ever devastated the earth hath not destroyed one thousandth part as many existences as the Lord Buddha."

"These are abstruse matters," said Euphronius, "and I lament that your stay in Berytus will not be long enough to instruct me adequately therein."

"Accompany us to India," said they, "and thou shalt receive instruction at the fountain head."

"I am old and feeble," apologised Euphronius, "and adjusted by long habit to my present environment. Nevertheless I will propound the enterprise to my pupils, only somewhat repressing their ardour, lest the volunteers should be inconveniently numerous."

When, however, the proposition was made not a soul responded; though Euphronius reproached his disciples severely, and desired them to compare their want of spirit with his own thirst for knowledge, which, when he was a young man, had taken him as far as Alexandria to hear a celebrated rhetorician. In the evening, however, two disciples came to him together, and professed their readiness to undertake the expedition, if promised a reward commensurate with its danger and difficulty.

"Ye would learn the secret of my celebrated dilemma," said he, "which no sophist can elude? 'Tis much; 'tis immoderate; 'tis enormous; nevertheless, bring the wisdom of India to Berytus, and the knowledge of the stratagem shall be yours."

"No, Master," they said, "it is not thy dilemma of which we are enamoured. It is thy daughter."

A vehement altercation ensued, but at length the old philosopher, who at the bottom of his heart was much readier to part with his daughter than his dilemma, was induced to promise her to whichever of the pupils should bring home the most satisfactory exposition of Indian metaphysics: provided always that during their absence he should not have been compelled to bestow her hand as the price of a quibble even more subtle than his own: but this he believed to be impossible.

Mnesitheus and Rufus accordingly travelled with the embassy to India, and arrived in safety at the metropolis of Palimbothra. They had wisely devoted themselves meanwhile to learning the language, and were now able to converse with some fluency.

On reaching their destination they were placed under the superintendence of competent instructors, who were commissioned to initiate them into the canon of Buddhist scriptures, comprising, to mention only a few of the principal, the Lalitavistara, the Dhammapada, the Kuddhapatha, the Palinokkha, the Uragavagga, the Kulavagga, the Mahavagga, the Atthakavagga, and the Upasampadakammavaca. These works, composed in dead languages, and written in strange and unknown characters, were further provided with commentaries more voluminous and inexplicable than the text.

"Heavens," exclaimed Mnesitheus and Rufus, "can the life of a man suffice to study all this?"

"Assuredly not," replied the Indians. "The diligent student will resume his investigations in a subsequent stage of existence, and, if endowed with eminent faculties, may hope to attain the end he proposes to himself at the fifteenth transmigration."

"The end we propose to ourselves," said the Greeks, "is to marry our master's daughter. Will the fair Euphronia also have undergone fifteen transmigrations, and will her charms have continued unimpaired?"

"It is difficult to pronounce," said they, "for should the maiden, through the exercise of virtue, have merited to be born as a white elephant, her transmigrations must in the order of nature be but few; whereas should she have unfortunately become and remained a rat, a frog, or other shortlived animal, they cannot but be exceedingly numerous."

"The prospect of wedding a frog at the end of fifteen transmigrations," said the youths, "doth not in any respect commend itself to us. Are there no means by which the course of study may be accelerated?"

"Undoubtedly," said the Indians, "by the practice of religious austerities."

"Of what nature are these?" inquired the young men.

"The intrepid disciple," said the sages, "may chain himself to a tree, and gaze upon the sun until he is deprived of the faculty of vision. He may drive an iron bar through his cheeks and tongue, thus preventing all misuse of the gift of speech. It is open to him to bury himself in the earth up to his waist, relying for his maintenance on the alms of pious donors. He may recline upon a couch studded with spikes, until from the induration of his skin he shall have merited the title of a rhinoceros among sages. As, however, these latter practices interfere with locomotion, and thus prevent his close attendance on his spiritual guide, it is rather recommended to him to elevate his arms above his head, and retain them in that position until, by the withering of the sinews, it is impossible for him to bring them down again."

"In that case," cried Rufus, "farewell philosophy! farewell Euphronia!"

There is reason to believe that Mnesitheus would have made exactly the same observation if Rufus had not been beforehand with him. The spirit of contradiction and the affectation of superiority, however, led him to reproach his rival with pusillanimity, and he went so far that at length he found himself committed to undergo the ordeal: merely stipulating that, in consideration of his being a foreigner, he should be permitted to elevate the right arm only.

The king of the country most graciously came to his assistance by causing him to be fastened to a tree, with his uplifted arm secured by iron bands above his head, a fan being put in his other hand to protect him against the molestations of gnats and mosquitoes. By this means, and with the assistance of the monks who continually recited and expounded the Buddhist scriptures in his ears, some time even before his arm had stiffened for ever, the doctrine of the misery of existence had become perfectly clear to him.

Released from his captivity, he hastened back to Europe to claim the guerdon of his sufferings. History is silent respecting his adventures until his arrival at Berytus, where the strange wild-looking man with the uplifted arm found himself the centre of a turbulent and mischievous rabble. As he seemed about to suffer severe ill-usage, a personage of dignified and portly appearance hastened up, and with his staff showered blows to right and left upon the rioters.

"Scoundrels," he exclaimed, "finely have ye profited by my precepts, thus to misuse an innocent stranger! But I will no longer dwell among such barbarians. I will remove my school to Tarsus!"

The mob dispersed. The victim and his deliverer stood face to face.

"Mnesitheus!"

"Rufus!"

"Call me Rufinianus," corrected the latter; "for such is the appellation which I have felt it due to myself to assume, since the enhancement of my dignity by becoming Euphronius's successor and son-in-law."

"Son-in-law! Am I to lose the reward of my incredible sufferings?"

"Thou forgettest," said Rufinianus, "that Euphronia's hand was not promised as the reward of any austerities, but as the meed of the most intelligent, that is, the most acceptable, account of the Indian philosophy, which in the opinion of the late eminent Euphronius, has been delivered by me. But come to my chamber, and let me minister to thy necessities."

These having been duly attended to, Rufinianus demanded Mnesitheus's history, and then proceeded to narrate his own.

"On my journey homeward," said he, "I reflected seriously on the probable purpose of our master in sending us forth, and saw reason to suspect that I had hitherto misapprehended it. For I could not remember that he had ever

admitted that he could have anything to learn from other philosophers, or
that he had ever exhibited the least interest in philosophic dogmas, excepting
his own. The system of the Indians, I thought, must be either inferior to that
of Euphronius, or superior. If the former, he will not want it: if the latter, he
will want it much less. I therefore concluded that our mission was partly
a concession to public opinion, partly to enable him to say that his name
was known, and his teaching proclaimed on the very banks of the Ganges.
I formed my plan accordingly, and disregarding certain indications that I
was neither expected nor wanted, presented myself before Euphronius with a
gladsome countenance, slightly overcast by sorrow on account of thee, whom
I affirmed to have been devoured by a tiger.

"'Well,' said Euphronius in a disdainful tone, 'and what about this vaunted
wisdom of the Indians?'

"'The wisdom of the Indians,' I replied, 'is entirely borrowed from
Pythagoras.'

"'Did I not tell you so?' Euphronius appealed to his disciples.

"'Invariably,' they replied.

"'As if a barbarian could teach a Greek!' said he.

"'It is much if he is able to learn from one,' said they.

"'Pythagoras, then,' said Euphronius addressing me, 'did not resort to
India to be instructed by the Gymnosophists?'

"'On the contrary,' I answered, 'he went there to teach them, and the little
knowledge of divine matters they possess is entirely derived from him. His
mission is recorded in a barbarous poem called the Ramayana, wherein he is
figuratively represented as allying himself with monkeys. He is worshipped
all over the country under the appellations of Siva, Kamadeva, Kali, Gautama
Buddha, and others too numerous to mention.'

"When I further proceeded to explain that a temple had been erected to
Euphronius himself on the banks of the Ganges, and that a festival, called
Durga Popja, or the Feast of Reason, had been instituted in his honour, his
good humour knew no bounds, and he granted me his daughter's hand
without difficulty. He died a few years ago, bequeathing me his celebrated
dilemma, and I am now head of his school and founder of the Rufinianian
philosophy. I am also the author of some admired works, especially a life of
Pythagoras, and a manual of Indian philosophy and religion. I hope for thy
own sake thou wilt forbear to contradict me: for no one will believe thee. I
trust also that thou wilt speedily overcome thy disappointment with respect
to Euphronia. I do most honestly and truthfully assure thee that for a one-
armed man like thee to marry her would be most inexpedient, inasmuch

as the defence of one's beard from her, when she is in a state of excitement, requires the full use of both hands, and of the feet also. But come with me to her chamber, and I will present thee to her. She is always taunting me with my inferiority to thee in personal attractions, and I promise myself much innocent amusement from her discomfiture when she finds thee as gaunt as a wolf and as black as a cinder. Only, as I have represented thee to have been devoured by a tiger, thou wilt kindly say that I saved thy life, but concealed the circumstance out of modesty."

"I have learned in the Indian schools," said Mnesitheus, "not to lie for the benefit of others. I will not see Euphronia; I would not disturb her ideal of me, nor mine of her. Farewell. May the Rufinianian sect flourish! and may thy works on Pythagoras and India instruct posterity to the tenth generation! I return to Palimbothra, where I am held in honour on the self-same account that here renders me ridiculous. It shall be my study to enlighten the natives respecting their obligations to Pythagoras, whose name I did not happen to hear while I abode among them."

# THE DUMB ORACLE[1]

Many the Bacchi that brandish the rod:
Few that be filled with the fire of the God.

## I

IN THE DAYS of King Attalus, before oracles had lost their credit, one of peculiar reputation, inspired, as was believed, by Apollo, existed in the city of Dorylseum, in Phrygia. Contrary to usage, its revelations were imparted through the medium of a male priest. It was rarely left unthronged by devout questioners, whose inquiries were resolved in writing, agreeably to the method delivered by the pious Lucian, in his work "Concerning False Prophecy."[2] Sometimes, on extraordinary occasions, a voice, evidently that of the deity, was heard declaring the response from the innermost recesses of the shrine. The treasure house of the sanctuary was stored with tripods and goblets, in general wrought from the precious metals; its coffers were loaded with coins and ingots; the sacrifices of wealthy suppliants and the copious offerings in kind of the country people provided superabundantly for the daily maintenance of the temple servitors; while a rich endowment in land maintained the dignity of its guardians, and of the officiating priest. The latter reverend personage was no less eminent for prudence than for piety; on which account the Gods had rewarded him with extreme obesity. At length he died, whether of excess in meat or in drink is not agreed among historians.

The guardians of the temple met to choose a successor, and, naturally desirous that the sanctity of the oracle should suffer no abatement, elected a young priest of goodly presence and ascetic life; the humblest, purest, most fervent, and most ingenuous of the sons of men. So rare a choice might well be expected to be accompanied by some extraordinary manifestation, and, in fact, a prodigy took place which filled the sacred authorities with dismay.

---

1   *The Dumb Oracle.*—Appeared in the *University Magazine* for June, 1878. The legend on which it is founded, a mediaeval myth here transferred to classical times, is also the groundwork of Browning's ballad, "The Boy and the Angel."
2   *Pseudomantis*, cap. 19–21.

The responses of the oracle ceased suddenly and altogether. No revelation was vouchsafed to the pontiff in his slumbers; no access of prophetic fury constrained him to disclose the secrets of the future; no voice rang from the shrine; and the unanswered epistles of the suppliants lay a hopeless encumbrance on the great altar. As a natural consequence they speedily ceased to arrive; the influx of offerings into the treasury terminated along with them; the temple-courts were bare of worshippers; and the only victims whose blood smoked within them were those slain by the priest himself, in the hope of appeasing the displeasure of Apollo. The modest hierophant took all the blame upon his own shoulders; he did not doubt that he had excited the Deity's wrath by some mysterious but heinous pollution; and was confirmed in this opinion by the unanimous verdict of all whom he approached.

One day as he sat sadly in the temple, absorbed in painful meditation, and pondering how he might best relieve himself of his sacred functions, he was startled by the now unwonted sound of a footstep, and, looking up, espied an ancient woman. Her appearance was rather venerable than prepossessing. He recognised her as one of the inferior ministers of the temple.

"Reverend mother," he addressed her, "doubtless thou comest to mingle with mine thy supplications to the Deity, that it may please him to indicate the cause, and the remedy of his wrath."

"No, son," returned the venerable personage, "I propose to occasion no such needless trouble to Apollo, or any other Divinity. I hold within mine own hand the power of reviving the splendour of this forsaken sanctuary, and for such consideration as thou wilt thyself pronounce equitable, I am minded to impart the same unto thee." And as the astonished priest made no answer, she continued:

"My price is one hundred pieces of gold."

"Wretch!" exclaimed the priest indignantly, "thy mercenary demand alone proves the vanity of thy pretence of being initiated into the secrets of the Gods. Depart my presence this moment!"

The old woman retired without a syllable of remonstrance, and the incident soon passed from the mind of the afflicted priest. But on the following day, at the same hour, the aged woman again stood before him, and said:

"My price is *two* hundred pieces of gold."

Again she was commanded to depart, and again obeyed without a murmur. But the adventure now occasioned the priest much serious reflection. To his excited fancy, the patient persistency of the crone began to assume something of a supernatural character. He considered that the ways of the Gods are not as our ways, and that it is rather the rule than the exception with them to accomplish their designs in the most circuitous manner, and by the most unlikely instruments. He also reflected upon the history of the Sibyl and her books, and shuddered to think that unseasonable obstinacy might in the end cost the temple the whole of its revenues. The result of his cogitations was a resolution, if the old woman should present herself on the following day, to receive her in a different manner.

Punctual to the hour she made her appearance, and croaked out, "My price is *three* hundred pieces of gold."

"Venerable ambassadress of Heaven," said the priest, "thy boon is granted thee. Relieve the anguish of my bosom as speedily as thou mayest."

The old woman's reply was brief and expressive. It consisted in extending her open and hollow palm, into which the priest counted the three hundred pieces of gold with as much expedition as was compatible with the frequent interruptions necessitated by the crone's depositing each successive handful in a leather pouch; and the scrutiny, divided between jealousy and affection, which she bestowed on each individual coin.

"And now," said the priest, when the operation was at length completed, "fulfil thy share of the compact."

"The cause of the oracle's silence," returned the old woman, "is the unworthiness of the minister."

"Alas! 'tis even as I feared," sighed the priest. "Declare now, wherein consists my sin?"

"It consists in this," replied the old woman, "that the beard of thy understanding is not yet grown; and that the egg-shell of thy inexperience is still sticking to the head of thy simplicity; and that thy brains bear no adequate proportion to the skull enveloping them; and in fine, lest I seem to speak overmuch in parables, or to employ a superfluity of epithets, that thou art an egregious nincompoop."

And as the amazed priest preserved silence, she pursued:

"Can aught be more shameful in a religious man than ignorance of the very nature of religion? Not to know that the term, being rendered into the language of truth, doth therein signify deception practised by the few wise upon the many foolish, for the benefit of both, but more particularly the former? O silly as the crowds who hitherto have brought their folly here, but now carry it elsewhere to the profit of wiser men than thou! O fool! to deem that oracles were rendered by Apollo! How should this be, seeing that there is no such person? Needs there, peradventure, any greater miracle for the decipherment of these epistles than a hot needle?[3] As for the supernatural voice, it doth in truth proceed from a respectable, and in some sense a sacred personage, being mine own when I am concealed within a certain recess prepared for me by thy lamented predecessor, whose mistress I was in youth, and whose coadjutor I have been in age. I am now ready to minister to thee in the latter capacity. Be ruled by me; exchange thy abject superstition for common sense; thy childish simplicity for discreet policy; thy unbecoming spareness for a majestic portliness; thy present ridiculous and uncomfortable situation for the repute of sanctity, and the veneration of men. Thou wilt own that this is cheap at three hundred pieces."

The young priest had hearkened to the crone's discourse with an expression of the most exquisite distress. When she had finished, he arose, and disregarding his repulsive companion's efforts to detain him, departed hastily from the temple.

## II

IT was the young priest's purpose, as soon as he became capable of forming one, to place the greatest possible distance between himself and the city of Dorylæum. The love of roaming insensibly grew upon him, and ere long his active limbs had borne him over a considerable portion of Asia. His simple wants were easily supplied by the wild productions of the country, supplemented when needful by the proceeds of light manual labour. By degrees the self-contempt which had originally stung him to desperation took the form of an ironical compassion for the folly of mankind, and the restlessness which had at first impelled him to seek relief in a change of scene gave place to a spirit of curiosity and observation. He learned to mix freely with all orders of men, save one, and rejoiced to find the narrow mysticism which he had imbibed from his previous education gradually yielding to contact with the great world. From one class of men, indeed, he learned nothing—the priests, whose society he eschewed with scrupulous vigilance, nor did he ever enter the temples of the Gods. Diviners, augurs, all that made any pretension whatever to a supernatural character, he held in utter abhorrence, and his ultimate return in the direction of his native country is attributed to his inability to persevere further in the path he was following without danger of encountering Chaldean soothsayers, or Persian magi, or Indian gymnosophists.

He cherished, however, no intention of returning to Phrygia, and was still at a considerable distance from that region, when one night, as he was sitting

---

3   Lucian.

in the inn of a small country town, his ear caught a phrase which arrested his attention.

"As true as the oracle of Dorylæum." The speaker was a countryman, who appeared to have been asseverating something regarded by the rest of the company as greatly in need of confirmation. The sudden start and stifled cry of the ex-priest drew all eyes to him, and he felt constrained to ask, with the most indifferent air he could assume:

"Is the oracle of Dorylæum, then, so exceedingly renowned for veracity?"

"Whence comest thou to be ignorant of that?" demanded the countryman, with some disdain. "Hast thou never heard of the priest Eubulides?"

"Eubulides!" exclaimed the young traveller, "that is my own name!"

"Thou mayest well rejoice, then," observed another of the guests, "to bear the name of one so holy and pure, and so eminently favoured by the happy Gods. So handsome and dignified, moreover, as I may well assert who have often beheld him discharging his sacred functions. And truly, now that I scan thee more closely, the resemblance is marvellous. Only that thy namesake bears with him a certain air of divinity, not equally conspicuous in thee."

"Divinity!" exclaimed another. "Aye, if Phœbus himself ministered at his own shrine, he could wear no more majestic semblance than Eubulides."

"Or predict the future more accurately," added a priest.

"Or deliver his oracles in more exquisite verse," subjoined a poet.

"Yet is it not marvellous," remarked another speaker, "that for some considerable time after his installation the good Eubulides was unable to deliver a single oracle?"

"Aye, and that the first he rendered should have foretold the death of an aged woman, one of the ministers of the temple."

"Ha!" exclaimed Eubulides, "how was that?"

"He prognosticated her decease on the following day, which accordingly came to pass, from her being choked with a piece of gold, not lawfully appertaining to herself, which she was endeavouring to conceal under the root of her tongue."

"The Gods be praised for that!" ejaculated Eubulides, under his breath. "Pshaw! as if there were Gods! If they existed, would they tolerate this vile mockery? To keep up the juggle—well, I know it must be so; but to purloin my name! to counterfeit my person! By all the Gods that are not, I will expose the cheat, or perish in the endeavour."

He arose early on the following morning and took his way towards the city of Dorylæum. The further he progressed in this direction, the louder became the bruit of the oracle of Apollo, and the more emphatic the testimonies to the piety, prophetic endowments, and personal attractions of the priest Eubulides; his own resemblance to whom was the theme of continual remark. On approaching the city, he found the roads swarming with throngs hastening to the temple, about to take part in a great religious ceremony to be held therein. The seriousness of worship blended delightfully with the glee of the festival, and Eubulides, who at first regarded the gathering with bitter scorn, found his moroseness insensibly yielding to the poetic charm of the scene. He could not but acknowledge that the imposture he panted to expose was at least the source of much innocent happiness, and almost wished that the importance of religion, considered as an engine of policy, had been offered to his contemplation from this point of view, instead of the sordid and revolting aspect in which it had been exhibited by the old woman.

In this ambiguous frame of mind he entered the temple. Before the high altar stood the officiating priest, a young man, the image, yet not the image, of himself. Lineament for lineament, the resemblance was exact, but over the stranger's whole figure was diffused an air of majesty, of absolute serenity and infinite superiority, which excluded every idea of deceit, and so awed the young priest that his purpose of rushing forward to denounce the impostor and drag him from the shrine was immediately and involuntarily relinquished. As he stood confounded and irresolute, the melodious voice of the hierophant rang through the temple:

"Let the priest Eubulides stand forth."

This summons naturally caused the greatest astonishment in every one but Eubulides, who emerged as swiftly as he could from the swaying and murmuring crowd, and confronted his namesake at the altar. A cry of amazement broke from the multitude as they beheld the pair, whose main distinction in the eyes of most was their garb. But, as they gazed, the form of the officiating priest assumed colossal proportions; a circle of beams, dimming sunlight, broke forth around his head; hyacinthine locks clustered on his shoulders, his eyes sparkled with supernatural radiance; a quiver depended at his back; an unstrung bow occupied his hand; the majesty and benignity of his presence alike seemed augmented tenfold. Eubulides and the crowd sank simultaneously on their knees, for all recognised Apollo.

All was silence for a space. It was at length broken by Phœbus.

"Well, Eubulides," inquired he, with the bland raillery of an Immortal, "has it at length occurred to thee that I may have been long enough away from Parnassus, filling thy place here while thou hast been disporting thyself amid heretics and barbarians?"

The abashed Eubulides made no response. The Deity continued:

"Deem not that thou hast in aught excited the displeasure of the Gods. In deserting their altars for Truth's sake, thou didst render them the most acceptable of sacrifices, the only one, it may be, by which they set much store. But, Eubulides, take heed how thou again sufferest the unworthiness of men to overcome the instincts of thine own nature. Thy holiest sentiments should not have been at the mercy of a knave. If the oracle of Dorylæum was an imposture, hadst thou no oracle in thine own bosom? If the voice of Religion was no longer breathed from the tripod, were the winds and waters silent, or had aught quenched the everlasting stars? If there was no power to impose its mandates from without, couldst thou be unconscious of a power within? If thou hadst nothing to reveal unto men, mightest thou not have found some-what to propound unto them? Know this, that thou hast never experienced a more truly religious emotion than that which led thee to form the design of overthrowing this my temple, the abode, as thou didst deem it, of fraud and superstition."

"But now, Phœbus," Eubulides ventured to reply, "shall I not return to the shrine purified by thy presence, and again officiate as thy unworthy minister?"

"No, Eubulides," returned Phœbus, with a smile; "silver is good, but not for ploughshares. Thy strange experience, thy long wanderings, thy lonely meditations, and varied intercourse with men, have spoiled thee for a priest, while, as I would fain hope, qualifying thee for a sage. Some worthy person may easily be found to preside over this temple; and by the aid of such inspiration as I may from time to time see meet to vouchsafe him, administer its affairs indifferently well. Do thou, Eubulides, consecrate thy powers to a more august service than Apollo's, to one that shall endure when Delphi and Delos know *his* no more."

"To whose service, Phœbus?" inquired Eubulides.

"To the service of Humanity, my son," responded Apollo.

# DUKE VIRGIL[1]

## I

THE CITIZENS OF Mantua were weary of revolutions. They had acknowledged the suzerainty of the Emperor Frederick and shaken it off. They had had a Podestà of their own and had shaken him off. They had expelled a Papal Legate, incurring excommunication thereby. They had tried dictators, consuls, prætors, councils of ten, and other numbers odd and even, and ere the middle of the thirteenth century were luxuriating in the enjoyment of perfect anarchy.

An assembly met daily in quest of a remedy, but its members were forbidden to propose anything old, and were unable to invent anything new.

"Why not consult Manto, the alchemist's daughter, our prophetess, our Sibyl?" the young Benedetto asked at last.

"Why not?" repeated Eustachio, an elderly man.

"Why not, indeed?" interrogated Leonardo, a man of mature years.

All the speakers were noble. Benedetto was Manto's lover; Eustachio her father's friend; Leonardo his creditor. Their advice prevailed, and the three were chosen as a deputation to wait on the prophetess. Before proceeding formally on their embassy the three envoys managed to obtain private interviews, the two elder with Manto's father, the youth with Manto herself. The creditor promised that if he became Duke by the alchemist's influence with his daughter he would forgive the debt; the friend went further, and vowed that he would pay it. The old man promised his good word to both, but when he went to confer with his daughter he found her closeted with Benedetto, and returned without disburdening himself of his errand. The youth had just risen from his knees, pleading with her, and drawing glowing pictures of their felicity when he should be Duke and she Duchess.

---

1 *Duke Virgil.*—The subject of this story is derived from Leopold Schefer's novel, "Die Sibylle von Mantua," though there is but little resemblance in the incidents. Schefer cites Friedrich von Quandt as his authority for the Mantuans having actually elected Virgil as their duke in the thirteenth century: but the notion seems merely founded upon the interpretation of the insignia accompanying a mediæval statue of the poet.

She answered, "Benedetto, in all Mantua there is not one man fit to rule another. To name any living person would be to set a tyrant over my native city. I will repair to the shades and seek a ruler among the dead."

"And why should not Mantua have a tyrant?" demanded Benedetto. "The freedom of the mechanic is the bondage of the noble, who values no liberty save that of making the base-born do his bidding. 'Tis hell to a man of spirit to be contradicted by his tailor. If I could see my heart's desire on the knaves, little would I reck submitting to the sway of the Emperor."

"I know that well, Benedetto," said Manto, "and hence will take good heed not to counsel Mantua to choose thee. No, the Duke I will give her shall be one without passions to gratify or injuries to avenge, and shall already be crowned with a crown to make the ducal cap as nothing in his eyes, if eyes he had."

Benedetto departed in hot displeasure, and the alchemist came forward to announce that the commissioners waited.

"My projection," he whispered, "only wants one more piece of gold to insure success, and Eustachio proffers thirty. Oh, give him Mantua in exchange for boundless riches!"

"And they call thee a philosopher and me a visionary!" said Manto, patting his cheek.

The envoys' commission having been unfolded, she took not a moment to reply, "Be your Duke Virgil."

The deputation respectfully represented that although Virgil was no doubt Mantua's greatest citizen, he laboured under the disqualification of having been dead more than twelve hundred years. Nothing further, however, could be extorted from the prophetess, and the ambassadors were obliged to withdraw.

The interpretation of Manto's oracle naturally provoked much diversity of opinion in the council.

"Obviously," said a poet, "the prophetess would have us confer the ducal dignity upon the contemporary bard who doth most nearly accede to the vestiges of the divine Maro; and he, as I judge, is even now in the midst of you."

"Virgil the poet," said a priest, who had long laboured under the suspicion of occult practices, "was a fool to Virgil the enchanter. The wise woman evidently demands one competent to put the devil into a hole[2]—an operation

2   *To put the devil into a hole.*—"Then sayd Virgilius, 'Shulde ye well passe in to the hole that ye cam out of?' 'Yea, I shall well,' sayd the devyl. 'I holde the best plegge that I have, that ye shall not do it.' 'Well,' sayd the devyll, 'thereto I consent.' And then the devyll wrange himselfe into

which I have striven to perform all my life."

"Canst thou balance our city upon an egg?" inquired Eustachio.[3]

"Better upon an egg than upon a quack!" retorted the priest.

But such was not the opinion of Eustachio himself, who privately conferred with Leonardo. Eustachio had a character, but no parts; Leonardo had parts, but no character.

"I see not why these fools should deride the oracle of the prophetess," he said. "She would doubtless impress upon us that a dead master is in divers respects preferable to a living one."

"Surely," said Eustachio, "provided always that the servant is a man of exemplary character, and that he presumes not upon his lord's withdrawal to another sphere, trusting thereby to commit malpractices with impunity, but doth, on the contrary, deport himself as ever in his great taskmaster's eye."

"Eustachio," said Leonardo, with admiration, "it is the misery of Mantua that she hath no citizen who can act half as well as thou canst talk. I would fain have further discourse with thee."

The two statesmen laid their heads together, and ere long the mob were crying, "A Virgil! a Virgil!"

The councillors reassembled and passed resolutions.

"But who shall be Regent?" inquired some one when Virgil had been elected unanimously.

"Who but we?" asked Eustachio and Leonardo. "Are we not the heads of the Virgilian party?"

Thus had the enthusiastic Manto, purest of idealists, installed in authority the two most unprincipled politicians in the republic; and she had lost her lover besides, for Benedetto fled the city, vowing vengeance.

Anyhow, the dead poet was enthroned Duke of Mantua; Eustachio and Leonardo became Regents, with the style of Consuls, and it was provided that in doubtful cases reference should be made to the Sortes Virgilianae. And truly, if we may believe the chronicles, the arrangement worked for a time surprisingly well. The Mantuans, in an irrational way, had done what it behoves all communities to do rationally if they can. They had sought for a good and worthy citizen to rule them; it was their misfortune that such an

---

the lytyll hole ageyne, and he was therein. Virgilius kyvered the hole ageyne with the borde close, and so was the devyll begyled, and myght nat there come out agen, but abideth shutte still therein" ("Romance of Virgilius").

3  *Ibid. Canst thou balance our city upon an egg?*—"Than he thought in his mynde to founde in the middle of the sea a fayre towne, with great landes belongynge to it, and so he did by his cunnynge, and called it Napells. And the foundacyon of it was of eggs" ("Romance of Virgilius").

one could only be found among the dead. They felt prouder of themselves
for being governed by a great man—one in comparison with whom kings
and pontiffs were the creatures of a day. They would not, if they could help
it, disgrace themselves by disgracing their hero; they would not have it said
that Mantua, which had not been too weak to bear him, had been too weak
to endure his government. The very hucksters and usurers among them
felt dimly that there was such a thing as an Ideal. A glimmering perception
dawned upon mailed, steel-fisted barons that there was such a thing as an
Idea, and they felt uneasily apprehensive, like beasts of prey who have for the
first time sniffed gunpowder. The railleries and mockeries of Mantua's neighbours, moreover, stimulated Mantua's citizens to persevere in their course,
and deterred them from doing aught to approve themselves fools. Were not
Verona, Cremona, Lodi, Pavia, Crema, cities that could never enthrone the
Virgil they had never produced, watching with undissembled expectation to
see them trip? The hollow-hearted Eustachio and the rapacious Leonardo,
their virtual rulers, might indeed be little sensible to this enthusiasm, but
they could not disregard the general drift of public opinion, which said
clearly: "Mantua is trying a great experiment. Woe to you if you bring it to
nought by your selfish quarrels!"

The best proof that there was something in Manto's idea was that after a
while the Emperor Frederick took alarm, and signified to the Mantuans that
they must cease their mumming and fooling and acknowledge him as their
sovereign, failing which he would besiege their city.

## II

MANTUA was girt by a zone of fire and steel. Her villas and homesteads
flamed or smoked; her orchards flared heavenward in a torrent of sparks or
stood black sapless trunks charred to their inmost pith; the promise of her
harvests lay as grey ashes over the land. But her ramparts, though breached
in places, were yet manned by her sons, and their assailants recoiled pierced
by the shafts or stunned by the catapults of the defence. Kaiser Frederick sat
in his tent, giving secret audience to one who had stolen in disguise over
from the city in the grey of the morning. By the Emperor's side stood a tall
martial figure, wearing a visor which he never removed.

"Your Majesty," Leonardo was saying, for it was he, "this madness will
soon pass away. The people will weary of sacrificing themselves for a dead
heathen."

"And Liberty?" asked the Emperor, "is not that a name dear to those misguided creatures?"

"So dear, please your Majesty, that if they have but the name they will per-fectly dispense with the thing. I do not advise that your imperial yoke should be too palpably adjusted to their stiff necks. Leave them in appearance the choice of their magistrate, but insure its falling upon one of approved fidelity, certain to execute obsequiously all your Majesty's mandates; such an one, in short, as your faithful vassal Leonardo. It would only be necessary to decapi-tate that dangerous revolutionist, Eustachio."

"And the citizens are really ready for this?"

"All the respectable citizens. All of whom your Majesty need take account. All men of standing and substance."

"I rejoice to hear it," said the Emperor, "and do the more readily credit thee inasmuch as a most virtuous and honourable citizen hath already been beforehand with thee, assuring me of the same thing, and affirming that but one traitor, whose name, methinks, sounded like thine, stands between me and the subjugation of Mantua."

And, withdrawing a curtain, he disclosed the figure of Eustachio.

"I thought he was asleep," muttered Eustachio.

"That noodle to have been beforehand with me!" murmured Leonardo.

"What perplexes me," continued Frederick, after enjoying the confusion of the pair for a few moments, "is that our masked friend here will have it that he is the man for the Dukedom, and offers to open the gates to me by a method of his own."

"By fair fighting, an' please my liege," observed the visored personage, "not by these dastardly treacheries."

"How inhuman!" sighed Eustachio.

"How old-fashioned!" sneered Leonardo.

"The truth is," continued Frederick, "he gravely doubts whether either of you possesses the influence which you allege, and has devised a method of putting this to the proof, which I trust will commend itself to you."

Leonardo and Eustachio expressed their readiness to submit their credit with their fellow-citizens to any reasonable trial.

"He proposes, then," pursued the Emperor, "that ye, disarmed and bound, should be placed at the head of the storming column, and in that situation should, as questionless ye would, exert your entire moral influence with your fellow-citizens to dissuade them from shooting you. If the column, thus shielded, enters the city without resistance, ye will both have earned the Dukedom, and the question who shall have it may be decided by single combat between yourselves. But should the people, rather than submit to our clemency, impiously slay their elected magistrates, it will be apparent that the methods of our martial friend are the only ones corresponding to the exigency of the case. Is the storming column ready?"

"All but the first file, please your Majesty," responded the man in the visor.

"Let it be equipped," returned Frederick, and in half-an-hour Eustachio and Leonardo, their hands tied behind them, were stumbling up the breach, impelled by pikes in the rear, and confronting the catapults, *chevaux de frise*, hidden pitfalls, Greek fire, and boiling water provided by their own direction, and certified to them the preceding evening as all that could be desired. They had, however, the full use of their voices, and this they turned to the best account. Never had Leonardo been so cogent, or Eustachio so pathetic. The Mantuans, already disorganised by the unaccountable disappearance of the Executive, were entirely irresolute what to do. As they hesitated the visored chief incited his followers. All seemed lost, when a tall female figure appeared among the defenders. It was Manto.

"Fools and cowards!" she exclaimed, "must ye learn your duty from a woman?"

And, seizing a catapult, she discharged a stone which laid the masked warrior stunned and senseless on the ground. The next instant Eustachio and Leonardo fell dead, pierced by showers of arrows. The Mantuans sallied forth. The dismayed Imperialists fled to their camp. The bodies of the fallen magistrates and of the unconscious chieftain in the mask were brought into the city. Manto herself undid the fallen man's visor, and uttered a fearful shriek as she recognised Benedetto.

"What shall be done with him, mistress?" they asked.

Manto long stood silent, torn by conflicting emotions. At length she said, in a strange, unnatural voice:

"Put him into the Square Tower."

"And now, mistress, what further? How to choose the new consuls?"

"Ask me no more," she said. "I shall never prophesy again. Virtue has gone away from me."

The leaders departed, to intrigue for the vacant posts, and devise tortures for Benedetto. Manto sat on the rampart, still and silent as its stones. Anon she rose, and roved about as if distraught, reciting verses from Virgil.

Night had fallen. Benedetto lay wakeful in his cell. A female figure stood before him bearing a lamp. It was Manto.

"Benedetto," she said, "I am a wretch, faithless to my country and to my master. I did but even now open his sacred volume at hazard, and on what did my eye first fall? Trojaque nunc stares, Priamique arx alta maneres. But I can no other. I am a woman. May Mantua never entrust her fortunes to the like of me again!

Come with me, I will release thee."

She unlocked his chains; she guided him through the secret passage under the moat; they stood at the exit, in the open air.

"Fly," she said, "and never again draw sword against thy mother. I will return to my house, and do that to myself which it behoved me to have done ere I released thee."

"Manto," exclaimed Benedetto "a truce to this folly! Forsake thy dead Duke, and that cheat of Liberty more crazy and fantastic still. Wed a living Duke in me!"

"Never!" exclaimed Manto. "I love thee more than any man living on earth, and I would not espouse thee if the earth held no other."

"Thou canst not help thyself," he rejoined; "thou hast revealed to me the secret of this passage. I hasten to the camp. I return in an hour with an army, and wilt thou, wilt thou not, to-morrow's sun shall behold thee the partner of my throne!"

Manto wore a poniard. She struck Benedetto to the heart, and he fell dead. She drew the corpse back into the passage, and hurried to her home. Opening her master's volume again, she read:

Tædet coeli convexa tueri.

A few minutes afterwards her father entered the chamber to tell her he had at last found the philosopher's stone, but, perceiving his daughter hanging by her girdle, he forbore to intrude upon her, and returned to his laboratory.

It was time. A sentinel of the besiegers had marked Benedetto's fall, and the disappearance of the body into the earth. A pool of blood revealed the entrance to the passage. Ere sunrise Mantua was full of Frederick's soldiers, full also of burning houses, rifled sanctuaries, violated damsels, children playing with their dead mothers' breasts, especially full of citizens protesting that they had ever longed for the restoration of the Emperor, and that this was the happiest day of their lives. Frederick waited till everybody was killed, then entered the city and proclaimed an amnesty. Virgil's bust was broken, and his writings burned with Manto's body. The flames glowed on the dead face, which gleamed as it were with pleasure. The old alchemist had been slain among his crucibles; his scrolls were preserved with jealous care.

But Manto found another father. She sat at Virgil's feet in Elysium; and as he stroked the fair head, now golden with perpetual youth, listened to his mild reproofs and his cheerful oracles. By her side stood a bowl filled with the untasted waters of Lethe.

"Woe," said Virgil—but his manner contradicted his speech—"woe to the idealist and enthusiast! Woe to them who live in the world to come! Woe to them who live only for a hope whose fulfilment they will not behold on earth! Drink not, therefore, of that cup, dear child, lest Duke Virgil's day should come, and thou shouldst not know it. For come it will, and all the sooner for thy tragedy and thy comedy."

# THE CLAW[1]

T HE BALM AND stillness of a summer's night enveloped a spacious piazza in the city of Shylock and Desdemona. The sky teemed with light drifting clouds through which the beaming of the full moon broke at intervals upon some lamp-lit palace, thronged and musical, for it was a night of festivity, or silvered the dull creeping waters. Ever and anon some richly attired young patrician descended the steps of one or other of these mansions, and hurried across the wide area to the canal stairs, where his gondola awaited him. Whoever did this could not but observe a tall female figure, which, cloaked and masked, walked backwards and forwards across the piazza, regarding no one, yet with an air that seemed to invite a companion.

More than one of the young nobles approached the presumably fair peripatetic, and, with courtesy commonly in inverse ratio to the amount of wine he was carrying home, proffered his escort to his gondola. Whenever this happened the figure removed her mask and unclasped her robe, and revealed a sight which for one moment rooted the young man to the earth and in the next sent him scampering to his bark. For the countenance was a death's head, and the breast was that of a mouldering skeleton.

At last, however, a youth presented himself who, more courageous or more tipsy than his fellows, or more helplessly paralysed with horror than they, did not decline the proffered caress, and suffered himself to be drawn within the goblin's accursed embrace. Valiant or pot-valiant, great was his relief at finding himself clasped, instead of by a loathsome spectre, by a silver-haired man of noble presence, yet with a countenance indescribably haggard and anxious.

"Come, my son," he cried, "hasten whither the rewards of thy intrepidity await thee. Impouch the purse of Fortunatus! Indue the signet of Solomon!"

The young man hesitated. "Is there nought else?" he cautiously demanded. "Needs it not that I should renounce my baptism? Must I not subscribe an infernal compact?"

---

1  *The Claw.*—Originally published in *The English Illustrated Magazine.*

"In thy own blood, my son," cheerfully responded the old gentleman.

"Peradventure," hesitatingly interrogated the youth, "peradventure you are *he*?"

"Not so, my son, upon honour," returned the mysterious personage. "I am but a distressed magician, at this present in fearful straits, from which I look to be delivered by thee."

The youth gazed some moments at his companion's head, and then still more earnestly at his feet. He then yielded his own hand to him, and the pair crossed the piazza, almost at a run, the magician ever ejaculating, "Speed! speed!"

They paused at the foot of a lofty tower, doorless and windowless, with no visible access of any kind. But the magician signed with his hand, pronounced some cabalistical words, and instantly stone and lime fell asunder and revealed an entrance through which they passed, and which immediately closed behind them. The youth quaked at finding himself alone in utter darkness with he knew not what, but the wizard whistled, and a severed hand appeared in air bearing a lamp which illuminated a long winding staircase. The old man motioned to the youth to precede him, nor dared he refuse, though feeling as though he would have given the world for the very smallest relic of the very smallest saint. The distorted shadows of the twain, dancing on stair and wall with the wavering lamp-shine, seemed phantoms capering in an infernal revel, and he glanced back ever and anon weening to see himself dogged by some frightful monster, but he saw only the silver hair and sable velvet of the dignified old man.

After the ascent of many steps a door opened before them, and they found themselves in a spacious chamber, brightly, yet from its size imperfectly illumined by a single large lamp. It was wainscoted with ebony, and the furniture was of the same. A long table was covered with scrolls, skulls, crucibles, crystals, star-charts, geomantic figures, and other appurtenances of a magician's calling. Tomes of necromantic lore lined the walls, which were yet principally occupied with crystal vessels, in which foul beings seemed dimly and confusedly to agitate themselves.

The magician signed to his visitor to be seated, sat down himself and began:

"Brave youth, ere entering upon the boundless power and riches that await thee, learn who I am and why I have brought thee here. Behold in me no vulgar wizard, no mere astrologer or alchemist, but a compeer of Merlin and Michael Scott, with whose name it may be the nurse of thy infancy hath oft-times quelled thy froward humours. I am Peter of Abano,[2] falsely believed to have lain two centuries buried in the semblance of a dog under a heap of stones hurled by the furious populace, but in truth walking earth to this day, in virtue of the compact now to be revealed to thee. Hearken, my son! Vain must be the machinations of my enemies, vain the onslaughts of the rabble, so long as I fulfil a certain contract registered in hell's chancery, as I have now done these three hundred years. And the condition is this, that every year I present unto the Demon one who hath at my persuasion assigned his soul to him in exchange for power, riches, knowledge, magical gifts, or whatever else his heart chiefly desireth; nor until this present year have I perilled the fulfilment of my obligation. Seest thou these scrolls? They are the assignments of which I have spoken. It would amaze thee to scan the subscriptions, and perceive in these the signatures of men exemplary in the eyes of their fellows, clothed with high dignities in Church and State—nay sometimes redolent of the very odour of sanctity. Never hath my sagacity deceived me until this year, when, smitten with the fair promise of a youth of singular impishness, I omitted to take due note of his consumptive habit, and have but this afternoon encountered his funeral. This is the last day of my year, and should my engagement be unredeemed when the sun attains the cusp of that nethermost house of heaven which he is even now traversing, I must become an inmate of the infernal kingdom. No time has remained for nice investigation. I have therefore proved the courage of the Venetian youth in the manner thou knowest, and thou alone hast sustained the ordeal. Fail not at my bidding, or thou quittest not this chamber alive. For when the Demon comes to bear me away, he will assuredly rend thee in pieces for being found in my company. Thou hast, therefore, everything to gain and nothing to lose by joining the goodly fellowship of my mates and partners. Delay not, time urges, night deepens, they that would drink thy blood are abroad. Hearest thou not the moaning and pelting of the rising storm, and the muttering and scraping of my imprisoned goblins? Save us,

---

2  *Peter of Abano.*—Pietro di Abano, who took his name from his birthplace, a village near Padua, was a physician contemporary with Dante, whose skill in medicine and astrology caused him to be accused of magic. It is nevertheless untrue that he was burned by the Inquisition or stoned by the populace; but after his death he was burned in effigy, his remains having been secretly removed by his friends. Honours were afterwards paid to his memory; and there seems no doubt that he was a man of great attainments, including a knowledge of Greek, and of unblemished character, if he had not sometimes sold his skill at too high a rate. For his authentic history, see the article in the *Biographie Universelle* by Ginguené; for the legendary, Tieck's romantic tale, "Pietro von Abano" (1825), which has been translated into English.

I entreat, I command, save us both!"

Screaming with agitation the aged sorcerer laid a scroll engrossed with fairly written characters before the youth, stabbed the latter's arm with a stylus that at once evoked and collected the crimson stream, thrust this into his hand and strove to guide it to the parchment, chanting at the same time litanies to the infernal powers. The crystal flagons rang like one great harmonica with shrill but spirit-stirring music; volumes of vaporous perfumes diffused themselves through the apartment, and an endless procession of treasure-laden figures defiled before the bewildered youth. He seemed buried in the opulence of the world, as he sat up to his waist in gold and jewels; all the earth's beauty gazed at him through eyes brilliant and countless as the stars of heaven; courtiers beckoned him to thrones; battle-steeds neighed and pawed for his mounting; laden tables allured every appetite; vassals bent in homage; slaves fell prostrate at his feet. Now he seemed to collect or disperse legions of spirits with the waving of a wand; anon, as he pronounced a spell, golden dragons glided away from boughs laden with golden fruits. Well for him, doubtless, that in him Nature had kneaded from ordinary clay as unimaginative a youth as could be found in Venice: yet even so, dazzled with glamour, intoxicated with illusion, less and less able to resist the cunningly mingled caresses, entreaties, and menaces of Abano, he could not refrain from tracing a few characters with the stylus, when, catching reflected in a mirror the old magician's expression of wolfish glee, he dropped the instrument from his grasp, and cast his eye upwards as if appealing to Heaven. But every drop of blood seemed frozen in his frame as he beheld an enormous claw thrust through the roof, member as it seemed of some being too gigantic to be contained in the chamber or the tower itself. Cold, poignant, glittering as steel, it rested upon a socket of the repulsive hue of jaundiced ivory, with no vestige of a foot or anything to relieve its naked horror as, rigid and lifeless, yet plainly with a mighty force behind it, it pointed at the magician's heart. As Abano, following the youth's eye, caught sight of the portent, his visage assumed an expression of frantic horror, his spells died upon his lips, and the gorgeous figures became grinning apes or blotchy toads: madly he seized the young man's hand, and strove to force him to complete his signature. The robust youth felt as an infant in his grasp, but ere the stylus could be again thrust upon him the first stroke of the midnight hour rang through the chamber, and instantly the gigantic talon pierced Abano from breast to back, projecting far beyond his shoulders, and swept him upwards to the roof, through which both disappeared without leaving a trace of their passage.

Horror and thankfulness rushed together into the young man's mind, and there contended for some brief instants: but as the last stroke sounded all the crystal vials shivered with a stunning crash, and their hellish inmates, rejoicing in their deliverance, swarmed into the chamber. All made for the youth, who, tugged, clawed, fondled, bitten, beslimed, blinded, deafened, beset in every way by creatures of indescribable loathsomeness, grasped frantically as his sole weapon, the stylus; but it had become a writhing serpent. This was too much, sense forsook him on the spot.

On recovering consciousness he found himself stretched on a pallet in the dungeons of the Inquisition. The Inquisitors sat on their tribunals; black-robed familiars flitted about, or waited attentive upon their orders; one expert in ecclesiastical jurisprudence proved the edge of an axe, and another heated pincers in a chafing-dish; dismal groans pierced the massy walls; two sturdy fellows, stripped to the waist, adjusted the rollers of a rack. A surgeon approached the bedside, bearing a phial and a lancet. The youth screamed and again became insensible.

But his affright was groundless. The Inquisitors had already taken cognisance of Abano's scrolls, and found that, touching these at least, he had spoken sooth. Besides kings, princes, ministers, magistrates, and other secular persons who had owed their success in life to dealings with the devil under his mediation, the infernal bondsmen included so many pillars of the Church and champions of the Faith; prelates plenty, abbots in abundance, cardinals not a few, a (some whispered *the*) Pope; above all, so many of the Inquisitors themselves, that further inquiry could evidently nowise conduce to edification. The surgeon, therefore, infused an opiate into the veins of the unconscious youth, and he came to himself upon a galley speeding him to the holy war in Cyprus, where he fell fighting the Turk.

# ALEXANDER THE RATCATCHER[1]

"Alexander Octavus mures, qui Urbem supra modum vexabant, anathemate perculit."—*Palatius. Fasti Cardinalium*, tom. v.p. 46.

## I

"ROME AND HER rats are at the point of battle!"

This metaphor of Menenius Agrippa's became, history records, matter of fact in 1689, when rats pervaded the Eternal City from garret to cellar, and Pope Alexander the Eighth seriously apprehended the fate of Bishop Hatto. The situation worried him sorely; he had but lately attained the tiara at an advanced age—the twenty-fourth hour, as he himself remarked in extenuation of his haste to enrich his nephews. The time vouchsafed for worthier deeds was brief, and he dreaded descending to posterity as the Rat Pope. Witty and genial, his sense of humour teased him with a full perception of the absurdity of his position. Peter and Pasquin concurred in forbidding him to desert his post; and he derived but small comfort from the ingenuity of his flatterers, who compared him to St. Paul contending with beasts at Ephesus.

It wanted three half-hours to midnight, as Alexander sat amid traps and ratsbane in his chamber in the Vatican, under the protection of two enormous cats and a British terrier. A silver bell stood ready to his hand, should the aid of the attendant chamberlains be requisite. The walls had been divested of their tapestries, and the floor gleamed with pounded glass. A tome of legendary lore lay open at the history of the Piper of Hamelin. All was silence, save for the sniffing and scratching of the dog and a sound of subterranean scraping and gnawing.

"Why tarries Cardinal Barbadico[2] thus?" the Pope at last asked himself

---

1   *Alexander the Ratcatcher.*—This story, to whose ground-work *History and Rabelais* have equally contributed, was first published in vol. xii. of *The Yellow Book*, January, 1897.

2   *Cardinal Barbadico.*—This cardinal was actually entrusted by Alexander VIII. with the commission of suppressing the rats; an occasion upon which the "sardonic grin" imputed to the Pope by a detractor may be conjectured to have been particularly apparent. Barbadico was a remarkable instance of a man "kicked upstairs." As Archbishop of Corfu he had had a

aloud. The inquiry was answered by a wild burst of squeaking and clattering and scurrying to and fro, as who should say, "We've eaten him! We've eaten him!"

But this exultation was at least premature, for just as the terrified Pope clutched his bell, the door opened to the narrowest extent compatible with the admission of an ecclesiastical personage of dignified presence, and Cardinal Barbadico hastily squeezed himself through.

"I shall hardly trust myself upon these stairs again," he remarked, "unless under the escort of your Holiness's terrier."

"Take him, my son, and a cruse of holy water to boot," the Pope responded. "Now, how go things in the city?"

"As ill as may be, your Holiness. Not a saint stirs a finger to help us. The country-folk shun the city, the citizens seek the country. The multitude of enemies increases hour by hour. They set at defiance the anathemas fulminated by your Holiness, the spiritual censures placarded in the churches, and the citation to appear before the ecclesiastical courts, although assured that their cause shall be pleaded by the ablest advocates in Rome. The cats, amphibious with alarm, are taking to the Tiber. Vainly the city reeks with toasted cheese, and the Commissary-General reports himself short of arsenic."

"And how are the people taking it?" demanded Alexander. "To what cause do they attribute the public calamity?"

"Generally speaking, to the sins of your Holiness," replied the Cardinal.

"Cardinal!" exclaimed Alexander indignantly.

"I crave pardon for my temerity," returned Barbadico. "It is with difficulty that I force myself to speak, but I am bound to lay the ungrateful truth before your Holiness. The late Pope, as all men know, was a personage of singular sanctity."

"Far too upright for this fallen world," observed Alexander with unction.

"I will not dispute," responded the Cardinal, "that the head of Innocent the Eleventh might have been more fitly graced by a halo than by a tiara. But the vulgar are incapable of placing themselves at this point of view. They know that the rats hardly squeaked under Innocent, and that they swarm under Alexander. What wonder if they suspect your Holiness of familiarity with Beelzebub, the patron of vermin, and earnestly desire that he would take you to himself? Vainly have I represented to them the unreasonableness of imposing upon him a trouble he may well deem superfluous, considering

violent dispute with the Venetian governor, and Innocent XI., equally unwilling to disown the representative of Papal authority or offend the Republic, recalled him to Rome and made him a Cardinal to keep him there.

your Holiness's infirm health and advanced age. Vainly, too, have I pointed out that your anathema has actually produced all the effect that could have been reasonably anticipated from any similar manifesto on your predecessor's part. They won't see it. And, in fact, might I humbly advise, it does appear impolitic to hurl anathemas unless your Holiness knows that some one will be hit. It might be opportune, for example, to excommunicate Father Molinos, now fast in the dungeons of St. Angelo, unless, indeed, the rats have devoured him there. But I question the expediency of going much further."

"Cardinal," said the Pope, "you think yourself prodigiously clever, but you ought to know that the state of public opinion allowed us no alternative. Moreover, I will give you a wrinkle, in case you should ever come to be Pope yourself. It is unwise to allow ancient prerogatives to fall entirely into desuetude. Far-seeing men prognosticate a great revival of sacerdotalism in the nineteenth century, and what is impotent in an age of sense may be formidable in an age of nonsense. Further, we know not from one day to another whether we may not be absolutely necessitated to excommunicate that fautor of Gallicanism, Louis the Fourteenth, and before launching our bolt at a king, we may think well to test its efficacy upon a rat. *Fiat experimentum.* And now to return to our rats, from which we have ratted. Is there indeed no hope?"

"*Lateat scintillula forsan,*" said the Cardinal mysteriously.

"Ha! How so?" eagerly demanded Alexander.

"Our hopes," answered the Cardinal, "are associated with the recent advent to this city of an extraordinary personage."

"Explain," urged the Pope.

"I speak," resumed the Cardinal, "of an aged man of no plebeian mien or bearing, albeit most shabbily attired in the skins, now fabulously cheap, of the vermin that torment us; who, professing to practise as an herbalist, some little time ago established himself in an obscure street of no good repute. A tortoise hangs in his needy shop, nor are stuffed alligators lacking. Understanding that he was resorted to by such as have need of philters and love-potions, or are incommoded by the longevity of parents and uncles, I was about to have him arrested, when I received a report which gave me pause. This concerned the singular intimacy which appeared to subsist between him and our enemies. When he left home, it was averred, he was attended by troops of them obedient to his beck and call, and spies had observed him banqueting them at his counter, the rats sitting erect and comporting themselves with perfect decorum. I resolved to investigate the matter for myself. Looking into his house through an unshuttered window, I perceived him in truth surrounded by feasting and gambolling rats; but when the door was opened in obedience to my attendants' summons, he appeared to be entirely alone. Laying down a pestle and mortar, he greeted me by name with an easy familiarity which for the moment quite disconcerted me, and inquired what had procured him the honour of my visit. Recovering myself, and wishing to intimidate him:

"'I desire in the first place,' I said, 'to point out to you your grave transgression of municipal regulations in omitting to paint your name over your shop.'

"'Call me Rattila,' he rejoined with unconcern, 'and state your further business.'

"I felt myself on the wrong tack, and hastened to interrogate him respecting his relations with our adversaries. He frankly admitted his acquaintance with rattery in all its branches, and his ability to deliver the city from this scourge, but his attitude towards your Holiness was so deficient in respect that I question whether I ought to report it."

"Proceed, son," said the Pope; "we will not be deterred from providing for the public weal by the ribaldry of a ratcatcher."

"He scoffed at what he termed your Holiness's absurd position, and affirmed that the world had seldom beheld, or would soon behold again, so ridiculous a spectacle as a Pope besieged by rats. 'I can help your master,' he continued, 'and am willing; but my honour, like his, is aspersed in the eyes of the multitude, and he must come to my aid, if I am to come to his.'

"I prayed him to be more explicit, and offered to be the bearer of any communication to your Holiness.

"'I will unfold myself to no one but the Pope himself,' he replied, 'and the interview must take place when and where I please to appoint. Let him meet me this very midnight, and alone, in the fifth chamber of the Appartamento Borgia.'

"'The Appartamento Borgia!' I exclaimed in consternation. 'The saloons which the wicked Pope Alexander the Sixth nocturnally perambulates, mingling poisons that have long lost their potency for Cardinals who have long lost their lives!'

"'Have a care!' he exclaimed sharply. 'You speak to his late Holiness's most intimate friend.'

"'Then,' I answered, 'you must obviously be the Devil, and I am not at present empowered to negotiate with your Infernal Majesty. Consider, however, the peril and inconvenience of visiting at dead of night rooms closed for generations. Think of the chills and cobwebs. Weigh the probability of his Holiness being devoured by rats.'

"'I guarantee his Holiness absolute immunity from cold,' he replied, 'and that none of my subjects shall molest him either going or returning.'

"'But,' I objected, 'granting that you are not the Devil, how the devil, let me ask, do you expect to gain admittance at midnight to the Appartamento Borgia?'

"'Think you I cannot pass through a stone wall?' answered he, and vanished in an instant. A tremendous scampering of rats immediately ensued, then all was silence.

"On recovering in some measure from my astounded condition, I caused strict search to be made throughout the shop. Nothing came to light but herbalists' stuff and ordinary medicines. And now, Holy Father, your Holiness's resolution? Reflect well. This Rattila may be the King of the Rats, or he may be Beelzebub in person."

Alexander the Eighth was principally considered by his contemporaries in the light of a venerable fox, but the lion had by no means been omitted from his composition.

"All powers of good forbid," he exclaimed, "that a Pope and a Prince should shrink from peril which the safety of the State summons him to encounter! I will confront this wizard, this goblin, in the place of his own appointing, under his late intimate friend's very nose. I am a man of many transgressions, but something assures me that Heaven will not deem this a fit occasion for calling them to remembrance. Time presses; I lead on; follow, Cardinal Barbadico, follow! Yet stay, let us not forget temporal and spiritual armouries."

And hastily providing himself with a lamp, a petronel, a bunch of keys, a crucifix, a vial of holy water, and a manual of exorcisms, the Pope passed through a secret door in a corner of his chamber, followed by the Cardinal bearing another lamp and a naked sword, and preceded by the dog and the two cats, all ardent and undaunted as champions bound to the Holy Land for the recovery of the Holy Sepulchre.

## II

THE wizard had kept his word. Not a rat was seen or heard upon the pilgrimage, which was exceedingly toilsome to the aged Pope, from the number of passages to be threaded and doors to be unlocked. At length the companions stood before the portal of the Appartamento Borgia.

"Your Holiness must enter alone," Cardinal Barbadico admonished, with manifest reluctance.

"Await my return," enjoined the Pontiff, in a tone of more confidence than he could actually feel, as, after much grinding and grating, the massive door swung heavily back, and he passed on into the dim, unexplored space beyond. The outer air, streaming in as though eager to indemnify itself for years of exile, smote and swayed the flame of the Pope's lamp, whose feeble ray flitted from floor to ceiling as the decrepit man, weary with the way he had traversed and the load he was bearing, tottered and stumbled painfully along, ever and anon arrested by a closed door, which he unlocked with prodigious difficulty. The cats cowered close to the Cardinal; the dog at first accompanied the Pope, but whined so grievously, as though he beheld a spirit, that Alexander bade him back.

Supreme is the spell of the *genius loci*. The chambers traversed by the Pope were in fact adorned with fair examples of the painter's art, mostly scriptural in subject, but some inspired with the devout Pantheism in which all creeds are reconciled. All were alike invisible to the Pontiff, who, with the dim flicker of his lamp, could no more discern Judaea wed with Egypt on the frescoed ceiling than, with the human limitation of his faculties, he could foresee that the ill-reputed rooms would one day harbour a portion of the Vatican Library, so greatly enriched by himself. Nothing but sinister memories and vague alarms presented themselves to his imagination. The atmosphere, heavy and brooding from the long exclusion of the outer air, seemed to weigh upon him with the density of matter, and to afford the stuff out of which phantasmal bodies perpetually took shape and, as he half persuaded himself, substance. Creeping and tottering between bowl and cord, shielding himself with lamp and crucifix from Michelotto's spectral poniard and more fearful contact with fleshless Vanozzas and mouldering Giulias, the Pope urged, or seemed to urge, his course amid phantom princes and cardinals, priests and courtesans, soldiers and serving-men, dancers, drinkers, dicers, Bacchic and Cotyttian workers of whatsoever least beseemed the inmates of a Pontifical household, until, arrived in the fifth chamber, close by the, to him, invisible picture of the Resurrection, he sank exhausted into a spacious chair that seemed placed for his reception, and for a moment closed his eyes. Opening them immediately afterwards, he saw with relief that the phantoms had vanished, and that he confronted what at least seemed a fellow-mortal, in the ancient ratcatcher, habited precisely as Cardinal Barbadico had described, yet, for all his mean apparel, wearing the air of one wont to confer with the potentates of the earth on other subjects than the extermination of rats.

"This is noble of your Holiness—really," he said, bowing with mock reverence. "A second Leo the Great!"

"I tell you what, my man," responded Alexander, feeling it very necessary to assert his dignity while any of it remained, "you are not to imagine that, because I have humoured you so far as to grant you an audience at an unusual place and time, I am going to stand any amount of your nonsense and impertinence. You can catch our rats, can you? Catch them then, and you need not fear that we shall treat you like the Pied Piper of Hamelin. You have committed sundry rascalities, no doubt? A pardon shall be made out for you. You want a patent or a privilege for your ratsbane? You shall have it. So to work, in the name of St. Muscipulus! and you may keep the tails and skins."

"Alexander," said the ratcatcher composedly, "I would not commend or disraise you unduly, but this I may say, that of all the Popes I have known you are the most exuberant in hypocrisy and the most deficient in penetration. The most hypocritical, because you well know, and know that I know that you know, that you are not conversing with an ordinary ratcatcher: had you deemed me such, you would never have condescended to meet me at this hour and place. The least penetrating, because you apparently have not yet discovered to whom you are speaking. Do you really mean to say that you do not know me?"

"I believe I have seen your face before," said Alexander, "and all the more likely as I was inspector of prisons when I was Cardinal."

"Then look yonder," enjoined the ratcatcher, as he pointed to the frescoed wall, at the same time vehemently snapping his fingers. Phosphoric sparks hissed and crackled forth, and coalesced into a blue lambent flame, which concentrated itself upon a depicted figure, whose precise attitude the rat-catcher assumed as he dropped upon his knees. The Pope shrieked with amazement, for, although the splendid Pontifical vestments had become ragged fur, in every other respect the kneeling figure was the counterpart of the painted one, and the painted one was Pinturicchio's portrait of Pope Alexander the Sixth kneeling as a witness of the Resurrection.

Alexander the Eighth would fain have imitated his predecessor's attitude, but terror bound him to his chair, and the adjuration of his patron St. Mark which struggled towards his lips never arrived there. The book of exorcisms fell from his paralysed hand, and the vial of holy water lay in shivers upon the floor. Ere he could collect himself, the dead Pope had seated himself beside the Pope with one foot in the grave, and, fondling a ferret-skin, proceeded to enter into conversation.

"What fear you?" he asked. "Why should I harm you? None can say that I ever injured any one for any cause but my own advantage, and to injure your Holiness now would be to obstruct a design which I have particularly at heart."

"I crave your Holiness's forgiveness," rejoined the Eighth Alexander, "but you must be aware that you left the world with a reputation which disqualifies you for the society of any Pope in the least careful of his character. It positively compromises me to have so much as the ghost of a person so universally decried as your Holiness under my roof, and you would infinitely oblige me by forthwith repairing to your own place, which I take to be about four thousand miles below where you are sitting. I could materially facilitate and accelerate your Holiness's transit thither if you would be so kind as to hand me that little book of exorcisms."

"How is the fine gold become dim!" exclaimed Alexander the Sixth. "Popes in bondage to moralists! Popes nervous about public opinion! Is there another judge of morals than the Pope speaking *ex cathedra*, as I always did? Is the Church to frame herself after the prescriptions of heathen philosophers and profane jurists? How, then, shall she be terrible as an army with banners? Did I concern myself with such pedantry when the Kings of Spain and Portugal came to me like cats suing for morsels, and I gave them the West and the East?"

"It is true," Alexander the Eighth allowed, "that the lustre of the Church hath of late been obfuscated by the prevalence of heresy."

"It isn't the heretics," Borgia insisted. "It is the degeneracy of the Popes. A shabby lot! You, Alexander, are about the best of them; but the least Cardinal about my Court would have thought himself bigger than you."

Alexander's spirit rose. "I would suggest," he said, "that this haughty style is little in keeping with the sordid garb wherein your Holiness, consistent after death as in your life, masquerades to the scandal and distress of the faithful."

"How can I other? Has your Holiness forgotten your Rabelais?"

"The works of that eminent Doctor and Divine," answered Alexander the Eighth, "are seldom long absent from my hands, yet I fail to remember in what manner they elucidate the present topic."

"Let me refresh your memory," rejoined Borgia, and, producing a volume of the Sage of Meudon, he turned to the chapter descriptive of the employments of various eminent inhabitants of the nether world, and pointed to the sentence:

"LE PAPE ALEXANDRE ESTOYT PRENEUR DE RATZ."[3]

---

3   *Pantagruel*, Book XI. ch. 30.

"Is this indeed sooth?" demanded his successor.

"How else should François Rabelais have affirmed it?" responded Borgia. "When I arrived in the subterranean kingdom, I found it in the same condition as your Holiness's dominions at the present moment, eaten up by rats. The attention which, during my earthly pilgrimage, I had devoted to the science of toxicology indicated me as a person qualified to abate the nuisance, which commission I executed with such success, that I received the appointment of Ratcatcher to his Infernal Majesty, and so discharged its duties as to merit a continuance of the good opinion which had always been entertained of me in that exalted quarter. After a while, however, interest began to be made for me in even more elevated spheres. I had not been able to cram Heaven with Spaniards, as I had crammed the Sacred College—on the contrary. Truth to speak, my nation has not largely contributed to the population of the regions above. But some of us are people of consequence. My great-grandson, the General of the Jesuits, who, as such, had the ear of St. Ignatius Loyola, represented that had I adhered strictly to my vows, he could never have come into existence, and that the Society would thus have wanted one of its brightest ornaments. This argument naturally had great weight with St. Ignatius, the rather as he, too, was my countryman. Much also was said of the charity I had shown to the exiled Jews, which St. Dominic was pleased to say made him feel ashamed of himself when he came to think of it; for my having fed my people in time of dearth, instead of contriving famines to enrich myself, as so many Popes' nephews have done since; and of the splendid order in which I kept the College of Cardinals. Columbus said a good word for me, and Savonarola did not oppose. Finally I was allowed to come upstairs, and exercise my profession on earth. But mark what pitfalls line the good man's path! I never could resist tampering with drugs of a deleterious nature, and was constantly betrayed by the thirst for scientific experiment into practices incompatible with the public health. The good nature which my detractors have not denied me was a veritable snare. I felt for youth debarred from its enjoyments by the unnatural vitality of age, and sympathised with the blooming damsel whose parent alone stood between her and her lover. I thus lived in constant apprehension of being ordered back to the Netherlands, and yearned for the wings of a dove, that I might flee away and be out of mischief. At last I discovered that my promotion to a higher sphere depended upon my obtaining a testimonial from the reigning Pope. Let a solemn procession be held in my honour, and intercession be publicly made for me, and I should ascend forthwith. I have consequently represented my case to many of your predecessors: but, O Alexander, you seventeenth-century Popes are a miserable breed! No fellow-feeling, no *esprit de corps. Heu pietas! heu prisca fides*! No one was so rude as your ascetic antecessor. The more of a saint, the less of a gentleman. Personally offensive, I assure you! But the others were nearly as bad. The haughty Paul, the fanatic Gregory, the worldly Urban, the austere Innocent the Tenth, the affable Alexander the Seventh, all concurred in assuring me that it was deeply to be regretted that I should ever have been emancipated from the restraints of the Stygian realm, to which I should do well to return with all possible celerity; that it would much conduce to the interests of the Church if my name could be forgotten; and that as for doing anything to revive its memory, they would just as soon think of canonising Judas Iscariot."

"And therefore your Holiness has brought these rats upon us, enlisted, I nothing doubt, in the infernal regions?"

"Precisely so: Plutonic, necyomantic, Lemurian rats, kindly lent by the Prince of Darkness for the occasion, and come dripping from Styx to squeak and gibber in the Capitol. But I note your Holiness's admission that they belong to a region exempt from your jurisdiction, and that, therefore, your measures against them, except as regards their status as belligerents, are for the most part illegitimate and *ultra vires*."

"I would argue that point," replied Alexander the Eighth, "if my lungs were as tough as when I pleaded before the Rota in Pope Urban's time. For the present I confine myself to formally protesting against your Holiness's unprecedented and parricidal conduct in invading your country at the head of an army of loathsome vermin."

"Unprecedented!" exclaimed Borgia. "Am I not the modern Coriolanus? Did Narses experience blacker ingratitude than I? Where would the temporal power be but for me? Who smote the Colonna? Who squashed the Orsini? Who gave the Popes to dwell quietly in their own house? Monsters of unthankfulness!"

"I am sure," said Alexander the Eighth soothingly, "that my predecessors' inability to comply with your Holiness's request must have cost them many inward tears, not the less genuine because entirely invisible and completely inaudible. A wise Pope will, before all things, consider the spirit of his age. The force of public opinion, which your Holiness lately appeared to disparage, was, in fact, as operative upon yourself as upon any of your successors. If you achieved great things in your lifetime, it was because the world was with you. Did you pursue the same methods now, you would soon discover that you had become an offensive anachronism. It will not have escaped your Holiness's penetration that what moralists will persist in terming the elevation of the standard of the Church, is the result of the so-called improvement of the world."

"There is a measure of truth in this," admitted Alexander the Sixth, "and the spirit of this age is a very poor spirit. It was my felicity to be a Pope of the Renaissance. Blest dispensation! when men's view of life was large and liberal; when the fair humanities flourished; when the earth yielded up her hoards of chiselled marble and breathing bronze, and new-found agate urns as fresh as day; when painters and sculptors vied with antiquity, and poets and historians followed in their path; when every benign deity was worshipped save Diana and Vesta; when the arts of courtship and cosmetics were expounded by archbishops; when the beauteous Imperia was of more account than the eleven thousand virgins; when obnoxious persons glided imperceptibly from the world; and no one marvelled if he met the Pope arm in arm with the Devil. How miserable, in comparison, is the present sapless age, with its prudery and its pedantry, and its periwigs and its painted coaches, and its urban Arcadias and the florid impotence and ostentatious inanity of what it calls its art! Pope Alexander! I see in the spirit the sepulchre destined for *you*, and I swear to you that my soul shivers in my ratskins! Come, now! I do not expect you to emulate the Popes of my time, but show that your virtues are your own, and your faults those of your epoch. Pluck up a spirit! Take bulls by the horns! Look facts in the face! Think upon the images of Brutus and Cassius! Recognise that you cannot get rid of me, and that the only safe course is to rehabilitate me. I am not a candidate for canonisation just now; but repair past neglect and appease my injured shade in the way you wot of. If this is done, I pledge my word that every rat shall forthwith evacuate Rome. Is it a bargain? I see it is; you are one of the good old sort, though fallen on evil days."

Renaissance or Rats, Alexander the Eighth yielded.

"I promise," he declared.

"Your hand upon it!"

Subduing his repugnance and apprehension by a strong effort, Alexander laid his hand within the spectre's clammy paw. An icy thrill ran through his veins, and he sank back senseless into his chair.

### III

WHEN the Pope recovered consciousness he found himself in bed, with slight symptoms of fever. His first care was to summon Cardinal Barbadico, and confer with him respecting the surprising adventures which had recently befallen them. To his amazement, the Cardinal's mind seemed an entire blank on the subject. He admitted having made his customary report to his Holiness the preceding night, but knew nothing of any supernatural ratcatcher, and nothing of any midnight rendezvous at the Appartamento Borgia. Investigation seemed to justify his nescience; no vestige of the man of rats or of his shop could be discovered; and the Borgian apartments, opened and carefully searched through, revealed no trace of having been visited for many years. The Pope's book of exorcisms was in its proper place, his vial of holy water stood unbroken upon his table; and his chamberlains deposed that they had consigned him to Morpheus at the usual hour. His illusion was at first explained as the effect of a peculiarly vivid dream; but when he declared his intention of actually holding a service and conducting a procession for the weal of his namesake and predecessor, the conviction became universal that the rats had effected a lodgement in his Holiness's upper storeys.

Alexander, notwithstanding, was resolute, and so it came to pass that on the same day two mighty processions encountered within the walls of Rome. As the assembled clergy, drawn from all the churches and monasteries in the city, the Pope in his litter in their midst, marched, carrying candles, intoning chants, and, with many a secret shrug and sneer, imploring Heaven for the repose of Alexander the Sixth, they were suddenly brought to bay by another procession precipitated athwart their track, disorderly, repulsive, but more grateful to the sight of the citizens than all the pomps and pageants of the palmiest days of the Papacy. Black, brown, white, grey; fat and lean; old and young; strident or silent; the whiskered legions tore and galloped along; thronging from every part of the city, they united in single column into an endless host that appeared to stretch from the rising to the setting of the sun. They seemed making for the Tiber, which they would have speedily choked; but ere they could arrive there a huge rift opened in the earth, down which they madly precipitated themselves. Their descent, it is affirmed, lasted as many hours as Vulcan occupied in falling from Heaven to Lemnos; but when the last tail was over the brink, the gulf closed as effectually as the gulf in the Forum closed over Marcus Curtius, not leaving the slightest inequality by which any could detect it.

Long ere this consummation had been attained, the Pope, looking forth from his litter, observed a venerable personage clad in ratskins, who appeared desirous of attracting his notice. Glances of recognition were exchanged, and instantly in place of the ratcatcher stood a tall, swarthy, corpulent, elderly man, with the majestic yet sensual features of Alexander the Sixth, accoutred with the official habiliments and insignia of a Pope, who rose slowly into the air as though he had been inflated with hydrogen.

"To your prayers!" cried Alexander the Eighth, and gave the example. The priesthood resumed its chants, the multitude dropped upon their knees. Their orisons seemed to speed the ascending figure, which was rising rapidly, when suddenly appeared in air Luxury, Simony, and Cruelty, contending which should receive the Holy Father into her bosom.[4] Borgia struck at them with his crozier, and seemed to be keeping them at bay, when a cloud wrapped the group from the sight of men. Thunder roared, lightning glared, the rush of waters blended with the ejaculations of the people and the yet more tempestuous rushing of the rats. Accompanied as he was, it is not probable that Alexander passed, like Dante's sigh, "beyond the sphere that doth all spheres enfold"; but, as he was never again seen on earth, it is not doubted that he attained at least as far as the moon.

---

4        Per aver riposo
       Portato fu fra l'anime beate
       Lo spirito di Alessandro glorioso;
       Del qual seguiro le sante pedate
       Tre sue familiari e care ancelle,
       Lussuria, Simonia, e Crudeltate.
           —MACHIAVELLI, *Decennale Primo.*

# THE REWARDS OF INDUSTRY[1]

IN CHINA, UNDER the Tang dynasty, early in the seventh century of the Christian era, lived a learned and virtuous, but poor mandarin who had three sons, Fu-su, Tu-sin, and Wang-li. Fu-su and Tu-sin were young men of active minds, always labouring to find out something new and useful. Wang-li was clever too, but only in games of skill, in which he attained great proficiency.

Fu-su and Tu-sin continually talked to each other of the wonderful inventions they would make when they arrived at man's estate, and of the wealth and renown they promised themselves thereby. Their conversation seldom reached the ears of Wang-li, for he rarely lifted his eyes from the chess-board on which he solved his problems. But their father was more attentive, and one day he said:

"I fear, my sons, that among your multifarious pursuits and studies you must have omitted to include that of the laws of your country, or you would have learned that fortune is not to be acquired by the means which you have proposed to yourselves."

"How so, father?" asked they.

"It hath been justly deemed by our ancestors," said the old man, "that the reverence due to the great men who are worshipped in our temples, by reason of our indebtedness to them for the arts of life, could not but become impaired if their posterity were suffered to eclipse their fame by new discoveries, or presumptuously amend what might appear imperfect in their productions. It is therefore, by an edict of the Emperor Suen, forbidden to invent anything; and by a statute of the Emperor Wu-chi it is further provided that nothing hitherto invented shall be improved. My predecessor in the small office I hold was deprived of it for saying that in his judgment money ought to be made round instead of square, and I have myself run risk of my life for seeking to combine a small file with a pair of tweezers."

"If this is the case," said the young men, "our fatherland is not the place for

---

1  *The Rewards of Industry.*—Appeared originally in *Atalanta* for August, 1888.

us." And they embraced their father, and departed. Of their brother Wang-li they took no farewell, inasmuch as he was absorbed in a chess problem. Before separating, they agreed to meet on the same spot after thirty years, with the treasure which they doubted not to have acquired by the exercise of their inventive faculties in foreign lands. They further covenanted that if either had missed his reward the other should share his possessions with him.

Fu-su repaired to the artists who cut out characters in blocks of hard wood, to the end that books may be printed from the same. When he had fathomed their mystery he betook himself to a brass-founder, and learned how to cast in metal. He then sought a learned man who had travelled much, and made himself acquainted with the Greek, Persian, and Arabic languages. Then he cast a number of Greek characters in type, and putting them into a bag and providing himself with some wooden letter-tablets of his own carving, he departed to seek his fortune. After innumerable hardships and perils he arrived in the land of Persia, and inquired for the great king.

"The great king is dead," they told him, "and his head is entirely separated from his body. There is now no king in Persia, great or small,"

"Where shall I find another great king?" demanded he.

"In the city of Alexandria," replied they, "where the Commander of the Faithful is busy introducing the religion of the Prophet."

Fu-su passed to Alexandria, carrying his types and tablets.

As he entered the gates he remarked an enormous cloud of smoke, which seemed to darken the whole city. Before he could inquire the reason, the guard arrested him as a stranger, and conducted him to the presence of the Caliph Omar.

"Know, O Caliph," said Fu-su, "that my countrymen are at once the wisest of mankind and the stupidest. They have invented an art for the preservation of letters and the diffusion of knowledge, which the sages of Greece and India never knew, but they have not learned to take, and they refuse to be taught how to take, the one little step further necessary to render it generally profitable to mankind."

And producing his tablets and types, he explained to the Caliph the entire mystery of the art of printing.

"Thou seemest to be ignorant," said Omar, "that we have but yesterday condemned and excommunicated all books, and banished the same from the face of the earth, seeing that they contain either that which is contrary to the Koran, in which case they are impious, or that which is agreeable to the Koran, in which case they are superfluous. Thou art further unaware, as it would seem, that the smoke which shrouds the city proceeds from the library of the unbelievers, consumed by our orders. It will be meet to burn thee along with it."

"O Commander of the Faithful," said an officer, "of a surety the last scroll of the accursed ceased to flame even as this infidel entered the city."

"If it be so," said Omar, "we will not burn him, seeing that we have taken away from him the occasion to sin. Yet shall he swallow these little brass amulets of his, at the rate of one a day, and then be banished from the country."

The sentence was executed, and Fu-su was happy that the Court physician condescended to accept his little property in exchange for emetics.

He begged his way slowly and painfully back to China, and arrived at the covenanted spot at the expiration of the thirtieth year. His father's modest dwelling had disappeared, and in its place stood a magnificent mansion, around which stretched a park with pavilions, canals, willow-trees, golden pheasants, and little bridges.

"Tu-sin has surely made his fortune," thought he, "and he will not refuse to share it with me agreeably to our covenant."

As he thus reflected he heard a voice at his elbow, and turning round perceived that one in a more wretched plight than himself was asking alms of him. It was Tu-sin.

The brothers embraced with many tears, and after Tu-sin had learned Fu-su's history, he proceeded to recount his own.

"I repaired," said he, "to those who know the secret of the grains termed fire-dust, which Suen has not been able to prevent us from inventing, but of which Wu-chi has taken care that we shall make no use, save only for fireworks. Having learned their mystery I deposited a certain portion of this fire-dust in hollow tubes which I had constructed of iron and brass, and upon it I further laid leaden balls of a size corresponding to the hollow of the tubes. I then found that by applying a light to the fire-dust at one end of the tube I could send the ball out at the other with such force that it penetrated the cuirasses of three warriors at once. I filled a barrel with the dust, and concealing it and the tubes under carpets which I laid upon the backs of oxen, I set out to the city of Constantinople. I will not at present relate my adventures on the journey. Suffice it that I arrived at last half dead from fatigue and hardship, and destitute of everything except my merchandise. By bribing an officer with my carpets I was admitted to have speech with the Emperor. I found him busily studying a problem in chess.

"I told him that I had discovered a secret which would make him the master of the world, and in particular would help him to drive away the Saracens, who threatened his empire with destruction.

"'Thou must perceive,' he said, 'that I cannot possibly attend to thee until I have solved this problem. Yet, lest any should say that the Emperor neglects his duties, absorbed in idle amusement, I will refer thy invention to the chief armourers of my capital. And he gave me a letter to the armourers, and returned to his problem. And as I quitted the palace bearing the missive, I came upon a great procession. Horsemen and running footmen, musicians, heralds, and banner-bearers surrounded a Chinaman who sat in the attitude of Fo under a golden umbrella upon a richly caparisoned elephant, his pigtail plaited with yellow roses. And the musicians blew and clashed, and the standard-bearers waved their ensigns, and the heralds proclaimed, 'Thus shall it be done to the man whom the Emperor delights to honour.' And unless I was very greatly mistaken, the face of the Chinaman was the face of our brother Wang-li.

"At another time I would have striven to find what this might mean, but my impatience was great, as also my need and hunger. I sought the chief armourers, and with great trouble brought them all together to give me audience, I produced my tube and fire-dust, and sent my balls with ease through the best armour they could set before me.

"'Who will want breast-plates now?' cried the chief breast-plate maker.

"'Or helmets?' exclaimed one who made armour for the head.

"'I would not have taken fifty bezants for that shield, and what good is it now?' said the head of the shield trade.

"'My swords will be of less account,' said a swordsmith.

"'My arrows of none,' lamented an arrow-maker.

"''Tis villainy,' cried one.

"''Tis magic,' shouted another.

"''Tis illusion, as I'm an honest tradesman,' roared a third, and put his integrity to the proof by thrusting a hot iron bar into my barrel. All present rose up in company with the roof of the building, and all perished, except myself, who escaped with the loss of my hair and skin. A fire broke out on the spot, and consumed one-third of the city of Constantinople.

"I was lying on a prison-bed some time afterwards, partly recovered of my hurts, dolefully listening to a dispute between two of my guards as to whether I ought to be burned or buried alive, when the Imperial order for my disposal came down. The gaolers received it with humility, and read 'Kick him out of the city.' Marvelling at the mildness of the punishment, they nevertheless executed it with so much zeal that I flew into the middle of the Bosphorus, where I was picked up by a fishing vessel, and landed on the Asiatic coast, whence I have begged my way home. I now propose that we appeal to the pity of the owner of this splendid mansion, who may compassionate us on hearing that we were reared in the Cottage which has been pulled down to make room for his palace."

They entered the gates, walked timidly up to the house, and prepared to fall at the feet of the master, but did not, for ere they could do so they recognised their brother Wang-li.

It took Wang-li some time to recognise them, but when at length he knew them he hastened to provide for their every want. When they had well eaten and drunk, and had been clad in robes of honour, they imparted their histories, and asked for his.

"My brothers," said Wang-li, "the noble game of chess, which was happily invented long before the time of the Emperor Suen, was followed by me solely for its pleasure, and I dreamed not of acquiring wealth by its pursuit until I casually heard one day that it was entirely unknown to the people of the West. Even then I thought not of gaining money, but conceived so deep a compassion for those forlorn barbarians that I felt I could know no rest until I should have enlightened them. I accordingly proceeded to the city of Constantinople, and was received as a messenger from Heaven. To such effect did I labour that ere long the Emperor and his officers of state thought of nothing else but playing chess all day and night, and the empire fell into entire confusion, and the Saracens mightily prevailed. In consideration of these services the Emperor was pleased to bestow those distinguished honours upon me which thou didst witness at his palace gate, dear brother.

"After, however, the fire which was occasioned through thy instrumentality, though in no respect by thy fault, the people murmured, and taxed the Emperor with seeking to destroy his capital in league with a foreign sorcerer, meaning thee. Ere long the chief officers conspired and entered the Emperor's apartment, purposing to dethrone him, but he declared that he would in nowise abdicate until he had finished the game of chess he was then playing with me. They looked on, grew interested, began to dispute with one another respecting the moves, and while they wrangled loyal officers entered and made them all captive. This greatly augmented my credit with the Emperor, which was even increased when shortly afterwards I played with the Saracen admiral blockading the Hellespont, and won of him forty corn-ships, which turned the dearth of the city into plenty.

"The Emperor bade me choose any favour I would, but I said his liberality had left me nothing to ask for except the life of a poor countryman of mine who I had heard was in prison for burning the city. The Emperor bade me write his sentence with my own hand. Had I known that it was thou,

Tu-sin, believe me I had shown more consideration for thy person. At length I departed for my native land, loaded with wealth, and travelling most comfortably by relays of swift dromedaries. I returned hither, bought our father's cottage, and on its site erected this palace, where I dwell meditating on the problems of chessplayers and the precepts of the sages, and persuaded that a little thing which the world is willing to receive is better than a great thing which it hath not yet learned to value aright. For the world is a big child, and chooses amusement before instruction."

"Call you chess an amusement?" asked his brothers.

# MADAM LUCIFER

LUCIFER SAT PLAYING chess with Man for his soul.

The game was evidently going ill for Man. He had but pawns left, few and straggling. Lucifer had rooks, knights, and, of course, bishops.

It was but natural under such circumstances that Man should be in no great hurry to move. Lucifer grew impatient.

"It is a pity," said he at last, "that we did not fix some period within which the player must move, or resign."

"Oh, Lucifer," returned the young man, in heart-rending accents, "it is not the impending loss of my soul that thus unmans me, but the loss of my betrothed. When I think of the grief of the Lady Adeliza, that paragon of terrestrial loveliness!" Tears choked his utterance; Lucifer was touched.

"Is the Lady Adeliza's loveliness in sooth so transcendent?" he inquired.

"She is a rose, a lily, a diamond, a morning star!"

"If that is the case," rejoined Lucifer, "thou mayest reassure thyself. The Lady Adeliza shall not want for consolation. I will assume thy shape and woo her in thy stead."

The young man hardly seemed to receive all the comfort from this promise which Lucifer no doubt designed. He made a desperate move. In an instant the Devil checkmated him, and he disappeared.


"UPON my word, if I had known what a business this was going to be, I don't think I should have gone in for it," soliloquised the Devil, as, wearing his captive's semblance and installed in his apartments, he surveyed the effects to which he now had to administer. They included coats, shirts, collars, neckties, foils, cigars, and the like *ad libitum*; and very little else except three challenges, ten writs, and seventy-four unpaid bills, elegantly disposed around the looking-glass. To the poor youth's praise be it said, there were no billets-doux, except from the Lady Adeliza herself.

Noting the address of these carefully, the Devil sallied forth, and nothing but his ignorance of the topography of the hotel, which made him take the back stairs, saved him from the clutches of two bailiffs lurking on the principal staircase. Leaping into a cab, he thus escaped a perfumer and a bootmaker, and shortly found himself at the Lady Adeliza's feet.

The truth had not been half told him. Such beauty, such wit, such correctness of principle! Lucifer went forth from her presence a love-sick fiend. Not Merlin's mother had produced half the impression upon him; and Adeliza on her part had never found her lover one-hundredth part so interesting as he seemed that morning.

Lucifer proceeded at once to the City, where, assuming his proper shape for the occasion, he negotiated a loan without the smallest difficulty. All debts were promptly discharged, and Adeliza was astonished at the splendour and variety of the presents she was constantly receiving.

Lucifer had all but brought her to name the day, when he was informed that a gentleman of clerical appearance desired to wait upon him.

"Wants money for a new church or mission, I suppose," said he. "Show him up."

But when the visitor was ushered in, Lucifer found with discomposure that he was no earthly clergyman, but a celestial saint; a saint, too, with whom Lucifer had never been able to get on. He had served in the army while on earth, and his address was curt, precise, and peremptory.

"I have called," he said, "to notify to you my appointment as Inspector of Devils."

"What!" exclaimed Lucifer, in consternation. "To the post of my old friend Michael!"

"Too old," said the Saint laconically. "Millions of years older than the world. About your age, I think?"

Lucifer winced, remembering the particular business he was then about. The Saint continued:

"I am a new broom, and am expected to sweep clean. I warn you that I mean to be strict, and there is one little matter which I must set right immediately. You are going to marry that poor young fellow's betrothed, are you? Now you know you cannot take his wife, unless you give him yours."

"Oh, my dear friend," exclaimed Lucifer, "what an inexpressibly blissful prospect you do open unto me!"

"I don't know that," said the Saint. "I must remind you that the dominion of the infernal regions is unalterably attached to the person of the present Queen thereof. If you part with her you immediately lose all your authority and possessions. I don't care a brass button which you do, but you must understand that you cannot eat your cake and have it too. Good morning!"

Who shall describe the conflict in Lucifer's bosom? If any stronger passion existed therein at that moment than attachment to Adeliza, it was aversion to his consort, and the two combined were well-nigh irresistible. But to disenthrone himself, to descend to the condition of a poor devil!

Feeling himself incapable of coming to a decision, he sent for Belial, unfolded the matter, and requested his advice.

"What a shame that our new inspector will not let you marry Adeliza!" lamented his counsellor. "If you did, my private opinion is that forty-eight hours afterwards you would care just as much for her as you do now for Madam Lucifer, neither more nor less. Are your intentions really honourable?"

"Yes," replied Lucifer, "it is to be a Lucifer match."

"The more fool you," rejoined Belial. "If you tempted her to commit a sin, she would be yours without any conditions at all."

"Oh, Belial," said Lucifer, "I cannot bring myself to be a tempter of so much innocence and loveliness."

And he meant what he said.

"Well then, let me try," proposed Belial.

"You?" replied Lucifer contemptuously; "do you imagine that Adeliza would look at *you*?"

"Why not?" asked Belial, surveying himself complacently in the glass.

He was humpbacked, squinting, and lame, and his horns stood up under his wig.

The discussion ended in a wager after which there was no retreat for Lucifer.

The infernal Iachimo was introduced to Adeliza as a distinguished foreigner, and was soon prosecuting his suit with all the success which Lucifer had predicted. One thing protected while it baffled him—the entire inability of Adeliza to understand what he meant. At length he was constrained to make the matter clear by producing an enormous treasure, which he offered Adeliza in exchange for the abandonment of her lover.

The tempest of indignation which ensued would have swept away any ordinary demon, but Belial listened unmoved. When Adeliza had exhausted herself he smilingly rallied her upon her affection for an unworthy lover, of whose infidelity he undertook to give her proof. Frantic with jealousy, Adeliza consented, and in a trice found herself in the infernal regions.

ADELIZA's arrival in Pandemonium, as Belial had planned, occurred immediately after the receipt of a message from Lucifer, in whose bosom love had finally gained the victory, and who had telegraphed his abdication and resignation of Madam Lucifer to Adeliza's betrothed. The poor young man had just been hauled up from the lower depths, and was beset by legions of demons obsequiously pressing all manner of treasures upon his acceptance. He stared, helpless and bewildered, unable to realise his position in the smallest degree. In the background grave and serious demons, the princes of the infernal realm, discussed the new departure, and consulted especially how to break it to Madam Lucifer—a commission of which no one seemed ambitious.

"Stay where you are," whispered Belial to Adeliza; "stir not; you shall put his constancy to the proof within five minutes."

Not all the hustling, mowing, and gibbering of the fiends would under ordinary circumstances have kept Adeliza from her lover's side: but what is all hell to jealousy?

In even less time than he had promised Belial returned, accompanied by Madam Lucifer. This lady's black robe, dripping with blood, contrasted agreeably with her complexion of sulphurous yellow; the absence of hair was compensated by the exceptional length of her nails; she was a thousand million years old, and, but for her remarkable muscular vigour, looked every one of them. The rage into which Belial's communication had thrown her was something indescribable; but, as her eye fell on the handsome youth, a different order of thoughts seemed to take possession of her mind.

"Let the monster go!" she exclaimed; "who cares? Come, my love, ascend the throne with me, and share the empire and the treasures of thy fond Luciferetta."

"If you don't, back you go," interjected Belial.

What might have been the young man's decision if Madam Lucifer had borne more resemblance to Madam Vulcan, it would be wholly impertinent to inquire, for the question never arose.

"Take me away!" he screamed, "take me away, anywhere I anywhere out of her reach! Oh, Adeliza!"

With a bound Adeliza stood by his side. She was darting a triumphant glance at the discomfited Queen of Hell, when suddenly her expression changed, and she screamed loudly. Two adorers stood before her, alike in every lineament and every detail of costume, utterly indistinguishable, even by the eye of Love.

Lucifer, in fact, hastening to throw himself at Adeliza's feet and pray her to defer his bliss no longer, had been thunderstruck by the tidings of her elopement with Belial. Fearing to lose his wife and his dominions along with his sweetheart, he had sped to the nether regions with such expedition that he had had no time to change his costume. Hence the equivocation which confounded Adeliza, but at the same time preserved her from being torn to pieces by the no less mystified Madam Lucifer.

Perceiving the state of the case, Lucifer with true gentlemanly feeling resumed his proper semblance, and Madam Lucifer's talons were immediately inserted into his whiskers.

"My dear! my love!" he gasped, as audibly as she would let him, "is this the way it welcomes its own Lucy-pucy?"

"Who is that person?" demanded Madam Lucifer.

"I don't know her," screamed the wretched Lucifer. "I never saw her before. Take her away; shut her up in the deepest dungeon!"

"Not if I know it," sharply replied Madam Lucifer, "You can't bear to part with her, can't you? You would intrigue with her under my nose, would you? Take that! and that! Turn them both out, I say! turn them both out!"

"Certainly, my dearest love, most certainly," responded Lucifer.

"Oh, Sire," cried Moloch and Beelzebub together, "for Heaven's sake let your Majesty consider what he is doing. The Inspector——"

"Bother the Inspector!" screeched Lucifer. "D'ye think I'm not a thousand times more afraid of your mistress than of all the saints in the calendar? There," addressing Adeliza and her betrothed, "be off! You'll find all debts paid, and a nice balance at the bank. Cut! Run!"

They did not wait to be told twice. Earth yawned. The gates of Tartarus stood wide. They found themselves on the side of a steep mountain, down which they scoured madly, hand linked in hand. But fast as they ran, it was long ere they ceased to hear the tongue of Madam Lucifer.

# THE TALISMANS[1]

W HAT A WONDROUS creature is man! What feats the humblest among us perform, which, if related of another order of beings, we should deem incredible!

By what magic could the young student escape the weary old professor, who was prosily proving Time merely a form of thought; a proposition of which, to judge by the little value he appeared to set on the subject of his discourse, he must himself have been fully persuaded? Without exciting his suspicions in the smallest degree, the student stole away to a region inconceivably remote, and presented himself at the portal of a magnificent palace, guarded by goblins, imps, lions, serpents, and monsters whose uncouthness forbids description.

A singular transformation seemed to have befallen the student. In the professor's class he had been noted as timid, awkward, and painfully respectful. He now strode up with an air of alacrity and defiance, brandishing a roll of parchments, and confronted the seven principal goblins, by whom he was successively interrogated.

"Hast thou undergone the seven probations?"

"Yes," said the student.

"Hast thou swallowed the ninety-nine poisons?"

"Ninety-nine times each," said the student.

"Hast thou wedded a Salamander, and divorced her?"

"I have," said the student.

"Art thou at this present time betrothed to a Vampire?"

"I am," said the student.

"Hast thou sacrificed thy mother and sister to the infernal powers?"

"Of course," said the student,

"Hast thou attestations of all these circumstances under the hands and seals of a thousand and one demons?"

The student displayed his parchments.

---

1   *The Talismans.*—First published in *Atlanta* for September, 1890.

"Thou hast undergone every trial," pronounced the seventh goblin; "thou hast won the right to enter the treasury of the treasurer of all things, and to choose from it any one talisman at thy liking."

The imps cheered, the goblins congratulated, the serpents shrank hissing away, the lions fawned upon the student, a centaur bore him upon his back to the treasurer's presence,

The treasurer, an old bent man, with a single lock of silvery hair, received the adventurer with civility.

"I have come," said the student, "for the talismans in thy keeping, to the choice among which I have entitled myself."

"Thou hast fairly earned them," replied the old man, "and I may not say thee nay. Thou canst, however, only possess any of them in the shape which it has received at my hands during the long period for which these have remained in my custody."

"I must submit to the condition," said the student.

"Behold, then, Aladdin's lamp," said the ancient personage, tendering a tiny vase hardly bigger than a pill-box, containing some grains of a coarse, rusty powder.

"Aladdin's lamp!" cried the student.

"All of it, at least, that I have seen fit to preserve," replied the old man. "Thou art but just in time for this even. It is proper to apprise thee that the virtues of the talisman having necessarily dwindled with its bulk, it is at present incompetent to evoke any Genie, and can at most summon an imp, of whose company thou wilt never be able to rid thyself, inasmuch as the least friction will inevitably destroy what little of the talisman remains."

"Confusion!" cried the young man, "Show me, then, Aladdin's ring."

"Here," replied the old man, producing a plain gold hoop,

"This, at least," asked the student, "is not devoid of virtue?"

"Assuredly not, if placed on the finger of some fair lady. For, its magic properties depending wholly upon certain engraved characters, which I have gradually obliterated, it is at present unadapted to any other use than that of a wedding-ring, which it would subserve to admiration."

"Produce another talisman," commanded the youth,

"These," said the ancient treasurer, holding up two shapeless pieces of leather, "are the shoes of swiftness, incomparable until I wore them out."

"This, at least, is bright and weighty," exclaimed the student, as the old man displayed the sword of sharpness.

"In truth a doughty weapon," returned the treasurer, "if wielded by a stronger arm than thine, for it will no longer fly in the air and smite off heads of its own accord, since the new blade hath been fitted to the new hilt."

After a hasty inspection of the empty frame of a magic mirror, and a fragment of the original setting of Solomon's seal, the youth's eye lighted upon a volume full of mysterious characters.

"Whose book is this?" he inquired. "Heavens, it is Michael Scott's!"

"Even so," returned the venerable man, "and its spells have lost nothing of their efficacy. But the last leaf, containing the formula for dismissing spirits after they have been summoned from the nether world, hath been removed by me. Inattention to this circumstance hath caused several most respectable magicians to be torn in pieces, and hath notably increased the number of demons at large."

"Thou old villain!" shouted the exasperated youth, "is this the way in which the treasures in thy custody are protected by thee? Deemest thou that I will brook being thus cheated of my dear-bought talisman? Nay, but I will deprive thee of thine. Give me that lock of hair."

"O good youth," supplicated the now terrified and humbled old man, "bereave me not of the source of all my power. Think, only think of the consequences!"

"I will not think," roared the youth. "Deliver it to me, or I'll rend it from thy head with my own hands."

With a heavy sigh, Time clipped the lock from his brow and handed it to the youth, who quitted the place unmolested by any of the monsters.


ENTERING the great city, the student made his way by narrow and winding streets until, after a considerable delay, he emerged into a large public square. It was crowded with people, gazing intently at the afternoon sky, and the air was rife with a confused murmur of altercations and exclamations.

"It is." "No, I tell you, it is impossible." "It cannot be." "I see it move." "No, it's only my eyes are dazzled." "Who could have believed it?" "Whatever will happen next?"

Following the gaze of the people, the youth discovered that the object of their attention was the sun, in whose aspect, however, he could discover nothing unusual.

"No," a man by him was saying, "it positively has not moved for an hour. I have my instruments by me. I cannot possibly be mistaken."

"It ought to have been behind the houses long ago," said another.

"What's o'clock?" asked a third. The inquiry made many turn their eyes towards the great clock in the square. It had stopped an hour ago. The hands were perfectly motionless. All who had watches simultaneously drew them from their pockets. The motion of each was suspended; so intense, in turn, was the hush of the breathless crowd, that you could have heard a single tick, but there was none to hear.

"Time is no more," proclaimed a leader among the people.

"I am a ruined man," lamented a watchmaker.

"And I," ejaculated a maker of almanacks.

"What of quarter-day?" inquired a landlord and a tenant simultaneously.

"We shall never see the moon again," sobbed a pair of lovers.

"It is well this did not happen at night," observed an optimist.

"Indeed?" questioned the director of a gas company.

"I told you the Last Day would come in our time," said a preacher.

It was still long before the people realised that the trance of Time had paralysed his daughter Mutability as well. Every operation depending on her silent processes was arrested. The unborn could not come to life. The sick could not die. The human frame could not waste. Every one in the enjoyment of health and strength felt assured of the perpetual possession of these blessings, unless he should meet with accident or violent death. But all growth ceased, and all dissolution was stayed. Mothers looked with despair on infants who could never be weaned or learn to walk. Expectant heirs gazed with dismay on immortal fathers and uncles. The reigning beauties, the fashionable boxers and opera dancers were in the highest feather. Nor did the intellectual less rejoice, counting on endless life and unimpaired faculties, and vowing to extend human knowledge beyond the conceivable. The poor and the outcast, the sick and the maimed, the broken-hearted and the dying made, indeed, a dismal outcry, the sincerity of which was doubted by some persons.

As for our student, forgetting his faithful Vampire, he made his way to a young lady of great personal attractions, to whom he had been attached in former days. The sight of her beauty, and the thought that it would be everlasting, revived his passion. To convince her of the perpetuity of her charms, and establish a claim upon her gratitude, he cautiously revealed to her that he was the author of this blissful state of things, and that Time's hair was actually in his possession.

"Oh, you dear good man!" she exclaimed, "how vastly I am obliged to you! Ferdinand will never forsake me now."

"Ferdinand! Leonora, I thought you cared for *me*."

"Oh!" she said, "you young men of science are so conceited!"

The discomfited lover fled from the house, and sought the treasurer's palace. It had vanished with all its monsters. Long did he roam the city ere he mixed again with the crowd, which an old meteorologist was addressing energetically.

"I ask you one thing," he was saying. "Will it ever rain again?"

"Certainly not," replied a geologist and a metaphysician together. "Rain being an agent of Time in the production of change, there can be no place for it under the present dispensation."

"Then will not the crops be burned up? Will the fruits mature? Are they not withering already? What of wells and rivers, and the mighty sea itself? Who will feed your cattle? And who will feed *you*?"

"This concerns us," said the butchers and bakers.

"Us also," added the fishmongers.

"I always thought," said a philosopher, "that this phenomenon must be the work of some malignant wizard."

"Show us the wizard that we may slay him," roared the mob.

Leonora had been communicative, and the student was immediately identified by twenty persons. The lock of hair was found upon him, and was held up in sight of the multitude.

"Kill him!"

"Burn him!"

"Crucify him!"

"It moves! it moves!" cried another division of the crowd. All eyes were bent on the hitherto stationary luminary. It was moving—no, it wasn't; yes, it certainly was. Dared men believe that their shadows were actually lengthening? Was the sun's rim really drawing nigh yonder great edifice? That muffled sound from the vast, silent multitude was, doubtless, the quick beating of innumerable hearts; but that sharper note? Could it be the ticking of watches? Suddenly all the public clocks clanged the first stroke of an hour—an absurdly wrong hour, but it was an hour. No mortal heard the second stroke, drowned in universal shouts of joy and gratitude. The student mingled with the mass, no man regarding him.

When the people had somewhat recovered from their emotion, they fell to disputing as to the cause of the last marvel. No scientific man could get beyond a working hypothesis. The mystery was at length solved by a very humble citizen, a barber.

"Why," he said, "the old gentleman's hair has grown again!"

And so it had! And so it was that the unborn came to life, the dying gave up the ghost, Leonora pulled out a grey hair, and the student told the professor his dream.

## THE ELIXIR OF LIFE[1]

T HE AGED PHILOSOPHER Aboniel inhabited a lofty tower in the city of Balkh, where he devoted himself to the study of chemistry and the occult sciences. No one was ever admitted to his laboratory. Yet Aboniel did not wholly shun intercourse with mankind, but, on the contrary, had seven pupils, towardly youths belonging to the noblest families of the city, whom he instructed at stated times in philosophy and all lawful knowledge, reserving the forbidden lore of magic and alchemy for himself.

But on a certain day he summoned his seven scholars to the mysterious apartment. They entered with awe and curiosity, but perceived nothing save the sage standing behind a table, on which were placed seven crystal phials, filled with a clear liquid resembling water.

"Ye know, my sons," he began, "with what ardour I am reputed to have striven to penetrate the hidden secrets of Nature, and to solve the problems which have allured and baffled the sages of all time. In this rumour doth not err: such hath ever been my object; but, until yesterday, my fortune hath been like unto theirs who have preceded me. The little I could accomplish seemed as nothing in comparison with what I was compelled to leave unachieved. Even now my success is but partial. I have not learned to make gold; the talisman of Solomon is not mine; nor can I recall the principle of life to the dead, or infuse it into inanimate matter. But if I cannot create, I can preserve. I have found the Elixir of Life."

The sage paused to examine the countenances of his scholars. Upon them he read extreme surprise, undoubting belief in the veracity of their teacher, and the dawning gleam of a timid hope that they themselves might become participators in the transcendent discovery he proclaimed. Addressing himself to the latter sentiment—"I am willing," he continued, "to communicate this secret to you, if such be your desire."

An unanimous exclamation assured him that there need be no uncertainty on this point.

1   *The Elixir of Life.*—Published July, 1881, in the third number of a magazine entitled *Our Times*, which blasted the elixir's character by expiring immediately afterwards.

"But remember," he resumed, "that this knowledge, like all knowledge, has its disadvantages and its drawbacks. A price must be paid, and when ye come to learn it, it may well be that it will seem too heavy. Understand that the stipulations I am about to propound are not of my imposing; the secret was imparted to me by spirits not of a benevolent order, and under conditions with which I am constrained strictly to comply. Understand also that I am not minded to employ this knowledge on my own behalf. My fourscore years' acquaintance with life has rendered me more solicitous for methods of abbreviating existence, than of prolonging it. It may be well for you if your twenty years' experience has led you to the same conclusion."

There was not one of the young men who would not readily have admitted, and indeed energetically maintained, the emptiness, vanity, and general unsatisfactoriness of life; for such had ever been the doctrine of their venerated preceptor. Their present behaviour, however, would have convinced him, had he needed conviction, of the magnitude of the gulf between theory and practice, and the feebleness of intellectual persuasion in presence of innate instinct. With one voice they protested their readiness to brave any conceivable peril, and undergo any test which might be imposed as a condition of participation in their master's marvellous secret.

"So be it," returned the sage, "and now hearken to the conditions.

"Each of you must select at hazard, and immediately quaff one of these seven phials, in one of which only is contained the Elixir of Life. Far different are the contents of the others; they are the six most deadly poisons which the utmost subtlety of my skill has enabled me to prepare, and science knows no antidote to any of them. The first scorches up the entrails as with fire; the second slays by freezing every vein, and benumbing every nerve; the third by frantic convulsions. Happy in comparison he who drains the fourth, for he sinks dead upon the ground immediately, smitten as it were with lightning. Nor do I overmuch commiserate him to whose lot the fifth may fall, for slumber descends upon him forthwith, and he passes away in painless oblivion. But wretched he who chooses the sixth, whose hair falls from his head, whose skin peels from his body, and who lingers long in excruciating agonies, a living death. The seventh phial contains the object of your desire. Stretch forth your hands, therefore, simultaneously to this table; let each unhesitatingly grasp and intrepidly drain the potion which fate may allot him, and be the quality of his fortune attested by the result."

The seven disciples contemplated each other with visages of sevenfold blankness. They next unanimously directed their gaze towards their preceptor, hoping to detect some symptom of jocularity upon his venerable features.

Nothing could be descried thereon but the most imperturbable solemnity, or, if perchance anything like an expression of irony lurked beneath this, it was not such irony as they wished to see. Lastly, they scanned the phials, trusting that some infinitesimal distinction might serve to discriminate the elixir from the poisons. But no, the vessels were indistinguishable in external appearance, and the contents of each were equally colourless and transparent.

"Well," demanded Aboniel at length, with real or assumed surprise, "wherefore tarry ye thus? I deemed to have ere this beheld six of you in the agonies of death!"

This utterance did not tend to encourage the seven waverers. Two of the boldest, indeed, advanced their hands half-way to the table, but perceiving that their example was not followed, withdrew them in some confusion.

"Think not, great teacher, that I personally set store by this worthless existence," said one of their number at last, breaking the embarrassing silence, "but I have an aged mother, whose life is bound up with mine."

"I," said the second, "have an unmarried sister, for whom it is meet that I should provide."

"I," said the third, "have an intimate and much-injured friend, whose cause I may in nowise forsake."

"And I an enemy upon whom I would fain be avenged," said the fourth.

"My life," said the fifth, "is wholly devoted to science. Can I consent to lay it down ere I have sounded the seas of the seven climates?"

"Or I, until I have had speech of the man in the moon?" inquired the sixth.

"I," said the seventh, "have neither mother nor sister, friends nor enemies, neither doth my zeal for science equal that of my fellows. But I have all the greater respect for my own skin; yea, the same is exceedingly precious in my sight."

"The conclusion of the whole matter, then," summed up the sage, "is that not one of you will make a venture for the cup of immortality?"

The young men remained silent and abashed, unwilling to acknowledge the justice of their master's taunt, and unable to deny it. They sought for some middle path, which did not readily present itself.

"May we not," said one at last, "may we not cast lots, and each take a phial in succession, as destiny may appoint?"

"I have nothing against this," replied Aboniel, "only remember that the least endeavour to contravene the conditions by amending the chance of any one of you, will ensure the discomfiture of all."

The disciples speedily procured seven quills of unequal lengths, and proceeded to draw them in the usual manner. The shortest remained in the hand of the holder, he who had pleaded his filial duty to his mother.

He approached the table with much resolution, and his hand advanced half the distance without impediment. Then, turning to the holder of the second quill; the man with the sister, he said abruptly:

"The relation between mother and son is notoriously more sacred and intimate than that which obtains between brethren. Were it not therefore fitting that thou shouldst encounter the first risk in my stead?"

"The relationship between an aged mother and an adult son," responded the youth addressed, in a sententious tone, "albeit most holy, cannot in the nature of things be durable, seeing that it must shortly be dissolved by death. Whereas the relationship between brother and sister may endure for many years, if such be the will of Allah. It is therefore proper that thou shouldst first venture the experiment."

"Have I lived to hear such sophistry from a pupil of the wise Aboniel!" exclaimed the first speaker, in generous indignation. "The maternal relationship—"

"A truce to this trifling," cried the other six; "fulfil the conditions, or abandon the task."

Thus urged, the scholar approached his hand to the table, and seized one of the phials. Scarcely, however, had he done so, when he fancied that he detected something of a sinister colour in the liquid, which distinguished it, in his imagination, from the innocent transparency of the rest. He hastily replaced it, and laid hold of the next. At that moment a blaze of light burst forth upon them, and, thunderstruck, the seven scholars were stretched senseless on the ground.

On regaining their faculties they found themselves at the outside of Aboniel's dwelling, stunned by the shock, and humiliated by the part they had played. They jointly pledged inviolable secrecy, and returned to their homes.

The secret of the seven was kept as well as the secret of seven can be expected to be; that is to say, it was not, ere the expiration of seven days, known to more than six-sevenths of the inhabitants of Balkh. The last of these to become acquainted with it was the Sultan, who immediately despatched his guards to apprehend the sage, and confiscate the Elixir. Failing to obtain admission at Aboniel's portal, they broke it open, and, on entering his chamber, found him in a condition which more eloquently than any profession bespoke his disdain for the life-bestowing draught. He was dead in his chair. Before him, on the table, stood the seven phials, six full as previously, the seventh empty. In his hand was a scroll inscribed as follows;

"Six times twice six years have I striven after knowledge, and I now bequeath to the world the fruit of my toil, being six poisons. One more deadly I might have added, but I have refrained,

"Write upon my tomb, that here he lies who forbore to perpetuate human affliction, and bestowed a fatal boon where alone it could be innoxious."

The intruders looked at each other, striving to penetrate the sense of Aboniel's last words. While yet they gazed, they were startled by a loud crash from an adjacent closet, and were even more discomposed as a large monkey bounded forth, whose sleek coat, exuberant playfulness, and preternatural agility convinced all that the deceased philosopher, under an inspiration of supreme irony, had administered to the creature every drop of the Elixir of Life.

# THE POET OF PANOPOLIS

## I

ALTHOUGH IN A manner retired from the world during the fifth and sixth Christian centuries, the banished Gods did not neglect to keep an eye on human affairs, interesting themselves in any movement which might seem to afford them a chance of regaining their lost supremacy, or in any person whose conduct evinced regret at their dethronement. They deeply sympathised with the efforts of their votary Pamprepius to turn the revolt of Illus to their advantage, and excused the low magical arts to which he stooped as a necessary concession to the spirit of a barbarous age. They ministered invisibly to Damascius and his companions on their flight into Persia, alleviating the hardships under which the frames of the veteran philosophers might otherwise have sunk. It was not, indeed, until the burning of the Alexandrian library that they lost all heart and lapsed into the chrysalis-like condition in which they remained until tempted forth by the young sunshine of the Renaissance.

Such a phenomenon for the fifth century as the Dionysiaca of Nonnus of Panopolis could not fail to excite their most lively interest. Forty-eight books of verse on the exploits of Bacchus in the age of pugnacious prelates and filthy coenobites, of imbecile rulers and rampant robbers, of the threatened dissolution of every tie, legal, social, or political; an age of earthquake, war, and famine! Bacchus, who is known from Aristophanes not to have excelled in criticism, protested that his laureate was greater than Homer; and, though Homer could not go quite so far as this, he graciously conceded that if he had himself been an Egyptian of the fifth century, with a faint glimmering of the poetical art, and encumbered with more learning than he knew how to use, he might have written almost as badly as his modern representative. More impartial critics judged Nonnus's achievement more favourably, and all agreed that his steadfastness in the faith deserved some special mark of distinction. The Muses under Pallas's direction (being themselves a little awkward in female accomplishments) embroidered him a robe; Hermes made a lyre, and Hephaestus forged a plectrum. Apollo added a chaplet of laurel, and

Bacchus one of ivy. Whether from distrust of Hermes' integrity, or wishing to make the personal acquaintance of his follower, Phœbus volunteered to convey the testimonial in person, and accordingly took his departure for the Egyptian Thebaid.

As Apollo fared through the sandy and rugged wilderness under the blazing sun of an African summer afternoon, he observed with surprise a vast crowd of strange figures swarming about the mouth of a cavern like bees clustering at the entrance to a hive. On a nearer approach he identified them as a posse of demons besetting a hermit. Words cannot describe the enormous variety of whatever the universe holds of most heterogeneous. Naked women of surpassing loveliness displayed their charms to the anchorite's gaze, sturdy porters bent beneath loads of gold which they heaped at his feet, other shapes not alien from humanity allured his appetite with costly dishes or cooling drinks, or smote at him with swords, or made feints at his eyes with spears, or burned sulphur under his nose, or displayed before him scrolls of poetry or learning, or shrieked blasphemies in his ears, or surveyed him from a little distance with glances of leering affection; while a motley crowd of goblins, wearing the heads of boars or lions, or whisking the tails of dragons, winged, or hoofed, or scaled, or feathered, or all at once, incessantly jostled and wrangled with each other and their betters, mopping and mowing, grunting and grinning, snapping, snarling, constantly running away and returning like gnats dancing over a marsh. The holy man sat doggedly at the entrance of his cavern, with an expression of fathomless stupidity, which seemed to defy all the fiends of the Thebaid to get an idea into his head, or make him vary his attitude by a single inch.

"These people did not exist in our time," said Apollo aloud, "or at least they knew their place, and behaved themselves."

"Sir," said a comparatively grave and respectable demon, addressing the stranger, "I should wish your peregrinity to understand that these imps are mere schoolboys—my pupils, in fact. When their education has made further progress they will be more mannerly, and will comprehend the folly of pestering an unintellectual old gentleman like this worthy Pachymius with beauty for which he has no eyes, and gold for which he has no use, and dainties for which he has no palate, and learning for which he has no head. But I'll wake him up!" And waving his pupils away, the paedagogic fiend placed himself at the anchorite's ear, and shouted into it—

"Nonnus is to be Bishop of Panopolis!"

The hermit's features were instantly animated by an expression of envy and hatred.

"Nonnus!" he exclaimed, "the heathen poet, to have the see of Panopolis, of which *I* was promised the reversion!"

"My dear sir," suggested Apollo, "it is all very well to enliven the reverend eremite; but don't you think it is rather a liberty to make such jokes at the expense of my good friend Nonnus?"

"There is no liberty," said the demon, "for there is no joke. Recanted on Monday. Baptized yesterday. Ordained to-day. To be consecrated to-morrow."

The anchorite poured forth a torrent of the choicest ecclesiastical curses, until he became speechless from exhaustion, and Apollo, profiting by the opportunity, addressed the demon:

"Would it be an unpardonable breach of politeness, respected sir, if I ventured to hint that the illusions your pupils have been trying to impose upon this venerable man have in some small measure impaired the confidence with which I was originally inspired by your advantageous personal appearance?"

"Not in the least," replied the demon, "especially as I can easily make my words good. If you and Pachymius will mount my back I will transport you to Panopolis, where you can verify my assertion for yourselves."

The Deity and the anchorite promptly consented, and seated themselves on the demon's shoulders. The shadow of the fiend's expanded wings fell black and vast on the fiery sand, but diminished and became invisible as he soared to a prodigious height, to escape observation from below. By-and-by the sun's glowing ball touched earth at the extremity of the horizon; it disappeared, the fires of sunset burned low in the west, and the figures of the demon and his freight showed like a black dot against a lake of green sky, growing larger as he cautiously stooped to earth. Grazing temples, skimming pyramids, the party came to ground in the precincts of Panopolis, just in time to avoid the rising moon that would have betrayed them. The demon immediately disappeared. Apollo hastened off to demand an explanation from Nonnus, while Pachymius repaired to a neighbouring convent, peopled, as he knew, by a legion of sturdy monks, ever ready to smite and be smitten in the cause of orthodoxy.

## II

Nonnus sat in his study, wrinkling his brow as he polished his verses by the light of a small lamp. A large scroll lay open on his knees, the contents of which seemed to afford him little satisfaction. Forty-eight more scrolls, resplendent with silver knobs and coquettishly tied with purple cord, reposed in an adjoining book-case; the forty-eight books, manifestly, of the

Panopolitan bard's Dionysiaca. Homer, Euripides, and other poets lay on the floor, having apparently been hurriedly dislodged to make room for divers liturgies and lives of the saints. A set of episcopal robes depended from a hook, and on a side table stood half-a-dozen mitres, which, to all appearance, the designated prelate had been trying on.

"Nonnus," said Phœbus, passing noiselessly through the unresisting wall, "the tale of thy apostasy is then true?"

It would be difficult to determine whether surprise, delight, or dismay preponderated in Nonnus's expression as he lifted up his eyes and recognised the God of Poetry. He had just presence of mind to shuffle his scroll under an enormous dictionary ere he fell at Apollo's feet.

"O Phœbus," he exclaimed, "hadst thou come a week ago!"

"It is true, then?" said Apollo. "Thou forsakest me and the Muses. Thou sidest with them who have broken our statues, unroofed our temples, desecrated our altars, and banished us from among mankind. Thou rejectest the glory of standing alone in a barbarous age as the last witness to culture and civilisation. Thou despisest the gifts of the Gods and the Muses, of which I am even now the bearer. Thou preferrest the mitre to the laurel chaplet, and the hymns of Gregory to the epics of Homer?"

"O Phœbus," replied Nonnus, "were it any God but thou, I should bend before him in silence, having nought to reply. But thou art a poet, and thou understandest the temper of a poet. Thou knowest how beyond other men he is devoured by the craving for sympathy. This and not vulgar vanity is his motive of action; his shaft is launched in vain unless he can deem it embedded in the heart of a friend. Thou mayest well judge what scoffings and revilings my Dionysiac epic has brought upon me in this evil age; yet, had this been all, peradventure I might have borne it. But it was not all. The gentle, the good, the affectionate, they who in happier times would have been my audience, came about me, saying, Nonnus, why sing the strains against which we must shut our ears? Sing what we may listen to, and we will love and honour thee. I could not bear the thought of going to my grave without having awakened an echo of sympathy, and weakly but not basely I have yielded, given them what they craved, and suffered them, since the Muses' garland is not theirs to bestow, to reward me with a mitre."

"And what demanded they?" asked Apollo.

"Oh, a mere romance! Something entirely fabulous."

"I must see it," persisted Apollo; and Nonnus reluctantly disinterred his scroll from under the big dictionary, and handed it up, trembling like a schoolboy who anticipates a castigation for a bad exercise.

"What trash have we here?" cried Phœbus—

>*Αχρονος ην, ακιχητος, εν αρρητω Λογος αρχη,*
>*Ίσοφυης Γενετηρος όμηλικος Τιος αμητωρ,*
>*Και Λογος αυτοφυτοιο Θεου, φως, εκ φαεος φως.*

"If it isn't the beginning of the Gospel of John! Thy impiety is worse than thy poetry!"

Apollo cast the scroll indignantly to the ground. His countenance wore an expression so similar to that with which he is represented in act to smite the Python, that Nonnus judged it prudent to catch up his manuscript and hold it shield-wise before his face.

"Thou doest well," said Apollo, laughing bitterly; "that rampart is indeed impenetrable to my arrows."

Nonnus seemed about to fall prostrate, when a sharp rap came to the door.

"That is the Governor's knock," he exclaimed. "Do not forsake me utterly, O Phœbus!" But as he turned to open the door, Apollo vanished. The Governor entered, a sagacious, good-humoured-looking man in middle life.

"Who was with thee just now?" he asked. "Methought I heard voices."

"Merely the Muse," explained Nonnus, "with whom I am wont to hold nocturnal communings."

"Indeed!" replied the Governor. "Then the Muse has done well to take herself off, and will do even better not to return. Bishops must have no flirtations with Muses, heavenly or earthly—not that I am now altogether certain that thou *wilt* be a bishop."

"How so?" asked Nonnus, not without a feeling of relief.

"Imagine, my dear friend," returned the Governor, "who should turn up this evening but that sordid anchorite Pachymius, to whom the see was promised indeed, but who was reported to have been devoured by vermin in the desert. The rumour seemed so highly plausible that it must be feared that sufficient pains were not taken to verify it—cannot have been, in fact; for, as I said, here he comes, having been brought, as he affirms, through the air by an angel. Little would it have signified if he had come by himself, but he is accompanied by three hundred monks carrying cudgels, who threaten an insurrection if he is not consecrated on the spot. My friend the Archbishop and I are at our wits' end: we have set our hearts on having a gentleman over the diocese, but we cannot afford to have tumults reported at Constantinople. At last, mainly through the mediation of a sable personage whom no one seems to know, but who approves himself most intelligent and obliging, the matter is put off till to-morrow, when them and Pachymius are to compete for the bishopric in public on conditions not yet settled, but which our swarthy friend undertakes to arrange to every one's satisfaction. So keep up a good heart, and don't run away in any case. I know thou art timid, but remember that there is no safety for thee but in victory. If thou yieldest thou wilt be beheaded by me, and if thou art defeated thou wilt certainly be burned by Pachymius."

With this incentive to intrepidity the Governor withdrew, leaving the poor poet in a pitiable state between remorse and terror. One thing alone somewhat comforted him! the mitres had vanished, and the gifts of the Gods lay on the table in their place, whence he concluded that a friendly power might yet be watching over him.

### III

NEXT morning all Panopolis was in an uproar. It was generally known that the pretensions of the candidates for the episcopate would be decided by public competition, and it was rumoured that this would partake of the nature of an ordeal by fire and water. Nothing further had transpired except that the arrangements had been settled by the Governor and Archbishop in concert with two strangers, a dingy Libyan and a handsome young Greek, neither of whom was known in the city, but in both of whom the authorities seemed to repose entire confidence. At the appointed time the people flocked into the theatre, and found the stage already occupied by the parties chiefly concerned. The Governor and the Archbishop sat in the centre on their tribunals: the competitors stood on each side, Pachymius backed by the demon, Nonnus by Apollo; both these supporters, of course, appearing to the assembly in the light of ordinary mortals. Nonnus recognised Apollo perfectly, but Pachymius's limited powers of intelligence seemed entirely engrossed by the discomfort visibly occasioned him by the proximity of an enormous brass vessel of water, close to which burned a bright fire. Nonnus was also ill at ease, and continually directed his attention to a large package, of the contents of which he seemed instinctively cognisant.

All being ready, the Governor rose from his seat, and announced that, with the sanction of his Grace the Archbishop, the invidious task of determining between the claims of two such highly qualified competitors had been delegated to two gentlemen in the enjoyment of his full confidence, who would proceed to apply fitting tests to the respective candidates. Should one fail and the other succeed, the victor would of course be instituted; should both undergo the probation successfully, new criterions of merit would be devised; should both fall short, both would be set aside, and the disputed mitre would be conferred elsewhere. He would first summon Nonnus, long their fellow-citizen, and now their fellow-Christian, to submit himself to the test proposed.

Apollo now rose, and proclaimed in an audible voice, "By virtue of the authority committed to me I call upon Nonnus of Panopolis, candidate for the bishopric of his native city, to demonstrate his fitness for the same by consigning to the flames with his own hands the forty-eight execrable books of heathen poetry composed by him in the days of his darkness and blindness, but now without doubt as detestable to him as to the universal body of the faithful." So saying, he made a sign to an attendant, the wrapping of the package fell away, and the forty-eight scrolls of the Dionysiaca, silver knobs, purple cords, and all, came to view.

"Burn my poem!" exclaimed Nonnus. "Destroy the labours of twenty-four years! Bereave Egypt of its Homer! Erase the name of Nonnus from the tablet of Time!"

"How so, while thou hast the Paraphrase of St. John?" demanded Apollo maliciously.

"Indeed, good youth," said the Governor, who wished to favour Nonnus, "methinks the condition is somewhat exorbitant. A single book might suffice, surely!"

"I am quite content," replied Apollo. "If he consents to burn any of his books he is no poet, and I wash my hands of him."

"Come, Nonnus," cried the Governor, "make haste; one book will do as well as another. Hand them up here."

"It must be with his own hands, please your Excellency," said Apollo.

"Then," cried the Governor, pitching to the poet the first scroll brought to him, "the thirteenth book. Who cares about the thirteenth book? Pop it in!"

"The thirteenth book!" exclaimed Nonnus, "containing the contest between wine and honey, without which my epic becomes totally and entirely unintelligible!"

"This, then," said the Governor, picking out another, which chanced to be the seventeenth,

"In my seventeenth book," objected Nonnus, "Bacchus plants vines in India, and the superiority of wine to milk is convincingly demonstrated."

"Well," rejoined the Governor, "what say you to the twenty-second?"

"With my Hamadryad! I can never give up my Hamadryad!"

"Then," said the Governor, contemptuously hurling the whole set in the direction of Nonnus, "burn which you will, only burn!"

The wretched poet sat among his scrolls looking for a victim. All his forty-eight children were equally dear to his parental heart. The cries of applause and derision from the spectators, and the formidable bellowings of the exasperated monks who surrounded Pachymius, did not tend to steady his nerves, or render the task of critical discrimination the easier.

"I won't! I won't!" he exclaimed at last, starting up defiantly. "Let the bishopric go to the devil! Any one of my similes is worth all the bishoprics in Egypt!"

"Out on the vanity of these poets!" exclaimed the disappointed Governor.

"It is not vanity," said Apollo, "it is paternal affection; and being myself a sufferer from the same infirmity, I rejoice to find him my true son after all."

"Well," said the Governor, turning to the demon: "it is thy man's turn now. Trot him out!"

"Brethren," said the demon to the assembly, "it is meet that he who aspires to the office of bishop should be prepared to give evidence of extraordinary self-denial. Ye have seen even our weak brother Nonnus adoring what he hath burned, albeit as yet unwilling to burn what he hath adored. How much more may be reasonably expected of our brother Pachymius, so eminent for sanctity! I therefore call upon him to demonstrate his humility and self-renunciation, and effectually mortify the natural man, by washing himself in this ample vessel provided for the purpose."

"Wash myself!" exclaimed Pacyhmius, with a vivacity of which he had previously shown no token. "Destroy at one splash the sanctity of fifty-seven years! Avaunt! thou subtle enemy of my salvation! I know thee who thou art, the demon who brought me hither on his back yesterday."

"I thought it had been an angel," said the Governor.

"A demon in the disguise of an angel of light," said Pachymius.

A tumultuous discussion arose among Pachymius's supporters, some extolling his fortitude, others blaming his wrongheadedness.

"What!" said he to the latter, "would ye rob me of my reputation? Shall it be written of me, The holy Pachymius abode in the precepts of the eremites so long as he dwelt in the desert where no water was, but as soon as he came within sight of a bath, he stumbled and fell?"

"Oh, father," urged they, "savoureth not this of vaingloriousness? The demon in the guise of an angel of light, as thou so well saidest even now. Be strong. Quit thyself valiantly. Think of the sufferings of the primitive confessors."

"St. John was cast into a caldron of boiling oil," said one.

"St. Apocryphus was actually drowned," said another.

"I have reason to believe," said a third, "that the loathsomeness of ablution hath been greatly exaggerated by the heretics."

"I know it has," said another. "I *have* washed myself once, though ye might not think it, and can assert that it is by no means as disagreeable as one supposes."

"That is just what I dread," said Pachymius. "Little by little, one might positively come to like it! We should resist the beginnings of evil."

All this time the crowd of his supporters had been pressing upon the anchorite, and had imperceptibly forced him nearer the edge of the vessel, purposing at a convenient season to throw him in. He was now near enough to catch a glimpse of the limpid element. Recoiling in horror, he collected all his energies, and with head depressed towards his chest, and hands thrust forth as if to ward off pollution—butting, kicking, biting the air—he rushed forwards, and with a preternatural force deserving to be enumerated among his miracles, fairly overthrew the enormous vase, the contents streaming on the crowd in front of the stage.

"Take me to my hermitage!" he screamed. "I renounce the bishopric. Take me to my hermitage!"

"Amen," responded the demon, and, assuming his proper shape, he took Pachymius upon his back and flew away with him amid the cheers of the multitude.

Pachymius was speedily deposited at the mouth of his cavern, where he received the visits of the neighbouring anchorites, who came to congratulate him on the constancy with which he had sustained his fiery, or rather watery trial. He spent most of his remaining days in the society of the devil, on which account he was canonised at his death.

"O Phœbus," said Nonnus, when they were alone, "impose upon me any penance thou wilt, so I may but regain thy favour and that of the Muses. But before all things let me destroy my paraphrase."

"Thou shalt not destroy it," said Phœbus, "Thou shalt publish it. That shall be thy penance."

AND so it is that the epic on the exploits of Bacchus and the paraphrase of St. John's Gospel have alike come down to us as the work of Nonnus, whose authorship of both learned men have never been able to deny, having regard to the similarity of style, but never could explain until the facts above narrated came to light in one of the Fayoum papyri recently acquired by the Archduke Rainer.

# THE PURPLE HEAD[1]

Half ignorant, they turned an easy wheel
That set sharp racks at work to pinch and peel.

## I

IN THE HEYDAY of the Emperor Aurelian's greatness, when his strong right arm propped Rome up, and hewed Palmyra down, when he surrounded his capital with walls fifty miles in circuit, and led Tetricus and Zenobia in triumph through its streets, and distributed elephants among the senators, and laid Etruria out in vineyards, and contemplated in leisure moments the suppression of Christianity as a subordinate detail of administration, a mere ripple on the broad ocean of his policy—at this period Bahram the First, King of Persia, naturally became disquieted in his mind.

"This upstart soldier of fortune," reflected he, "has an unseemly habit of overcoming and leading captive legitimate princes; thus prejudicing Divine right in the eyes of the vulgar. The skin of his predecessor Valerian, curried and stuffed with straw, hangs to this hour in the temple at Ctesiphon, a pleasing spectacle to the immortal gods. How would my own skin appear in the temple of Jupiter Capitolinus? This must not be. I will send an embassy to him, and impress him with my greatness. But how?"

He accordingly convoked his counsellors; the viziers, the warriors, the magi, the philosophers; and addressed them thus:

"The king deigns to consult ye touching a difficult matter. I would flatter the pride of Rome, without lowering the pride of Persia. I would propitiate Aurelian, and at the same time humble him. How shall this be accomplished?"

The viziers, the warriors, and the magi answered not a word. Unbroken silence reigned in the assembly, until the turn came to the sage Marcobad, who, prostrating himself, said, "O king, live for ever! In ancient times, as hath been delivered by our ancestors, Persians were instructed in three accomplishments—to ride, to draw the bow, and to speak the truth. Persia still rides

---

1  *The Purple Head.*—Appeared originally in *Fraser's Magazine* for August, 1877.

and shoots; truth-speaking (praised be Ormuzd!) she hath discontinued as unbefitting an enlightened nation. Thou needest not, therefore, scruple to circumvent Aurelian. Offer him that which thou knowest will not be found in his treasury, seeing that it is unique in thine own; giving him, at the same time, to understand that it is the ordinary produce of thy dominions. So, while rejoicing at the gift, shall he be abashed at his inferiority. I refer to the purple robe of her majesty the queen, the like of which is not to be found in the whole earth, neither do any know where the dye that tinges it is produced, save that it proceeds from the uttermost parts of India."

"I approve thy advice," replied Bahram, "and in return will save thy life by banishing thee from my dominions. When my august consort shall learn that thou hast been the means of depriving her of her robe, she will undoubtedly request that thou mayest be flayed, and thou knowest that I can deny her nothing. I therefore counsel thee to depart with all possible swiftness. Repair to the regions where the purple is produced, and if thou returnest with an adequate supply, I undertake that my royal sceptre shall be graciously extended to thee."

The philosopher forsook the royal presence with celerity, and his office of chief examiner of court spikenard was bestowed upon another; as also his house and his garden, his gold and his silver, his wives and his concubines, his camels and his asses, which were numerous.

While the solitary adventurer wended his way eastward, a gorgeous embassy travelled westward in the direction of Rome.

Arrived in the presence of Aurelian, and at the conclusion of his complimentary harangue, the chief envoy produced a cedar casket, from which he drew a purple robe of such surpassing refulgence, that, in the words of the historian who has recorded the transaction, the purple of the emperor and of the matrons appeared ashy grey in comparison.[2] It was accompanied by a letter thus conceived:

"Bahram to Aurelian: health! Receive such purple as we have in Persia."

"Persia, forsooth!" exclaimed Sorianus, a young philosopher versed in natural science, "this purple never was in Persia, except as a rarity. Oh, the mendacity and vanity of these Orientals!"

The ambassador was beginning an angry reply, when Aurelian quelled the dispute with a look, and with some awkwardness delivered himself of a brief oration in acknowledgment of the gift. He took no more notice of the matter

2  *The purple of the emperor and of the matrons appeared ashy grey in comparison.* "Cineris specie decolorari videbantur caeterae divini comparatione fulgoris" (Vopiscus, in Vita Aureliani, cap. xxix.).

until nightfall, when he sent for Sorianus, and inquired where the purple actually was produced.

"In the uttermost parts of India," returned the philosopher.

"Well," rejoined Aurelian, summing up the matter with his accustomed rapidity and clearness of head, "either thou or the Persian king has lied to me, it is plain, and, by the favour of the Gods, it is immaterial which, seeing that my ground for going to war with him is equally good in either case. If he has sought to deceive me, I am right in punishing him; if he possesses what I lack, I am justified in taking it away. It would, however, be convenient to know which of these grounds to inscribe in my manifesto; moreover, I am not ready for hostilities at present; having first to extirpate the Blemmyes, Carpi, and other barbarian vermin. I will therefore despatch thee to India to ascertain by personal examination the truth about the purple. Do not return without it, or I shall cut off thy head. My treasury will charge itself with the administration of thy property during thy absence. The robe shall meanwhile be deposited in the temple of Jupiter Capitolinus. May he have it and thee in his holy keeping!"

Thus, in that age of darkness, were two most eminent philosophers reduced to beggary, and constrained to wander in remote and insalubrious regions; the one for advising a king, the other for instructing an emperor. But the matter did not rest here. For Aurelian, having continued the visible deity of half the world for one hundred and fifty days after the departure of Sorianus, was slain by his own generals. To him succeeded Tacitus, who sank oppressed by the weight of rule; to him Probus, who perished in a military tumult; to him Carus, who was killed by lightning; to him Carinus, who was assassinated by one whom he had wronged; to him Diocletian, who, having maintained himself for twenty years, wisely forbore to tempt Nemesis further, and retired to plant cabbages at Salona. All these sovereigns,[3] differing from each other in every other respect, agreed in a common desire to possess the purple dye, and when the philosopher returned not, successively despatched new emissaries in quest of it. Strange was the diversity of fate which befell these envoys. Some fell into the jaws of lions, some were crushed by monstrous serpents, some trampled by elephants at the command of native princes, some perished of hunger, and some of thirst; some, encountering smooth-browed and dark-tressed girls wreathing their hair with the champak blossom or bathing by moonlight in lotus-mantled tanks, forsook their

---

3    *All these sovereigns.*—"Diligentissime et Aurelianus et Probus et proxime Diocletianus missis diligentissimis confectoribus requisiverunt tale genus purpurae, nec tamen invenire potuerunt" (Vopiscus, *loc. cit.*).

quest, and led thenceforth idyllic lives in groves of banian and of palm. Some
became enamoured of the principles of the Gymnosophists, some couched
themselves for uneasy slumber upon beds of spikes, weening to wake in the
twenty-second heaven. All which romantic variety of fortune was the work
of a diminutive insect that crawled or clung heedless of the purple it was
weaving into the many-coloured web of human life.


II

SOME thirty years after the departure of the Persian embassy to Aurelian,
two travellers met at the bottom of a dell in trans-Gangetic India, having
descended the hill-brow by opposite paths. It was early morning; the sun
had not yet surmounted the timbered and tangled sides of the little valley,
so that the bottom still lay steeped in shadow, and glittering with large pearls
of limpid dew, while the oval space of sky circumscribed by the summit
glowed with the delicate splendour of the purest sapphire. Songs of birds
resounded through the brake, and the water lilies which veiled the rivulet
trickling through the depths of the retreat were unexpanded still. One of the
wayfarers was aged, the other a man of the latest period of middle life. Their
raiment was scanty and soiled; their frames and countenances alike bespoke
fatigue and hardship; but while the elder one moved with moderate alacrity,
the other shuffled painfully along by the help of a staff, shrinking every time
that he placed either of his feet on the ground.

They exchanged looks and greetings as they encountered, and the more
active of the two, whose face was set in an easterly direction, ventured a compassionate allusion to the other's apparent distress.

'I but suffer from the usual effects of crucifixion,' returned the other; and
removing his sandals, displayed two wounds, completely penetrating each
foot.

The Cross had not yet announced victory to Constantine, and was as yet
no passport to respectable society. The first traveller drew back hastily, and
regarded his companion with surprise and suspicion.

"I see what is passing in thy mind," resumed the latter, with a smile; "but
be under no apprehension. I have not undergone the censure of any judicial
tribunal. My crucifixion was merely a painful but necessary incident in my
laudable enterprise of obtaining the marvellous purple dye, to which end I
was despatched unto these regions by the Emperor Aurelian."

"The purple dye!" exclaimed the Persian, for it was he. "Thou hast obtained
it?"

"I have. It is the product of insects found only in a certain valley eastward from hence, to obtain access to which it is before all things needful to elude the vigilance of seven dragons."

"Thou didst elude them? and afterwards?" inquired Marcobad, with eagerness.

"Afterwards," repeated Sorianus, "I made my way into the valley, where I descried the remains of my immediate predecessor prefixed to a cross."

"Thy predecessor?"

"He who had last made the attempt before me. Upon any one's penetrating the Valley of Purple, as it is termed, with the design I have indicated, the inhabitants, observant of the precepts of their ancestors, append him to a cross by the feet only, confining his arms by ropes at the shoulders, and setting vessels of cooling drink within his grasp. If, overcome with thirst, he partakes of the beverage, they leave him to expire at leisure; if he endures for three days, he is permitted to depart with the object of his quest. My predecessor, belonging, as I conjecture, to the Epicurean persuasion, and consequently unable to resist the allurements of sense, had perished in the manner aforesaid. I, a Stoic, refrained and attained."

"Thou didst bear away the tincture? thou hast it now?" impetuously interrogated the Persian.

"Behold it!" replied the Greek, exhibiting a small flask filled with the most gorgeous purple liquid. "What seest thou here?" demanded he triumphantly, holding it up to the light. "To me this vial displays the University of Athens, and throngs of fair youths hearkening to the discourse of one who resembles myself."

"To my vision," responded the Persian, peering at the vial, "it rather reveals a palace, and a dress of honour. But suffer me to contemplate it more closely, for my eyes have waxed dim by over application to study."

So saying, he snatched the flask from Sorianus, and immediately turned to fly. The Greek sprang after his treasure, and failing to grasp Marcobad's wrist, seized his beard, plucking the hair out by handfuls. The infuriated Persian smote him on the head with the crystal flagon. It burst into shivers, and the priceless contents gushed forth in a torrent over the uncovered head and uplifted visage of Sorianus, bathing every hair and feature with the most vivid purple.

The aghast and thunderstricken philosophers remained gazing at each other for a moment.

"It is indelible!" cried Sorianus in distraction, rushing down, however, to the brink of the little stream, and plunging his head beneath the waters. They carried away a cloud of purple, but left the purple head stained as before.

The philosopher, as he upraised his glowing and dripping countenance from the brook, resembled Silenus emerging from one of the rivers which Bacchus metamorphosed into wine during his campaign in India. He resorted to attrition and contrition, to maceration and laceration; he tried friction with leaves, with grass, with sedge, with his garments; he regarded himself in one crystal pool after another, a grotesque anti-Narcissus. At last he flung himself on the earth, and gave free course to his anguish.

The grace of repentance is rarely denied us when our misdeeds have proved unprofitable. Marcobad awkwardly approached.

"Brother," he whispered, "I will restore the tincture of which I have deprived thee, and add thereto an antidote, if such may be found. Await my return under this camphor tree."

So saying, he hastened up the path by which Sorianus had descended, and was speedily out of sight.

### III

SORIANUS tarried long under the camphor tree, but at last, becoming weary, resumed his travels, until emerging from the wilderness he entered the dominions of the King of Ayodhya. His extraordinary appearance speedily attracted the attention of the royal officers, by whom he was apprehended and brought before his majesty.

"It is evident," pronounced the monarch, after bestowing his attention on the case, "that thou art in possession of an object too rare and precious for a private individual, of which thou must accordingly be deprived. I lament the inconvenience thou wilt sustain. I would it had been thy hand or thy foot."

Sorianus acknowledged the royal considerateness, but pleaded the indefeasible right of property which he conceived himself to have acquired in his own head.

"In respect," responded the royal logician, "that thy head is conjoined to thy shoulders, it is thine; but in respect that it is purple, it is mine, purple being a royal monopoly. Thy claim is founded on anatomy, mine on jurisprudence. Shall matter prevail over mind? Shall medicine, the most uncertain of sciences, override law, the perfection of human reason? It is but to the vulgar observation that thou appearest to have a head at all; in the eye of the law thou art acephalous."

"I would submit," urged the philosopher, "that the corporal connection of my head with my body is an essential property, the colour of it a fortuitous accident."

"Thou mightest as well contend," returned the king, "that the law is bound to regard thee in thy abstract condition as a human being, and is disabled from taking cognisance of thy acquired capacity of smuggler—rebel, I might say, seeing that thou hast assumed the purple."

"But the imputation of cruelty which might attach to your majesty's proceedings?"

"There can be no cruelty where there is no injustice. If any there be, it must be on thy part, since, as I have demonstrated, so far from my despoiling thee of thy head, it is thou who iniquitously withholdest mine. I will labour to render this even clearer to thy apprehension. Thou art found, as thou must needs admit, in possession of a contraband article forfeit to the crown by operation of law. What then? Shall the intention of the legislature be frustrated because thou hast insidiously rendered the possession of *my* property inseparable from the possession of *thine*? Shall I, an innocent proprietor, be mulcted of my right by thy fraud and covin? Justice howls, righteousness weeps, integrity stands aghast at the bare notion. No, friend, thy head has not a leg to stand on. Wouldst thou retain it, it behoves thee to show that it will be more serviceable to the owner, namely, myself, upon thy shoulders than elsewhere. This may well be. Hast thou peradventure any subtleties in perfumery? any secrets in confectionery? any skill in the preparation of soup?"

"I have condescended to none of these frivolities, O king. My study hath ever consisted in divine philosophy, whereby men are rendered equal to the gods."

"And yet long most of all for purple!" retorted the monarch, "as I conclude from perceiving thou hast after all preferred the latter. Thy head must indeed be worth the taking."

"Thy taunt is merited, O king! I will importune thee no longer. Thou wilt indeed render me a service in depriving me of this wretched head, hideous without, and I must fear, empty within, seeing that it hath not prevented me from wasting my life in the service of vanity and luxury. Woe to the sage who trusts his infirm wisdom and frail integrity within the precincts of a court! Yet can I foretell a time when philosophers shall no longer run on the futile and selfish errands of kings, and when kings shall be suffered to rule only so far as they obey the bidding of philosophers. Peace, Knowledge, Liberty—"

The King of Ayodhya possessed, beyond all princes of his age, the art of gracefully interrupting an unseasonable discourse. He slightly signed to a courtier in attendance, a scimitar flashed for a moment from its scabbard, and the head of Sorianus rolled on the pavement; the lips murmuring as though still striving to dwell with inarticulate fondness upon the last word of hope for mankind.

It soon appeared that the principle of life was essential to the resplendence of the Purple Head. Within a few minutes it had assumed so ghastly a hue that the Rajah himself was intimidated, and directed that it should be consumed with the body.

The same full-moon that watched the white-robed throng busied with the rites of incremation in a grove of palms, beheld also the seven dragons contending for the body of Marcobad. But, for many a year, the maids and matrons of Rome were not weary of regarding, extolling, and coveting the priceless purple tissue that glowed in the fane of Jupiter Capitolinus.

# THE FIREFLY

A certain Magician had retired for the sake of study to a cottage in a forest. It was summer in a hot country. In the trees near the cottage dwelt a most beautiful Firefly. The light she bore with her was dazzling, yet soft and palpitating, as the evening star, and she seemed a single flash of fire as she shot in and out suddenly from under the screen of foliage, or like a lamp as she perched panting upon some leaf, or hung glowing from some bough; or like a wandering meteor as she eddied gleaming over the summits of the loftiest trees; as she often did, for she was an ambitious Firefly. She learned to know the Magician, and would sometimes alight and sit shining in his hair, or trail her lustre across his book as she crept over the pages. The Magician admired her above all things:

"What eyes she would have if she were a woman!" thought he.

Once he said aloud;

"How happy you must be, you rare, beautiful, brilliant creature!"

"I am not happy," rejoined the Firefly; "what am I, after all, but a flying beetle with a candle in my tail? I wish I were a star."

"Very well," said the Magician, and touched her with his wand, when she became a beautiful star in the twelfth degree of the sign Pisces.

After some nights the Magician asked her if she was content.

"I am not," replied she. "When I was a Firefly I could fly whither I would, and come and go as I pleased. Now I must rise and set at certain times, and shine just so long and no longer. I cannot fly at all, and only creep slowly across the sky. In the day I cannot shine, or if I do no one sees me. I am often darkened by rain, and mist, and cloud. Even when I shine my brightest I am less admired than when I was a Firefly, there are so many others like me. I see, indeed, people looking up from the earth by night towards me, but how do I know that they are looking at me?"

"The laws of nature will have it so," returned the Magician.

"Don't talk to me of the laws of Nature," rejoined the Firefly. "I did not make them, and I don't see why I should be compelled to obey them. Make me something else."

"What would you be?" demanded the accommodating Magician.

"As I creep along here," replied the Star, "I see such a soft pure track of light. It proceeds from the lamp in your study. It flows out of your window like a river of molten silver, both cool and warm. Let me be such a lamp."

"Be it so," answered the Magician: and the star became a lovely alabaster lamp, set in an alcove in his study. Her chaste radiance was shed over his page as long as he continued to read. At a certain hour he extinguished her and retired to rest.

Next morning the Lamp was in a terrible humour.

"I don't choose to be blown out," she said.

"You would have gone out of your own accord else," returned the Magician.

"What!" exclaimed the Lamp, "am I not shining by my own light?"

"Certainly not: you are not now a Firefly or a Star. You must now depend upon others. You would be dark for ever if I did not rekindle you by the help of this oil."

"What!" cried the Lamp, "not shine of my own accord! Never! Make me an everlasting lamp, or I will not be one at all."

"Alas, poor friend," returned the Magician sadly, "there is but one place where aught is everlasting. I can make thee a lamp of the sepulchre."

"Content," responded the Lamp. And the Magician made her one of those strange occult lamps which men find ever and anon when they unseal the tombs of ancient kings and wizards, sustaining without nutriment a perpetual flame. And he bore her to a sepulchre where a great king was lying embalmed and perfect in his golden raiment, and set her at the head of the corpse. And whether the poor fitful Firefly found at last rest in the grave, we may know when we come thither ourselves. But the Magician closed the gates of the sepulchre behind him, and walked thoughtfully home. And as he approached his cottage, behold another Firefly darting and flashing in and out among the trees, as brilliantly as ever the first had done. She was a wise Firefly, well satisfied with the world and everything in it, more particularly her own tail. And if the Magician would have made a pet of her no doubt she would have abode with him. But he never looked at her.

# PAN'S WAND[1]

**I**RIDION HAD BROKEN her lily. A misfortune for any rustic nymph, but especially for her, since her life depended upon it.

From her birth the fate of Iridion had been associated with that of a flower of unusual loveliness—a stately, candid lily, endowed with a charmed life, like its possessor. The seasons came and went without leaving a trace upon it; innocence and beauty seemed as enduring with it, as evanescent with the children of men. In equal though dissimilar loveliness its frolicsome young mistress nourished by its side. One thing alone, the oracle had declared, could prejudice either, and this was an accident to the flower. From such disaster it had long been shielded by the most delicate care; yet in the inscrutable counsels of the Gods, the dreaded calamity had at length come to pass. Broken through the upper part of the stem, the listless flower drooped its petals towards the earth, and seemed to mourn their chastity, already sullied by the wan flaccidity of decay. Not one had fallen as yet, and Iridion felt no pain or any symptom of approaching dissolution, except, it may be, the unwonted seriousness with which, having exhausted all her simple skill on behalf of the languishing plant, she sat down to consider its fate in the light of its bearing upon her own.

Meditation upon an utterly vague subject, whether of apprehension or of hope, speedily lapses into reverie. To Iridion, Death was as indefinable an object of thought as the twin omnipotent controller of human destiny, Love. Love, like the immature fruit on the bough, hung unsoliciting and unsolicited as yet, but slowly ripening to the maiden's hand. Death, a vague film in an illimitable sky, tempered without obscuring the sunshine of her life. Confronted with it suddenly, she found it, in truth, an impalpable cloud, and herself as little competent as the gravest philosopher to answer the self-suggested inquiry, "What shall I be when I am no longer Iridion?" Superstition might have helped her to some definite conceptions, but superstition did not exist in her time. Judge, reader, of its remoteness.

---

1 *Pan's Wand.*—Published originally in a Christmas number of The *Illustrated London News.*

The maiden's reverie might have terminated only with her existence, but for the salutary law which prohibits a young girl, not in love or at school, from sitting still more than ten minutes. As she shifted her seat at the expiration of something like this period, she perceived that she had been sitting on a goatskin, and with a natural association of ideas—

"I will ask Pan," she exclaimed.

Pan at that time inhabited a cavern hard by the maiden's dwelling, which the judicious reader will have divined could only have been situated in Arcadia. The honest god was on excellent terms with the simple people; his goats browsed freely along with theirs, and the most melodious of the rustic minstrels attributed their proficiency to his instructions. The maidens were on a more reserved footing of intimacy—at least so they wished it to be understood, and so it was understood, of course. Iridion, however, decided that the occasion would warrant her incurring the risk even of a kiss, and lost no time in setting forth upon her errand, carrying her poor broken flower in its earthen vase. It was the time of day when the god might be supposed to be arousing himself from his afternoon's siesta. She did not fear that his door would be closed against her, for he had no door.

The sylvan deity stood, in fact, at the entrance of his cavern, about to proceed in quest of his goats. The appearance of Iridion operated a change in his intention, and he courteously escorted her to a seat of turf erected for the special accommodation of his fair visitors, while he placed for himself one of stone.

"Pan," she began, "I have broken my lily."

"That is a sad pity, child. If it had been a reed, now, you could have made a flute of it."

"I should not have time, Pan," and she recounted her story. A godlike nature cannot confound truth with falsehood, though it may mistake falsehood for truth. Pan therefore never doubted Iridion's strange narrative, and, having heard it to the end, observed, "You will find plenty more lilies in Elysium."

"Common lilies, Pan; not like mine."

"You are wrong. The lilies of Elysium—asphodels as they call them there—are as immortal as the Elysians themselves. I have seen them in Proserpine's hair at Jupiter's entertainment; they were as fresh as she was. There is no doubt you might gather them by handfuls—at least if you had any hands—and wear them to your heart's content, if you had but a heart."

"That's just what perplexes me, Pan. It is not the dying I mind, it's the living. How am I to live without anything alive about me? If you take away my hands, and my heart, and my brains, and my eyes, and my ears, and above all my tongue, what is left me to live in Elysium?"

As the maiden spake a petal detached itself from the emaciated lily, and she pressed her hand to her brow with a responsive cry of pain.

"Poor child!" said Pan compassionately, "you will feel no more pain by-and-by."

"I suppose not, Pan, since you say so. But if I can feel no pain, how can I feel any pleasure?

"In an incomprehensible manner," said Pan.

"How can I feel, if I have no feeling? and what am I to do without it?"

"You can think!" replied Pan. "Thinking (not that I am greatly given to it myself) is a much finer thing than feeling; no right-minded person doubts that. Feeling, as I have heard Minerva say, is a property of matter, and matter, except, of course, that appertaining to myself and the other happy gods, is vile and perishable—quite immaterial, in fact. Thought alone is transcendent, incorruptible, and undying!"

"But, Pan, how can any one think thoughts without something to think them with? I never thought of anything that I have not seen, or touched, or smelt, or tasted, or heard about from some one else. If I think with nothing, and about nothing, is that thinking, do you think?"

"I think," answered Pan evasively, "that you are a sensationalist, a materialist, a sceptic, a revolutionist; and if you had not sought the assistance of a god, I should have said not much better than an atheist. I also think it is time I thought about some physic for you instead of metaphysics, which are bad for my head, and for your soul." Saying this, Pan, with rough tenderness, deposited the almost fainting maiden upon a couch of fern, and, having supported her head with a bundle of herbs, leaned his own upon his hand, and reflected with all his might. The declining sun was now nearly opposite the cavern's mouth, and his rays, straggling through the creepers that wove their intricacies over the entrance, chequered with lustrous patches the forms of the dying girl and the meditating god. Ever and anon, a petal would drop from the flower; this was always succeeded by a shuddering tremor throughout Iridion's frame and a more forlorn expression on her pallid countenance: while Pan's jovial features assumed an expression of deeper concern as he pressed his knotty hand more resolutely against his shaggy forehead, and wrung his dexter horn with a more determined grasp, as though he had caught a burrowing idea by the tail.

"Aha!" he suddenly exclaimed, "I have it!"

"What have you, Pan?" faintly lisped the expiring Iridion.

Instead of replying, Pan grasped a wand that leaned against the wall of his grot, and with it touched the maiden and the flower. O strange meta-morphosis! Where the latter had been pining in its vase, a lovely girl, the image of Iridion, lay along the ground with dishevelled hair, clammy brow, and features slightly distorted by the last struggles of death. On the ferny couch stood an earthen vase, from which rose a magnificent lily, stately, with unfractured stem, and with no stain or wrinkle on its numerous petals.

"Aha!" repeated Pan; "I think we are ready for him now." Then, having lifted the inanimate body to the couch, and placed the vase, with its contents, on the floor of his cavern, he stepped to the entrance, and shading his eyes with his hand, seemed to gaze abroad in quest of some anticipated visitor.

The boughs at the foot of the steep path to the cave divided, and a figure appeared at the foot of the rock. The stranger's mien was majestic, but the fitness of his proportions diminished his really colossal stature to something more nearly the measure of mortality. His form was enveloped in a sweeping sad-coloured robe; a light, thin veil resting on his countenance, mitigated, without concealing, the not ungentle austerity of his marble features. His gait was remarkable; nothing could be more remote from every indication of haste, yet such was the actual celerity of his progression, that Pan had scarcely beheld him ere he started to find him already at his side.

The stranger, without disturbing his veil, seemed to comprehend the whole interior of the grotto with a glance; then, with the slightest gesture of recognition to Pan, he glided to the couch on which lay the metamorphosed lily, upraised the fictitious Iridion in his arms with indescribable gentleness, and disappeared with her as swiftly and silently as he had come. The discreet Pan struggled with suppressed merriment until the stranger was fairly out of hearing, then threw himself back upon his seat and laughed till the cave rang.

"And now," he said, "to finish the business." He lifted the transformed maiden into the vase, and caressed her beauty with an exulting but careful hand. There was a glory and a splendour in the flower such as had never until then been beheld in any earthly lily. The stem vibrated, the leaves shook in unison, the petals panted and suspired, and seemed blanched with a white-ness intense as the core of sunlight, as they throbbed in anticipation of the richer existence awaiting them.

Impatient to complete his task, Pan was about to grasp his wand when the motion was arrested as the sinking beam of the sun was intercepted by a gigantic shadow, and the stranger again stood by his side. The unbidden guest uttered no word, but his manner was sufficiently expressive of wrath as he disdainfully cast on the ground a broken, withered lily, the relic of what had bloomed with such loveliness in the morning, and had since for a brief space been arrayed in the vesture of humanity. He pointed imperiously to the gorgeous tenant of the vase, and seemed to expect Pan to deliver it forthwith.

"Look here," said Pan, with more decision than dignity, "I am a poor country god, but I know the law. If you can find on this plant one speck, one stain, one token that you have anything to do with her, take her, and welcome. If you cannot, take yourself off instead."

"Be it so," returned the stranger, haughtily declining the proffered inspection. "You will find it is ill joking with Death."

So saying, he quitted the cavern.

Pan sat down chuckling, yet not wholly at ease, for if the charity of Death is beautiful even to a mortal, his anger is terrible, even to a god. Anxious to terminate the adventure, he reached towards the charmed wand by whose wonderful instrumentality the dying maiden had already become a living flower, and was now to undergo a yet more delightful metamorphosis.

Wondrous wand! But where was it? For Death, the great transfigurer of all below this lunar sphere, had given Pan a characteristic proof of his superior cunning. Where the wand had reposed writhed a ghastly worm, which, as Pan's glance fell upon it, glided towards him, uplifting its head with an aspect of defiance. Pan's immortal nature sickened at the emblem of corruption; he could not for all Olympus have touched his metamorphosed treasure. As he shrank back the creature pursued its way towards the vase; but a marvellous change befell it as it came under the shadow of the flower. The writhing body divided, end from end, the sordid scales sank indiscernibly into the dust, and an exquisite butterfly, arising from the ground, alighted on the lily, and remained for a moment fanning its wings in the last sunbeam, ere it unclosed them to the evening breeze. Pan, looking eagerly after the Psyche in its flight, did not perceive what was taking place in the cavern; but the magic wand, now for ever lost to its possessor, must have cancelled its own spell, for when his gaze reverted from the ineffectual pursuit, the living lily had disappeared, and Iridion lay a corpse upon the ground, the faded flower of her destiny reposing upon her breast.

Death now stood for a third time upon Pan's threshold, but Pan heeded him not.

# A PAGE FROM THE BOOK OF FOLLY[1]

"That owned the virtuous ring and glass."
—*Il Penseroso.*

## I

"AURELIA!"

"Otto!"

"Must we then part?"

They were folded in each other's arms. There never was such kissing.

"How shall we henceforth exchange the sweet tokens of our undying affection, my Otto?"

"Alas, my Aurelia, I know not! Thy Otto blushes to acquaint thee that he cannot write."

"Blush not, my Otto, thou needest not reproach thyself. Even couldest thou write, thy Aurelia could not read. Oh these dark ages!"

They remained some minutes gazing on each other with an expression of fond perplexity. Suddenly the damsel's features assumed the aspect of one who experiences the visitation of a happy thought. Gently yet decidedly she pronounced:

"We will exchange rings."

They drew off their rings simultaneously. "This, Aurelia, was my grandfather's."

"This, Otto, was my grandmother's, which she charged me with her dying breath never to part with save to him whom alone I loved."

"Mine is a brilliant, more radiant than aught save the eyes of my Aurelia."

And, in fact, Aurelia's eyes hardly sustained the comparison. A finer stone could not easily be found.

"Mine is a sapphire, azure as the everlasting heavens, and type of a constancy enduring as they."

In truth, it was of a tint seldom to be met with in sapphires.

---

1  *A Page from the Book of Folly.*—Appeared in *Temple Bar* for 1871.

The exchange made, the lady seemed less anxious to detain her lover.

"Beware, Otto!" she cried, as he slid down the cord, which yielded him an oscillatory transit from her casement to the moat, where he alighted knee-deep in mud. "Beware!—if my brother should be gazing from his chamber on the resplendent moon!"

But that ferocious young baron was accustomed to spend his time in a less romantic manner; and so it came to pass that Otto encountered him not.

II

Days, weeks, months had passed by, and Otto, a wanderer in a foreign land, had heard no tidings of his Aurelia. Ye who have loved may well conceive how her ring was all in all to him. He divided his time pretty equally between gazing into its cerulean depths, as though her lovely image were mirrored therein, and pressing its chilly surface to his lips, little as it recalled the warmth and balminess of hers.

The burnished glow of gold, the chaste sheen of silver, the dance and sparkle of light in multitudinous gems, arrested his attention as he one evening perambulated the streets of a great city. He beheld a jeweller's shop. The grey-headed, spectacled lapidary sat at a bench within, sedulously polishing a streaked pebble by the light of a small lamp. A sudden thought struck Otto; he entered the shop, and, presenting the ring to the jeweller, inquired in a tone of suppressed exultation:

"What hold you for the worth of this inestimable ring?"

The jeweller, with no expression of surprise or curiosity, received the ring from Otto, held it to the light, glanced slightly at the stone, somewhat more carefully at the setting, laid the ring for a moment in a pair of light scales, and, handing it back to Otto, remarked with a tone and manner of the most entire indifference:

"The worth of this inestimable ring is one shilling and sixpence."

"Caitiff of a huckster!" exclaimed Otto, bringing down his fist on the bench with such vigour that the pebbles leaped up and fell rattling down: "Sayest thou this of a gem framed by genii in the bowels of the earth?"

"Nay, friend," returned the jeweller with the same imperturbable air, "that thy gem was framed of earth I in nowise question, seeing that it doth principally consist of sand. But when thou speakest of genii and the bowels of the earth, thou wilt not, I hope, take it amiss if I crave better proof than thy word that the devil has taken to glass-making. For glass, and nothing else, credit me, thy jewel is."

"And the gold?" gasped Otto.

"There is just as much gold in thy ring as sufficeth to gild handsomely a like superficies of brass, which is not saying much."

And, applying a sponge dipped in some liquid to a small part of the hoop, the jeweller disclosed the dull hue of the baser metal so evidently that Otto could hardly doubt longer. He doubted no more when the lapidary laid his ring in the scales against another of the same size and make, and pointed to the inequality of the balance.

"Thou seest," he continued, "that in our craft a very little gold goes a very great way. It is far otherwise in the world, as thou, albeit in no sort eminent for sapience, hast doubtless ere this ascertained for thyself. Thou art evidently a prodigious fool!"

This latter disparaging observation could be safely ventured upon, as Otto had rushed from the shop, speechless with rage.

Was Aurelia deceiver or deceived? Should he execrate her, or her venerable grandmother, or some unknown person? The point was too knotty to be solved in the agitated state of his feelings. He decided it provisionally by execrating the entire human race, not forgetting himself.

In a mood like Otto's a trifling circumstance is sufficient to determine the quality of action. The ancient city of which he was at the time an inhabitant was traversed by a large river spanned by a quaint and many-arched bridge, to which his frantic and aimless wanderings had conducted him. Spires and gables and lengthy façades were reflected in the water, blended with the shadows of boats, and interspersed with the mirrored flames of innumerable windows on land, or of lanterns suspended from the masts or sterns of the vessels. The dancing ripples bickered and flickered, and seemed to say, "Come hither to us," while the dark reaches of still water in the shadow of the piers promised that whatever might be entrusted to them should be faithfully retained. Swayed by a sudden impulse, Otto drew his ring from his finger. It gleamed an instant aloft in air; in another the relaxation of his grasp would have consigned it to the stream.

"Forbear!"

Otto turned, and perceived a singular figure by his side. The stranger was tall and thin, and attired in a dusky cloak which only partially concealed a flame-coloured jerkin. A cock's feather peaked up in his cap; his eyes were piercingly brilliant; his nose was aquiline; the expression of his features sinister and sardonic. Had Otto been more observant, or less preoccupied, he might have noticed that the stranger's left shoe was of a peculiar form, and that he limped some little with the corresponding foot.

"Forbear, I say; thou knowest not what thou doest."

"And what skills what I do with a piece of common glass?"

"Thou errest, friend; thy ring is not common glass. Had thy mistress surmised its mystic virtues, she would have thought oftener than twice ere exchanging it for thy diamond."

"What may these virtues be?" eagerly demanded Otto.

"In the first place, it will show thee when thy mistress may chance to think of thee, as it will then prick thy finger."

"Now I know thee for a lying knave," exclaimed the youth indignantly. "Learn, to thy confusion, that it hath not pricked me once since I parted from Aurelia."

"Which proves that she has never once thought of thee."

"Villain!" shouted Otto, "say that again, and I will transfix thee."

"Thou mayest if thou canst," rejoined the stranger, with an expression of such cutting scorn that Otto's spirit quailed, and he felt a secret but overpowering conviction of his interlocutor's veracity. Rallying, however, in some measure, he exclaimed:

"Aurelia is true! I will wager my soul upon it!"

"Done!" screamed the stranger in a strident voice of triumph, while a burst of diabolical laughter seemed to proceed from every cranny of the eaves and piers of the old bridge, and to be taken up by goblin echoes from the summits of the adjacent towers and steeples.

Otto's blood ran chill, but he mustered sufficient courage to inquire hoarsely:

"What of its further virtues?"

"When it shall have pricked thee," returned the mysterious personage, "on turning it once completely round thy finger thou wilt see thy mistress wherever she may be. If thou turnest it the second time, thou wilt know what her thought of thee is; and, if the third time, thou wilt find thyself in her presence. But I give thee fair warning that by doing this thou wilt place thyself in a more disastrous plight than any thou hast experienced hitherto. And now farewell."

The speaker disappeared. Otto stood alone upon the bridge. He saw nothing around him but the stream, with its shadows and lights, as he slowly and thoughtfully turned round to walk to his lodgings.

### III

YE who have loved, et cetera, as aforesaid, will comprehend the anxiety with which Otto henceforth consulted his ring. He was continually adjusting it to his finger in a manner, as he fancied, to render the anticipated puncture more perceptible when it should come at last. He would have worn it on all his fingers in succession had the conformation of his robust hand admitted of its being placed on any but the slenderest. Thousands of times he could have sworn that he felt the admonitory sting; thousands of times he turned the trinket round and round with desperate impatience; but Aurelia's form remained as invisible, her thoughts as inscrutable, as before. His great dread was that he might be pricked in his sleep, on which account he would sit up watching far into the morn. For, as he reasoned, not without plausibility, when could he more rationally hope for a place in Aurelia's thoughts than at that witching and suggestive period? She might surely think of him when she had nothing else to do! Had she really nothing else to do? And Otto grew sick and livid with jealousy. It of course frequently occurred to him to doubt and deride the virtues of the ring, and he was several times upon the point of flinging it away. But the more he pondered upon the appearance and manner of the stranger, the less able he felt to resist the conviction of his truthfulness.

At last a most unmistakable puncture! the distinct, though slight, pang of a miniature wound. A crimson bead of blood rose on Otto's finger, swelled to its due proportion, and became a trickling blot.

"She is thinking of me!" cried he rapturously, as if this were an instance of the most signal and unforeseen condescension. All the weary expectancy of the last six months was forgotten. He would have railed at himself had the bliss of the moment allowed him to remember that he had ever railed at her.

Otto turned his ring once, and Aurelia became visible in an instant. She was standing before the mercer's booth in the chief street of the little town which adjoined her father's castle. Her gaze was riveted on a silk mantle, trimmed with costly furs, which depended from a hook inside the doorway. Her lovely features wore an expression of extreme dissatisfaction. She was replacing a purse, apparently by no means weighty, in her embroidered girdle.

Otto turned the ring the second time, and Aurelia's silvery accents immediately became audible to the following effect:

"If that fool Otto were here, he would buy it for me."

She turned away, and walked down the street. Otto uttered a cry like the shriek of an uprooted mandrake. His hand was upon the ring to turn it for the third time; but the stranger's warning occurred to him, and for a moment he forbore. In that moment the entire vision vanished from before his eyes.

What boots it to describe Otto's feelings upon this revelation of Aurelia's sentiments? For lovers, description would be needless; to wiser people, incomprehensible. Suffice it to say, that as his lady deemed him a fool he appeared bent on proving that she did not deem amiss.

A long space of time elapsed without any further admonition from the ring. Perhaps Aurelia had no further occasion for his purse; perhaps she had found another pursebearer. The latter view of the case appeared the more plausible to Otto, and it hugely aggravated his torments.

At last the moment came. It was the hour of midnight. Again Otto felt the sharp puncture, again the ruby drop started from his finger, again he turned the ring, and again beheld Aurelia. She was in her chamber, but not alone. Her companion was a youth of Otto's age. She was in the act of placing Otto's brilliant upon his finger. Otto turned his own ring, and heard her utter, with singular distinctness:

"This ring was given me by the greatest fool I ever knew. Little did he imagine that it would one day be the means of procuring me liberty, and bliss in the arms of my Arnold. My venerable grandmother—"

The voice expired upon her lips, for Otto stood before her.

Arnold precipitated himself from the window, carrying the ring with him. Otto, glaring at his faithless mistress, stood in the middle of the apartment with his sword unsheathed. Was he about to use it? None can say; for at this moment the young Baron burst into the room, and, without the slightest apology for the liberty he was taking, passed his sword through Otto's body.

Otto groaned, and fell upon his face. He was dead. The young Baron ungently reversed the position of the corpse, and scanned its features with evident surprise and dissatisfaction.

"It is not Arnold, after all!" he muttered. "Who would have thought it?"

"Thou seest, brother, how unjust were thy suspicions," observed Aurelia, with an air of injured but not implacable virtue. "As for this abominable ravisher——" Her feelings forbade her to proceed.

The brother looked mystified. There was something beyond his comprehension in the affair; yet he could not but acknowledge that Otto was the person who had rushed by him as he lay in wait upon the stairs. He finally determined that it was best to say nothing about the matter: a resolution the easier of performance as he was not wont to be lavish of his words at any time. He wiped his sword on his sister's curtains, and was about to withdraw, when Aurelia again spoke:

"Ere thou departest, brother, have the goodness to ring the bell, and desire the menials to remove this carrion from my apartment."

The young Baron sulkily complied, and retreated growling to his chamber.

The attendants carried Otto's body forth. To the honour of her sex be it recorded, that before this was done Aurelia vouchsafed one glance to the corpse of her old lover. Her eye fell on the brazen ring. "And he has actually worn it all this time!" thought she.

"Would have outraged my daughter, would he?" said the old Baron, when the transaction was reported to him. "Let him be buried in a concatenation accordingly."

"What the guy dickens be a concatrenation, Geoffrey?" interrogated Giles.

"Methinks it is Latin for a ditch," responded Geoffrey.

This interpretation commending itself to the general judgment of the retainers, Otto was interred in the shelving bank of the old moat, just under Aurelia's window. A rough stone was laid upon the grave. The magic ring, which no one thought worth appropriating, remained upon the corpse's finger. Thou mayest probably find it there, reader, if thou searchest long enough.

The first visitor to Otto's humble sepulchre was, after all, Aurelia herself, who alighted thereon on the following night after letting herself down from her casement to fly with Arnold. Their escape was successfully achieved upon a pair of excellent horses, the proceeds of Otto's diamond, which had become the property of a Jew.

On the third night an aged monk stood by Otto's grave, and wept plentifully. He carried a lantern, a mallet, and a chisel. "He was my pupil," sobbed the good old man. "It were meet to contribute what in me lies to the befitting perpetuation of his memory."

Setting down the lantern, he commenced work, and with pious toil engraved on the stone in the Latin of the period:

"HAC MAGNUS STULTUS JACET IN FOSSA SEPULTUS.
MULIER CUI CREDIDIT MORTUUM ILLUM REDDIDIT."

Here he paused, at the end of his strength and of his Latin.

"Beshrew my old arms and brains!" he sighed.

"Hem!" coughed a deep voice in his vicinity.

The monk looked up. The personage in the dusky cloak and flame-coloured jerkin was standing over him.

"Good monk," said the fiend, "what dost thou here?"

"Good fiend," said the monk, "I am inscribing an epitaph to the memory of a departed friend. Thou mightest kindly aid me to complete it."

"Truly," rejoined the demon, "it would become me to do so, seeing that I have his soul here in my pocket. Thou wilt not expect me to employ the language of the Church. Nathless, I see not wherefore the vernacular may not serve as well."

And, taking the mallet and chisel, he completed the monk's inscription with the supplementary legend:

"SERVED HIM RIGHT."

# THE BELL OF SAINT EUSCHEMON

T HE TOWN OF Epinal, in Lorraine, possessed in the Middle Ages a peal
of three bells, respectively dedicated to St. Eulogius, St. Eucherius, and
St. Euschemon, whose tintinnabulation was found to be an effectual
safeguard against all thunderstorms. Let the heavens be ever so murky, it
was merely requisite to set the bells ringing, and no lightning flashed and no
thunder peal broke over the town, nor was the neighbouring country within
hearing of them ravaged by hail or flood.

One day the three saints, Eulogius, Eucherius, and Euschemon, were
sitting together, exceedingly well content with themselves and everything
around them, as indeed they had every right to be, supposing that they were
in Paradise. We say supposing, not being for our own part entirely able to
reconcile this locality with the presence of certain cans and flagons, which
had been fuller than they were.

"What a happy reflection for a Saint," said Eulogius, who was rapidly passing from the mellow stage of good fellowship to the maudlin, "that even after
his celestial assumption he is permitted to continue a source of blessing and
benefit to his fellow-creatures as yet dwelling in the shade of mortality! The
thought of the services of my bell, in averting lightning and inundation from
the good people of Epinal, fills me with indescribable beatitude."

"*Your* bell!" interposed Eucherius, whose path had lain through the
mellow to the quarrelsome. "*Your* bell, quotha! You had as good clink this
cannakin" (suiting the action to the word) "as your bell. It's my bell that does
the business."

"I think you might put in a word for *my* bell," interposed Euschemon, a
little squinting saint, very merry and friendly when not put out, as on the
present occasion.

"Your bell!" retorted the big saints, with incredible disdain; and, forgetting
their own altercation, they fell so fiercely on their little brother that he ran
away, stopping his ears with his hands, and vowing vengeance.

A short time after this fracas, a personage of venerable appearance presented himself at Epinal, and applied for the post of sacristan and bell-ringer,

at that time vacant. Though he squinted, his appearance was far from dis-agreeable, and he obtained the appointment without difficulty. His deport-ment in it was in all respects edifying; or if he evinced some little remissness in the service of Saints Eulogius and Eucherius, this was more than compen-sated by his devotion to the hitherto somewhat slighted Saint Euschemon. It was indeed observed that candles, garlands, and other offerings made at the shrines of the two senior saints were found to be transferred in an unac-countable and mystical manner to the junior, which induced experienced persons to remark that a miracle was certainly brewing. Nothing, however, occurred until, one hot summer afternoon, the indications of a storm became so threatening that the sacristan was directed to ring the bells. Scarcely had he begun than the sky became clear, but instead of the usual rich volume of sound the townsmen heard with astonishment a solitary tinkle, sounding quite ridiculous and unsatisfactory in comparison. St. Euschemon's bell was ringing by itself.

In a trice priests and laymen swarmed to the belfry, and indignantly demanded of the sacristan what he meant.

"To enlighten you," he responded. "To teach you to give honour where honour is due. To unmask those canonised impostors."

And he called their attention to the fact that the clappers of the bells of Eulogius and Eucherius were so fastened up that they could not emit a sound, while that of Euschemon vibrated freely.

"Ye see," he continued, "that these sound not at all, yet is the tempest stayed. Is it not thence manifest that the virtue resides solely in the bell of the blessed Euschemon?"

The argument seemed conclusive to the majority, but those of the clergy who ministered at the altars of Eulogius and Eucherius stoutly resisted, maintaining that no just decision could be arrived at until Euschemon's bell was subjected to the same treatment as the others. Their view even-tually prevailed, to the great dismay of Euschemon, who, although firmly convinced of the virtue of his own bell, did not in his heart disbelieve in the bells of his brethren. Imagine his relief and amazed joy when, upon his bell being silenced, the storm, for the first time in the memory of the oldest inhabitant, broke with full fury over Epinal, and, for all the frantic pealing of the other two bells, raged with unspeakable fierceness until his own was brought into requisition, when, as if by enchantment, the rain ceased, the thunder-clouds dispersed, and the sun broke out gloriously from the blue sky.

"Carry him in procession!" shouted the crowd.

"Amen, brethren; here I am," rejoined Euschemon, stepping briskly into the midst of the troop.

"And why in the name of Zernebock should we carry *you?*" demanded some, while others ran off to lug forth the image, the object of their devotion.

"Why, verily," Euschemon began, and stopped short. How indeed was he to prove to them that he *was* Euschemon? His personal resemblance to his effigy, the work of a sculptor of the idealistic school, was in no respect remarkable; and he felt, alas! that he could no more work a miracle than you or I. In the sight of the multitude he was only an elderly sexton with a cast in his eye, with nothing but his office to keep him out of the workhouse. A further and more awkward question arose, how on earth was he to get back to Paradise? The ordinary method was not available, for he had already been dead for several centuries; and no other presented itself to his imagination.

Muttering apologies, and glad to be overlooked, Euschemon shrank into a corner, but slightly comforted by the honours his image was receiving at the hands of the good people of Epinal. As time wore on he became pensive and restless, and nothing pleased him so well as to ascend to the belfry on moonlight nights, scribbling disparagement on the bells of Eulogius and Eucherius, which had ceased to be rung, and patting and caressing his own, which now did duty for all three. With alarm he noticed one night an incipient crack, which threatened to become a serious flaw.

"If this goes on," said a voice behind him, "I shall get a holiday."

Euschemon turned round, and with indescribable dismay perceived a gigantic demon, negligently resting his hand on the top of the bell, and looking as if it would cost him nothing to pitch it and Euschemon together to the other side of the town.

"Avaunt, fiend," he stammered, with as much dignity as he could muster, "or at least remove thy unhallowed paw from my bell."

"Come, Eusky," replied the fiend, with profane familiarity, "don't be a fool. You are not really such an ass as to imagine that your virtue has anything to do with the virtue of this bell?"

"Whose virtue then?" demanded Euschemon.

"Why truly," said the demon, "mine! When this bell was cast I was imprisoned in it by a potent enchanter, and so long as I am in it no storm can come within sound of its ringing. I am not allowed to quit it except by night, and then no further than an arm's length: this, however, I take the liberty of measuring by my own arm, which happens to be a long one. This must continue, as I learn, until I receive a kiss from some bishop of distinguished sanctity. Thou hast done some bishoping in thy time, peradventure?"

Euschemon energetically protested that he had been on earth but a simple laic, which was indeed the fact, and was also the reason why Eulogius and Eucherius despised him, but which, though he did not think it needful to tell the demon, he found a singular relief under present circumstances.

"Well," continued the fiend, "I wish he may turn up shortly, for I am half deaf already with the banging and booming of this infernal clapper, which seems to have grown much worse of late; and the blessings and the crossings and the aspersions which I have to go through are most repugnant to my tastes, and unsuitable to my position in society. Bye-bye, Eusky; come up to-morrow night." And the fiend slipped back into the bell, and instantly became invisible.

The humiliation of poor Euschemon on learning that he was indebted for his credit to the devil is easier to imagine than to describe. He did not, however, fail at the rendezvous next night, and found the demon sitting outside the bell in a most affable frame of mind. It did not take long for the devil and the saint to become very good friends, both wanting company, and the former being apparently as much amused by the latter's simplicity as the latter was charmed by the former's knowingness. Euschemon learned numbers of things of which he had not had the faintest notion. The demon taught him how to play cards (just invented by the Saracens), and initiated him into divers "arts, though unimagined, yet to be," such as smoking tobacco, making a book on the Derby, and inditing queer stories for Society journals. He drew the most profane but irresistibly funny caricatures of Eulogius and Eucherius, and the rest of the host of heaven. He had been one of the demons who tempted St. Anthony, and retailed anecdotes of that eremite which Euschemon had never heard mentioned in Paradise. He was versed in all scandal respecting saints in general, and Euschemon found with astonishment how much about his own order was known downstairs. On the whole he had never enjoyed himself so much in his life; he became proficient in all manner of minor devilries, and was ceasing to trouble himself about his bell or his ecclesiastical duties, when an untoward incident interrupted his felicity.

It chanced that the Bishop of Metz, in whose diocese Epinal was situated, finding himself during a visitation journey within a short distance of the town, determined to put, up there for the night. He did not arrive until nightfall, but word of his intention having been sent forward by a messenger the authorities, civil and ecclesiastical, were ready to receive him. When, escorted in state, he had arrived at the house prepared for his reception, the Mayor ventured to express a hope that everything had been satisfactory to his Lordship.

"Everything," said the bishop emphatically. "I did indeed seem to remark one little omission, which no doubt may be easily accounted for."

"What was that, my Lord?"

"It hath," said the bishop, "usually been the practice to receive a bishop with the ringing of bells. It is a laudable custom, conducive to the purification of the air and the discomfiture of the prince of the powers thereof. I caught no sound of chimes on the present occasion, yet I am sensible that my hearing is not what it was."

The civil and ecclesiastical authorities looked at each other. "That graceless knave of a sacristan!" said the Mayor.

"He hath indeed of late strangely neglected his charge," said a priest.

"Poor man, I doubt his wits are touched," charitably added another.

"What!" exclaimed the bishop, who was very active, very fussy, and a great stickler for discipline. "This important church, so renowned for its three miraculous bells, confided to the tender mercies of an imbecile rogue who may burn it down any night! I will look to it myself without losing a minute."

And in spite of all remonstrances, off he started. The keys were brought, the doors flung open, the body of the church thoroughly examined, but neither in nave, choir, or chancel could the slightest trace of the sacristan be found.

"Perhaps he is in the belfry," suggested a chorister.

"We'll see," responded the bishop, and bustling nimbly up the ladder, he emerged into the open belfry in full moonlight.

Heavens! what a sight met his eye! The sacristan and the devil sitting *vis-a-vis* close by the miraculous bell, with a smoking can of hot spiced wine between them, finishing a close game of cribbage.

"Seven," declared Euschemon.

"And eight are fifteen," retorted the demon, marking two.

"Twenty-three and pair," cried Euschemon, marking in his turn.

"And seven is thirty."

"Ace, thirty-one, and I'm up."

"It *is* up with you, my friend," shouted the bishop, bringing his crook down smartly on Euschemon's shoulders.

"Deuce!" said the devil, and vanished into his bell.

When poor Euschemon had been bound and gagged, which did not take very long, the bishop briefly addressed the assembly. He said that the accounts of the bell which had reached his ears had already excited his apprehensions. He had greatly feared that all could not be right, and now his anxieties were but too well justified. He trusted there was not a man before him who would not suffer his flocks and his crops to be destroyed by tempest fifty times over rather than purchase their safety by unhallowed means. What had been done had doubtless been done in ignorance, and could be made good by a mulct to the episcopal treasury. The amount of this he would carefully consider, and the people of Epinal might rest assured that it should not be too light to entitle them to the benefit of a full absolution. The bell must go to his cathedral city, there to be examined and reported on by the exorcists and inquisitors. Meanwhile he would himself institute a slight preliminary scrutiny.

The bell was accordingly unhung, tilted up, and inspected by the combined beams of the moonlight and torchlight. Very slight examination served to place the soundness of the bishop's opinion beyond dispute. On the lip of the bell were engraven characters unknown to every one else, but which seemed to affect the prelate with singular consternation.

"I hope," he exclaimed, "that none of you know anything about these characters! I earnestly trust that none can read a single one of them. If I thought anybody could I would burn him as soon as look at him!"

The bystanders hastened to assure him that not one of them had the slightest conception of the meaning of the letters, which had never been observed before.

"I rejoice to hear it," said the bishop. "It will be an evil day for the church when these letters are understood."

And next morning he departed, carrying off the bell, with the invisible fiend inside it; the cards, which were regarded as a book of magic; and the luckless Euschemon, who shortly found himself in total darkness, the inmate of a dismal dungeon.

It was some time before Euschemon became sensible of the presence of any partner in his captivity, by reason of the trotting of the rats. At length, however, a deep sigh struck upon his ear.

"Who art thou?" he exclaimed.

"An unfortunate prisoner," was the answer.

"What is the occasion of thy imprisonment?"

"Oh, a mere trifle. A ridiculous suspicion of sacrificing a child to Beelzebub. One of the little disagreeables that must occasionally occur in our profession."

"*Our* profession!" exclaimed Euschemon.

"Art thou not a sorcerer?" demanded the voice.

"No," replied Euschemon, "I am a saint."

The warlock received Euschemon's statement with much incredulity, but becoming eventually convinced of its truth—

"I congratulate thee," he said. "The devil has manifestly taken a fancy to thee, and he never forgets his own. It is true that the bishop is a great favourite with him also. But we will hope for the best. Thou hast never practised riding a broomstick? No? 'Tis pity; thou mayest have to mount one at a moment's notice."

This consolation had scarcely been administered ere the bolts flew back, the hinges grated, the door opened, and gaolers bearing torches informed the sorcerer that the bishop desired his presence.

He found the bishop in his study, which was nearly choked up by Euschemon's bell. The prelate received him with the greatest affability, and expressed a sincere hope that the very particular arrangements he had enjoined for the comfort of his distinguished prisoner had been faithfully carried out by his subordinates. The sorcerer, as much a man of the world as the bishop, thanked his Lordship, and protested that he had been perfectly comfortable.

"I have need of thy art," said the bishop, coming to business. "I am exceedingly bothered—flabbergasted were not too strong an expression—by this confounded bell. All my best exorcists have been trying all they know with it, to no purpose. They might as well have tried to exorcise my mitre from my head by any other charm than the offer of a better one. Magic is plainly the only remedy, and if thou canst disenchant it, I will give thee thy freedom."

"It will be a tough business," observed the sorcerer, surveying the bell with the eye of a connoisseur. "It will require fumigations."

"Yes," said the bishop, "and suffumigations."

"Aloes and mastic," advised the sorcerer.

"Aye," assented the bishop, "and red sanders."

"We must call in Primeumaton," said the warlock.

"Clearly," said the bishop, "and Amioram."

"Triangles," said the sorcerer.

"Pentacles," said the bishop.

"In the hour of Methon," said the sorcerer.

"I should have thought Tafrac," suggested the bishop, "but I defer to your better judgment."

"I can have the blood of a goat?" queried the wizard.

"Yes," said the bishop, "and of a monkey also."

"Does your Lordship think that one might venture to go so far as a little unweaned child?"

"If absolutely necessary," said the bishop.

"I am delighted to find such liberality of sentiment on your Lordship's part," said the sorcerer. "Your Lordship is evidently of the profession."

"These are things which stuck by me when I was an inquisitor," explained the bishop, with some little embarrassment.

Ere long all arrangements were made. It would be impossible to enumerate half the crosses, circles, pentagrams, naked swords, cross-bones, chafing-dishes, and vials of incense which the sorcerer found to be necessary. The child was fortunately deemed superfluous. Euschemon was brought up from his dungeon, and, his teeth chattering with fright and cold, set beside his bell to hold a candle to the devil. The incantations commenced, and speedily gave evidence of their efficacy. The bell trembled, swayed, split open, and a female figure of transcendent loveliness attired in the costume of Eve stepped forth and extended her lips towards the bishop. What could the bishop do but salute them? With a roar of triumph the demon resumed his proper shape. The bishop swooned. The apartment was filled with the fumes of sulphur. The devil soared majestically out of the window, carrying the sorcerer under one arm and Euschemon under the other.

It is commonly believed that the devil good-naturedly dropped Euschemon back again into Paradise, or wheresoever he might have come from. It is even added that he fell between Eulogius and Eucherius, who had been arguing all the time respecting the merits of their bells, and resumed his share in the discussion as if nothing had happened. Some maintain, indeed, that the devil, chancing to be in want of a chaplain, offered the situation to Euschemon, by whom it was accepted. But how to reconcile this assertion with the undoubted fact that the duties of the post in question are at present ably discharged by the Bishop of Metz, in truth we see not. One thing is certain: thou wilt not find Euschemon's name in the calendar, courteous reader.

The mulct to be imposed upon the parish of Epinal was never exacted. The bell, ruptured beyond repair by the demon's violent exit, was taken back and deposited in the museum of the town. The bells of Eulogius and Eucherius were rung freely on occasion; but Epinal has not since enjoyed any greater immunity from storms than the contiguous districts. One day an aged traveller, who had spent many years in Heathenesse and in whom some discerned a remarkable resemblance to the sorcerer, noticed the bell, and asked permission to examine it. He soon discovered the inscription, recognised the mysterious characters as Greek, read them without the least difficulty—

"Μη κινει Καμαριναν ακινητος γαρ αμεινων—"

and favoured the townsmen with this free but substantially accurate translation:—

"CAN'T YOU LET WELL ALONE?"

# BISHOP ADDO AND BISHOP GADDO

MIDDAY, MIDSUMMER, MIDDLE of the dark ages. Fine healthy weather at the city of Biserta in Barbary. Wind blowing strong from the sea, roughening the dark blue waters, and fretting their indigo with foam, as though the ocean's coursers champed an invisible curb. On land tawny sand whirling, green palm-fans swaying and whistling, men abroad in the noonday blaze rejoicing in the unwonted freshness.

"She is standing in," they cried, "and, by the Prophet, she seemeth not a ship of the true believers."

She was not, but she bore a flag of truce. Pitching and rearing, the little bark bounded in, and soon was fast in harbour. Ere long messengers of peace had landed, bearing presents and a letter from the Bishop of Amalfi to the Emir of Biserta. The presents consisted of fifty casks of Lacrima Christi, and of a captive, a tall, noble-looking man, in soiled ecclesiastical costume, and disfigured by the loss of his left eye, which seemed to have been violently plucked out.

"HEALTH to the Emir!" ran the letter. "I send thee my captive, Gaddo, sometime Bishop of Amalfi, now an ejected intruder. For what saith the Scripture? 'When a strong man armed keepeth his palace, his goods are in peace; but if one stronger than he cometh, he divideth the spoils.' Moreover it is written: 'His bishopric let another take.' Having solemnly sworn that I would not kill or blind or maim my enemy, or imprison him in a monastery, and the price of absolution from an oath in this corrupt age exceeding all reason and Christian moderation, I knew not how to take vengeance on him, until a sagacious counsellor represented that a man cannot be said to be blinded so long as he is deprived of only one eye. This I accordingly eradicated, and now, being restrained from imprisoning him, and fearing to release him, I send him to thee, to retain in captivity on my behalf; in return for which service, receive fifty casks of the choicest Lacrima Christi, which shall not fail to be sent thee yearly, so long as Gaddo continues in thy custody.

"+ Addo, by Divine permission Bishop of Amalfi."

"First," said the Emir, "I would be certified whether this vintage is indeed of such excellence as to prevail upon a faithful Mussulman to jeopard Paradise, the same being forbidden by his law."

Experiments were instituted forthwith, and the problem was resolved in the affirmative.

"This being so," declared the Emir, "honour and good faith towards Bishop Addo require that Bishop Gaddo be kept captive with all possible strictness. Yet bolts may be burst, fetters may be filed, walls may be scaled, doors may be broken through. Better to enchain the captive's soul, binding him with invisible bonds, and searing out of him the very wish to escape. Embrace the faith of the Prophet," continued he, addressing Gaddo; "become a Mollah."

"No," said the deposed Bishop, "my inclination hath ever been towards a military life. At present, mutilated and banished as I am, I rather affect the crown of martyrdom."

"Thou shalt receive it by instalments," said the Emir. "Thou shalt work at the new pavilion in my garden."

Unceasing toil under the blazing sun, combined with the discipline of the overseers, speedily wore down Gaddo's strength, already impaired by captivity and ill-treatment. Unable to drag himself away after his fellow-workmen had ceased from their labours, he lay one evening, faint and almost senseless, among the stones and rubbish of the unfinished edifice. The Emir's daughter passed by. Gaddo was handsome and wretched, the Princess was beautiful and compassionate. Conveyed by her fair hands, a cup of Bishop Addo's wine saved Bishop Gaddo's life.

The next evening Gaddo again lingered behind, and the Princess spoke to him out of her balcony. The third evening they encountered in an arbour. The next meeting took place in her chamber, where her father discovered them.

"I will tear thee to pieces with pincers," shouted he to Gaddo.

"Your Highness will not be guilty of that black action," responded Gaddo resolutely.

"No?" roared the Emir. "No? and what shall hinder me?"

"The Lacrima Christi will hinder your Highness," returned the far-seeing Gaddo. "Deems your Highness that Bishop Addo will send another cupful, once he is assured of my death?"

"Thou sayest well," rejoined the Emir. "I may not slay thee. But my daughter is manifestly most inflammable, wherefore I will burn her."

"Were it not better to circumcise me?" suggested Gaddo.

Many difficulties were raised, but Ayesha's mother siding with Gaddo, and promising a more amicable deportment for the future towards the other lights of the harem, the matter was arranged, and Gaddo recited the Mahometan profession of faith, and became the Emir's son-in-law. The execrable social system under which he had hitherto lived thus vanished like a nightmare from an awakened sleeper. Wedded to one who had saved his life by her compassion, and whose life he had in turn saved by his change of creed, adoring her and adored by her, with the hope of children, and active contact with multitudes of other interests from which he had hitherto been estranged, he forgot the ecclesiastic in the man; his intellect expanded, his ideas multiplied, he cleared his mind of cant, and became an eminent philosopher.

"Dear son," said the Emir to him one day, "the Lacrima is spent, we thirst, and the tribute of that Christian dog, the Bishop of Amalfi, tarries to arrive. We will presently fit out certain vessels, and thou shalt hold a visitation of thine ancient diocese."

"Methinks I see a ship even now," said Gaddo; and he was right. She anchored, the ambassadors landed and addressed the Emir:

"Prince, we bring thee the stipulated tribute, yet not without a trifling deduction."

"Deduction!" exclaimed the Emir, bending his brows ominously.

"Highness," they represented, "by reason of the deficiency of last year's vintage it hath not been possible to provide more than forty-nine casks, which we crave to offer thee accordingly."

"Then," pronounced the Emir sententiously, "the compact is broken, the ship is confiscated, and war is declared."

"Not so, Highness," said they, "for the fiftieth cask is worth all the rest."

"Let it be opened," commanded the Emir.

It was accordingly hoisted out, deposited on the quay, and prized open; and from its capacious interior, in a deplorable plight from hunger, cramp, and sea-sickness, was extracted—Bishop Addo.

"We have," explained the deputation, "wearied of our shepherd, who, shearing his flock somewhat too closely, hath brought the wolf to light. We therefore desire thee to receive him at our hands in exchange for our good Bishop Gaddo, promising one hundred casks of Lacrima Christi as yearly tribute for the future."

"He stands before you," answered the Emir; "take him, an ye can prevail upon him to return with you."

The eyes of the envoys wandered hopelessly from one whiskered, turbaned, caftaned, and yataghaned figure to another. They could not discover that any of the Paynim present looked more or less like a bishop than his fellows.

"Brethren," said Gaddo, taking compassion on their bewilderment, "behold me! I thank you for your kindly thought of me, but how to profit by it I see not. I have become a Saracen. I have pronounced the Mahometan confession. I am circumcised. I am known by the name of Mustapha."

"We acknowledge the weight of your Lordship's objections," they said, "and do but venture to hint remotely that the times are hard, and that the Holy Father is grievously in want of money."

"I have also taken a wife," said Gaddo.

"A wife!" exclaimed they with one consent. "If it had been a concubine! Let us return instantly."

They gathered up their garments and spat upon the ground.

"A bishop, then," inquired Gaddo, "may be guilty of any enormity sooner than wedlock, which money itself cannot expiate?"

"Such," they answered, "is the law and the prophets."

"Unless," added one of benignant aspect, "he sew the abomination up in a sack and cast her into the sea, then peradventure he may yet find place for repentance."

"Miserable blasphemers!" exclaimed Gaddo. "But why," continued he, checking himself, "do I talk of what none will understand for five hundred years, which to understand myself I was obliged to become a Saracen? Addo," he pursued, addressing his dejected competitor, "bad as thou art, thou art good enough for the world as it is. I spare thy life, restore thy dignity, and, to prove that the precepts of Christ may be practised under the garb of Mahomet, will not even exact eye for eye. Yet, as a wholesome admonition to thee that treachery and cruelty escape not punishment even in this life, I will that thou do presently surrender to me thy left ear. Restore my eye and I will return it immediately. And ye," addressing the envoys, "will for the future pay one hundred casks tribute, unless ye would see my father-in-law's galleys on your coasts."

So Addo returned to his bishopric, leaving his ear in Gaddo's keeping. The Lacrima was punctually remitted, and as punctually absorbed by the Emir and his son-in-law, with some little help from Ayesha. Gaddo's eye never came back, and Addo never regained his ear until, after the ex-prelate's death in years and honour, he ransomed it from his representatives. It became a relic, and is shown in Addo's cathedral to this day in proof of his inveterate enmity to the misbelievers, and of the sufferings he underwent at their hands. But Gaddo trumped him, the entry after his name in the episcopal register, "Fled to the Saracens," having been altered into "Flayed by the Saracens" by a later bishop, jealous of the honour of the diocese.

# THE PHILOSOPHER AND THE BUTTERFLIES[1]

THE SCENE WAS in a garden on a fine summer morning, brilliant with slants of sunshine, yet chequered with clouds significant of more than a remote possibility of rain. All the animal world was astir. Birds flitted or hopped from spray to spray; butterflies eddied around flowers within or upon which bees were bustling; ants and earwigs ran nimbly about on the mould; a member of the Universal Knowledge Society perambulated the gravel path.

The Universal Knowledge Society, be it understood, exists for the dissemination and not for the acquisition of knowledge. Our philosopher, therefore, did not occupy himself with considering whether in that miniature world, with its countless varieties of animal and vegetable being, something might not be found with which he was himself unacquainted; but, like the honey-freighted bee, rather sought an opportunity of disburdening himself of his stores of information than of adding to them. But who was to profit by his communicativeness? The noisy birds could not hear themselves speak, much less him; he shrewdly distrusted his ability to command the attention of the busy bees; and even a member of the Universal Knowledge Society may well be at a loss for a suitable address to an earwig. At length he determined to accost a Butterfly who, after sipping the juice of a flower, remained perched indolently upon it, apparently undecided whither to direct his flight.

"It seems likely to rain," he said, "have you an umbrella?"

The Butterfly looked curiously at him, but returned no answer.

"I do not ask," resumed the Philosopher, "as one who should imply that the probability of even a complete saturation ought to appal a ratiocinative being, endowed with wisdom and virtue. I rather designed to direct your attention to the inquiry whether these attributes are, in fact, rightly predicable of Butterflies."

Still no answer.

"An impression obtains among our own species," continued the

---

1   *The Philosopher and the Butterflies.*—One of the contributions by various writers to "The New Amphion," a little book prepared for sale at the Fancy Fair got up by the students of the University of Edinburgh in 1886.

Philosopher, "that you Butterflies are deficient in foresight and providence to a remarkable, I might almost say a culpable degree. Pardon me if I add that this suspicion is to some extent confirmed by my finding you destitute of protection against imbriferous inclemency under atmospheric conditions whose contingent humidity should be obvious to a being endowed with the most ordinary allotment of meteorological prevision."

The Butterfly still left all the talk to the Philosopher. This was just what the latter desired.

"I greatly fear," he continued, "that the omission to which I have reluctantly adverted is to a certain extent typically characteristic of the entire political and social economy of the lepidopterous order. It has even been stated, though the circumstance appears scarcely credible, that your system of life does not include the accumulation of adequate resources against the inevitable exigencies of winter."

"What is winter?" asked the Butterfly, and flew off without awaiting an answer.

The Philosopher remained for a moment speechless, whether from amazement at the Butterfly's nescience or disgust at his ill-breeding. Recovering himself immediately, he shouted after the fugitive:

"Frivolous animal!" "It is this levity," continued he, addressing a group of butterflies who had gradually assembled in the air, attracted by the conversation, "it is this fatal levity that constrains me to despair wholly of the future of you insects. That you should persistently remain at your present depressed level! That you should not immediately enter upon a process of self-development! Look at the Bee! How did she acquire her sting, think you? Why cannot you store up honey, as she does?"

"We cannot build cells," suggested a Butterfly.

"And how did the Bee learn, do you suppose, unless by imbuing her mind with the elementary principles of mathematics? Know that time has been when the Bee was as incapable of architectural construction as yourselves, when you and she alike were indiscriminable particles of primary protoplasm. (I suppose you know what that is.) One has in process of time exalted itself to the cognition of mathematical truth, while the other—Pshaw! Now, really, my friends, I must beg you to take my observations in good part. I do not imply, of course, that any endeavours of yours in the direction I have indicated could benefit any of you personally, or any of your posterity for numberless generations. But I really do consider that after a while its effects would be very observable—that in twenty millions of years or so, provided no geological cataclysm supervened, you Butterflies, with your innate genius for mimicry, might be conformed in all respects to the hymenopterous model, or perhaps carry out the principle of development into novel and unheard-of directions. You should derive much encouragement from the beginning you have made already."

"How a beginning?" inquired a Butterfly.

"I am alluding to your larval constitution as Caterpillars," returned the Philosopher. "Your advance upon that humiliating condition is, I admit, remarkable. I only wonder that it should not have proceeded much further. With such capacity for development, it is incomprehensible that you should so long have remained stationary. You ought to be all toads by this time, at the very least."

"I beg your pardon," civilly interposed the Butterfly. "To what condition were you pleased to allude?"

"To that of a Caterpillar," rejoined the Philosopher.

"Caterpillar!" echoed the Butterfly, and "Caterpillar!" tittered all his volatile companions, till the air seemed broken into little silvery waves of fairy laughter. "Caterpillar! he positively thinks we were once Caterpillars! He! he! he!"

"Do you actually mean to say you don't know that?" responded the Philosopher, scandalised at the irreverence of the insects, but inwardly rejoicing at the prospect of a controversy in which he could not be worsted.

"We know nothing of the sort," rejoined a Butterfly.

"Can you possibly be plunged into such utter oblivion of your embryonic antecedents?"

"We do not understand you. All we know is that we have always been Butterflies."

"Sir," said a large, dull-looking Butterfly with one wing in tatters, crawling from under a cabbage, and limping by reason of the deficiency of several legs, "let me entreat you not to deduce our scientific status from the inconsiderate assertions of the unthinking vulgar. I am proud to assure you that our race comprises many philosophical reasoners—mostly indeed such as have been disabled by accidental injuries from joining in the amusements of the rest. The Origin of our Species has always occupied a distinguished place in their investigations. It has on several occasions engaged the attention of our profoundest thinkers for not less than two consecutive minutes. There is hardly a quadruped on the land, a bird in the air, or a fish in the water to which it has not been ascribed by some one at some time; but never, I am rejoiced to say, has any Butterfly ever dreamed of attributing it to the obnoxious thing to which you have unaccountably made reference."

"We should rather think not," chorussed all the Butterflies.

"Look here," said the Philosopher, picking up and exhibiting a large hairy Caterpillar of very unprepossessing appearance. "Look here, what do you call this?"

"An abnormal organisation," said the scientific Butterfly.

"A nasty beast," said the others.

"Heavens," exclaimed the Philosopher, "the obtuseness and arrogance of these creatures! No, my poor friend," continued he, addressing the Caterpillar, "disdain you as they may, and unpromising as your aspect certainly is at present, the time is at hand when you will prank it with the gayest of them all."

"I cry your mercy," rejoined the Caterpillar somewhat crossly, "but I was digesting a gooseberry leaf when you lifted me in that abrupt manner, and I did not quite follow your remarks. Did I understand you to mention my name in connection with those flutterers?"

"I said the time would arrive when you would be even as they."

"I," exclaimed the Caterpillar, "I retrograde to the level of a Butterfly! Is not the ideal of creation impersonated in me already?"

"I was not aware of that," replied the Philosopher, "although," he added in a conciliatory tone, "far be it from me to deny you the possession of many interesting qualities."

"You probably refer to my agility," suggested the Caterpillar; "or perhaps to my abstemiousness?"

"I was not referring to either," returned the Philosopher.

"To my utility to mankind?"

"Not by any manner of means."

"To what then?"

"Well, if you must know, the best thing about you appears to me to be the prospect you enjoy of ultimately becoming a Butterfly."

The Caterpillar erected himself upon his tail, and looked sternly at the Philosopher. The Philosopher's countenance fell. A thrush, darting from an adjacent tree, seized the opportunity and the insect, and bore the latter away in his bill. At the same moment the shower prognosticated by the Sage burst forth, scattering the Butterflies in all directions, drenching the Philosopher, whose foresight had not assumed the shape of an umbrella, and spoiling his new hat. But he had ample consolation in the superiority of his head. And the Caterpillar was right too, for after all he never did become a Butterfly.

# TRUTH AND HER COMPANIONS

*Jupiter.* Daughter Truth, is this a befitting manner of presenting yourself before your divine father? You are positively dripping; the floor of my celestial mansion would be a swamp but for your praiseworthy economy in wearing apparel. Whence, in the name of the Naiads, do you come?

*Truth.* From the bottom of a well, father.

*Jupiter.* I thought, my daughter, that you had descended upon earth in the capacity of a benefactress of men rather than of frogs.

*Truth.* Such, indeed, was my purpose, father, and I accordingly repaired to the great city.

*Jupiter.* The city of the Emperor Apollyon?

*Truth.* The same; and I there obtained an audience of the monarch.

*Jupiter.* What passed?

*Truth.* I took the liberty of observing to him, father, that, having obtained his throne by perjury, and cemented it by blood, and maintained it by hypocrisy, he could entertain no hope of preserving it unless the collective baseness of his subjects should be found to exceed his own, which was not probable.

*Jupiter.* What reply did he vouchsafe to these admonitions?

*Truth.* He threatened to cut out my tongue. Perceiving that this would interfere with my utility to mankind, I retired somewhat precipitately from the Imperial presence, marvelling that I should ever have been admitted, and resolved never to be found there for the future. I then proceeded to the Nobles.

*Jupiter.* What said you to them?

*Truth.* I represented to them that they were, as a class, both arrogant and luxurious, and would, indeed, have long ago become insupportable, only that the fabric which their rapacity was for ever striving to erect, their extravagance as perpetually undermined. I further commented upon the insecurity of any institution dependent solely upon prescription. Finding these suggestions unpalatable, I next addressed myself to the priesthood.

*Jupiter.* Those holy men, my daughter, must have rejoiced at the opportunity of learning from you which portion of their traditions was impure or fabricated, and which authentic and sublime.

*Truth.* The value they placed upon my instructions was such that they wished to reserve them exclusively for themselves, and proposed that they should be delivered within the precincts of a certain subterranean apartment termed a dungeon, the key of which should be kept by one of their order. Whereupon I betook myself to the philosophers.

*Jupiter.* Your reception from these professed lovers of wisdom, my daughter, was, no doubt, all that could be expected.

*Truth.* It was all that could be expected, my father, from learned and virtuous men, who had already framed their own systems of the universe without consulting me.

*Jupiter.* You probably next addressed yourself to the middling orders of society?

*Truth.* I can scarcely say that I did, father; for although I had much to remark concerning their want of culture, and their servility, and their greed, and the absurdity of many of their customs, and the rottenness of most of their beliefs, and the thousand ways in which they spoiled lives that might have been beautiful and harmonious, I soon discovered that they were so absolutely swayed by the example of the higher orders that it was useless to expostulate with them until I should have persuaded the latter.

*Jupiter.* You returned, then, to the latter with this design?

*Truth.* On the contrary, I hastened to the poor and needy, whom I fully acquainted with the various wrongs and oppressions which they underwent at the hands of the powerful and the rich. And here, for the first time, I found myself welcome. All listened with gratitude and assent, and none made any endeavour to stone me or imprison me, as those other unprincipled persons had done.

*Jupiter.* That was indeed satisfactory, daughter. But when you proceeded to point out to these plebeians how much of their misery arose from their own idleness, and ignorance, and dissoluteness, and abasement before those higher in station, and jealousy of the best among themselves—what said they to that?

*Truth.* They expressed themselves desirous of killing me, and indeed would have done so if my capital enemies, the priests, had not been beforehand with them.

*Jupiter.* What did they?

*Truth.* Burned me.

*Jupiter.* Burned you?

*Truth*. Burned me in the market-place. And, but for my peculiar property of reviving from my ashes, I should not be here now. Upon reconsolidating myself, I felt in such a heat that I was fain to repair to the bottom of the nearest well. Finding myself more comfortable there than I had ever yet been on earth, I have come to ask permission to remain.

*Jupiter*. It does not appear to me, daughter, that the mission you have undertaken on behalf of mankind can be efficiently discharged at the bottom of a well.

*Truth*. No, father, nor in the middle of a fire either.

*Jupiter*. I fear that you are too plain and downright in your dealings with men, and deter where you ought to allure.

*Truth*. I were not Truth, else, but Flattery. My nature is a mirror's—to exhibit reality with plainness and faithfulness.

*Jupiter*. It is no less the nature of man to shatter every mirror that does not exhibit to him what he wishes to behold.

*Truth*. Let me, therefore, return to my well, and let him who wishes to behold me, if such there be, repair to the brink and look down.

*Jupiter*. No, daughter, you shall not return to your well. I have already perceived that you are not of yourself sufficient for the office I have assigned to you, and I am about to provide you with two auxiliaries. You are Truth. Tell me how this one appears to you.

*Truth*. Oh, father, the beautiful nymph! how mature, and yet how comely! how good-humoured, yet how gentle and grave! Her robe is closely zoned; her upraised finger approaches her lip; her foot falls soft as snow. What is her name?

*Jupiter*. Discretion. And this other?

*Truth*. Oh, father! the cordial look, the blooming cheek, the bright smile that is almost a laugh, the buoyant step, and the expansive bosom! What name bears she?

*Jupiter*. Good Nature. Return, my daughter, to earth; continue to enlighten man's ignorance and to reprove his folly; but let Discretion suggest the occasion, and Good Nature inspire the wording of your admonitions. I cannot engage that you may not, even with these precautions, sometimes pay a visit to the stake; and if, when an adventure of this sort appears imminent, Discretion should counsel a temporary retirement to your well, I am sure Good Nature will urge nothing to the contrary.

# THE THREE PALACES[1]

THREE PAIRS OF young people, each a youth with his bride, came together along a road to the point where it divided to the right and left. On one side was inscribed, "To the Palace of Truth," and on the other, "To the Palace of Illusion."

"This way, my beauty!" cried one of the youths, drawing his companion in the direction of the Palace of Truth. "To the place where and where alone thy perfections may be beheld as they are!"

"And my imperfections!" whispered the young spouse, but her tone was airy and confident.

"Well," said the second youth, "does the choice beseem you upon whom the moon of your nuptials is beaming still. My beloved and I are riper in Hymen's lore by not less, I ween, than one fortnight. Prudence impels us towards the Palace of Illusion."

"Thy will is mine, Alonso," said his lady.

"I," said the third youth, "will seek neither; for I would not be wise over-much, while of what I deem myself to know I would be well assured. Happy am I, and bless my lot, yet have I beheld a red mouse in closer contiguity to my beloved than I could bring myself to approve, albeit it leapt not from her mouth as they do sometimes. Yet do I know it for a red mouse and nothing worse; had I inhabited the Palace of Illusion haply I had deemed it a rat. And, it being a red mouse as it indubitably was, to what end fancy it a tawny-throated nightingale?"

While, therefore, the other pairs proceeded on the paths they had respectively chosen, this sage youth and his bride settled themselves at the parting of the ways, built their cot, tended their garden, tilled their field and raised fruits around them, including children.

The preparation of a cheerful repast was one day well advanced, when, lifting up their eyes, the pair beheld a haggard and emaciated couple tottering

---

1  *The Three Palaces.*—Published originally on a similar occasion to the last story, in "A Volunteer Haversack," an extensive repertory of miscellaneous contributions in prose and verse, printed and sold at Edinburgh for a benevolent purpose in 1902.

along the road that led from the Palace of Illusion.

"Heavens!" exclaimed they simultaneously, "no! yes! 'tis surely they!" O friends! whence this forlorn semblance? whence this osseous condition?"

"Of them anon," replied the attenuated youth, "but, before all things, dinner!"

The restorative was speedily administered, and the pilgrim commenced his narration.

"Guarded," he said, "though the Palace of Illusion was by every species of hippogriffic chimaera, my bride and I experienced no difficulty in penetrating inside its precincts. The giants lifted us in their arms, the dragons carried us on their backs, fairy bridges spanned the moats, golden ladders inclined against the ramparts, we scaled the towers and trod the courts securely, though constructed to all seeming of dissolving cloud. Delicate fare loaded every dish; smiling companions invited to every festivity; perfumes caressed our nostrils; music enwrapped our ears.

"But while all else charmed and allured, one fact intruded of which we could not pretend unconsciousness, the intensity of our aversion for each other. Never could I behold my Imogene without marvelling whatever could have induced me to wed her, and she has acknowledged that she laboured under the like perplexity. On the other hand, our good opinion of ourselves had grown prodigiously. The other's dislike appeared to each an insane delusion, and we seriously questioned whether it could be right to mate longer with a being so destitute of true aesthetic feeling. We confided these scruples to each other, with the result of a most tempestuous altercation.

"As this was attaining its climax, one of the inmates of the Palace, a pert forward boy, resembling a page out of livery, passed by, and ironically, as I thought, congratulated us on the strength of our mutual attachment. 'Never,' exclaimed he, 'have I beheld the like here before, and I am the oldest inhabitant.'

"As this felicitation was proffered at the precise moment when I was engaged in staunching a rent in my cheek with a handful of my wife's hair, I was constrained to regard it as unseasonable, and expressed myself to that effect.

"'What!' exclaimed he, with equal surprise, 'know ye not that this is the Palace of Illusion, where everything is inverted and appears the reverse of itself? Intense indeed must be the affection which can thus drive you to fisticuffs! Had I beheld you billing and cooing, truly I had counselled a judicial separation!'

"My wife and I looked at each other, and by a common impulse made at our utmost speed for the gate of the Palace of Illusion.

"Alas! it is one thing to enter and another to quit that domain of enchantment. The golden clouds enwrapt us still, cates and dainties tempted us as of old, the most bewitching strains detained us spellbound. The giant and dragon warders, indeed, offered no violent resistance, they simply turned into open portals which appeared to yield us egress, but proved entrances to interminable labyrinthine mazes. At last we escaped by resolutely, following the exact opposite track to that which we observed to be taken by a poet, who was chasing a phantom of Fame with a scroll of unintelligible and inharmonious verse.

"The moment that we emerged from the enchanted castle we knew ourselves and each other for what we were, and fell weeping into each other's arms. So feeble were we that we could hardly move, nevertheless we have made a shift to crawl hither, trusting to your hospitality to recruit us from the sawdust and ditch-water which we vehemently suspect to have been our diet during the whole of our residence."

"Eat and drink without stint and without ceremony," rejoined their host, "provided only that somewhat remain for the guests whom I see approaching."

And in a few moments the fugitives from the Palace of Illusion were reinforced by travellers from the Palace of Truth, whose backs were most determinately turned to that august edifice.

"My friends," said the youth last arrived, when the first greetings were over, "Truth's Palace might be a not ineligible residence were not the inmates necessitated not merely to know the truth but to speak it, and did not all innocent embellishments of her majestic person become entirely inefficient and absolutely nugatory. For example, the number of my wife's grey hairs speedily confounded me; and how should it be otherwise, when the excellent dye she had brought with her had completely lost its virtues? She on her part found herself continually obliged to acquaint me with the manifold defects she was daily discovering in my mind and person, which I was unable to deny, frequently as I opened my mouth for that purpose. It is true that I had the satisfaction of pointing out equal defects in herself; but this could not be considered a great satisfaction, seeing that every such discovery impugned my taste and judgment, and impaired the worth of my most cherished possession. At length we resolved that Truth and we were not made for each other, and, having verified the accuracy of this conclusion by uttering it unrebuked in Truth's own palace, quitted the unblest spot with all possible expedition. No sooner were we outside than our tenderness revived, and, the rites of reconciliation duly performed, my wife found nothing more urgent than to try whether her dye had recovered its natural properties, which, as ye may perceive, proved to be the case. We are now bound for the Palace of Illusion."

"Nay," said he who had escaped thence, "if my experience suffices not to deter you, learn that they who have known Truth can never taste of Illusion. Illusion is for life's golden prime, its fanes and pavilions may be reared but by the magic wand of Youth. The maturity that would recreate them builds not for Illusion but for Deceit. Yet, lest mortality should despair, there exists, as I have learned, yet another palace, founded midway between that of Illusion and that of Truth, open to those who are too soft for the one and too hard for the other. Thither, indeed, the majority of mankind in this age resort, and there appear to find themselves comfortable."

"And this palace is?" inquired Truth's runaways simultaneously.

"The Palace of Convention," replied the youth.

# NEW READINGS IN BIOGRAPHY[1]

### I.—TIMON OF ATHENS

NO, IT WAS not true that Timon was dead, and buried on the sea-shore. So the first party discovered that hastened to his cave at the tidings, thinking to seize his treasure, and had their heads broken for their pains. But the second party fared better; for these were robbers, captained by Alcibiades, who had taken to the road, as many a man of spirit, has done before and since. They took Timon's gold, and left him bound in his chair. But on the way home the lesser thieves mysteriously disappeared, and the gold became the sole property of Alcibiades. As it is written, "The tools to him that can handle them."

Timon sat many hours in an uncomfortable position, and though, in a general way, he abhorred the face of man, he was not displeased when a gentleman of bland appearance entered the cavern, and made him a low obeisance. And perceiving that Timon was bound, the bland man exclaimed with horror, and severed his bonds, ere one could say Themistocles. And in an instant the cavern was filled with Athenian senators.

"Hail," they cried, "to Timon the munificent! Hail to Timon the compassionate! Hail to Timon the lover of his kind!"

"I am none of these things," said Timon. "I am Timon the misanthrope."

"This must be my Lord's wit and playfulness," said the bland man, "for how else should the Senate and the people have passed a decree, indited by myself, ordering an altar to be raised to Timon the Benefactor, and appointing him chief archon? But come, hand over thy treasure, that thy installation may take effect with due observance."

"I have been deprived of my treasure," said Timon.

But the ambassadors gave him no credit until they had searched every chink and crevice in the cavern, and dug up all the earth round the entrance. They then regarded each other with blank consternation.

"Let us leave him as we found him," said one.

1  *New Readings in Biography.*—Originally published in *The Scots Observer* in 1889.

"Let us hang him up," said another.

"Let us sell him into captivity," said a third.

"Nay, friends," said the bland gentleman, "such confession of error would impeach our credit as statesmen. Moreover, should the people learn that Timon has lost his money, they will naturally conclude that we have taken it. Let us, therefore, keep this misfortune from their knowledge, and trust for relief to the chapter of accidents, as usual in State affairs."

They therefore robed Timon in a dress of honour, and conducted him to Athens, where half the inhabitants were awaiting him. Two triumphal arches spanned the principal street, and on one was inscribed "Timon the Benefactor," and on the other "Timon the Friend of Humanity." And all along, far as the eye could reach, stood those whom his bounty, as was stated, had rescued from perdition, the poor he had relieved, the sick he had medicined, the orphans he had fathered, the poets and painters he had patronised, all lauding and thanking him, and soliciting a continuance of his liberality. And the rabble cried "Largesse, largesse!" and horsemen galloped forth, casting among them nuts enveloped in silver-leaf and apples and comfits and trinkets and brass farthings in incredible quantities. At which the people murmured somewhat, and spoke amiss respecting Timon and the senators who escorted him, and the bland gentleman strove to keep Timon between himself and the populace. While Timon was pondering what the end of these things should be, his mob encountered another cheering for Alcibiades, and playing pitch and toss with drachmas and didrachmas and tetradrachmas, yea, even with staters and darics.

"Long live Alcibiades," cried Timon's followers, as they attacked Alcibiades's supporters to get their share.

"Long live Timon," cried Alcibiades's party, as they defended themselves.

Timon and Alcibiades extricated themselves from the scuffle, and walked away arm in arm.

"My dear friend," said Timon, "how inexpressibly beholden I am to you for taking the burden of my wealth upon yourself! There is nothing I would not do to evince my gratitude."

"Nothing?" queried Alcibiades.

"Nothing," persisted Timon.

"Then," said Alcibiades, "I will thank thee to relieve me of Timandra, who is as tired of me as I am of her."

Timon winced horribly, but his word was his bond, and Timandra accompanied him to his cavern, where at first she suffered much inconvenience from the roughness of the accommodation. But Timon, though a misanthrope, was not a brute; and when in process of time Timandra's health required special care, rugs and pillows were provided for her, and also for Timon; for he saw that he could no longer pass for a churl if he made his wife more comfortable than himself. And, though he counted gold as dross, yet was he not dissatisfied that Timandra had saved the gold he had given her formerly against a rainy day. And when a child was born, Timon was at his wits' end, and blessed the old woman who came to nurse it. And she admonished him of his duty to the Gods, which meant sacrifice, which meant merry-making. And the child grew, and craved food and drink, and Timon possessed himself of three acres and a cow. And not being able to doubt his child's affection for him, he came to believe in Timandra's also. And when the tax-gatherer oppressed his neighbours, he pleaded their cause, which was also his own, in the courts of Athens, and gained it by the interest of Alcibiades. And his neighbours made him demarch, and he feasted them. And Apemantus came to deride him, and Timon bore with him; but he was impertinent to Timandra, and Timon beat him.

And in fine, Timon became very like any other Attic country gentleman, save that he always maintained that a young man did well to be a misanthrope until he got a loving and sensible wife, which, as he observed, could but seldom happen. And the Gods looked down upon him with complacency, and deferred the ruin of Athens until he should be no more.

## II.—NAPOLEON'S SANGAREE

NAPOLEON BUONAPARTE sat in his garden at St. Helena, in the shadow of a fig-tree. Before him stood a little table, and upon the table stood a glass of sangaree. The day was hot and drowsy; the sea boomed monotonously on the rocks; the broad fig-leaves stirred not; great flies buzzed heavily in the sultry air. Napoleon wore a loose linen coat and a broad brimmed planter's hat, and looked as red as the sangaree, but nowise as comfortable.

"To think," he said aloud, "that I should end my life here, with nothing to sweeten my destiny but this lump of sugar!"

And he dropped it into the sangaree, and little ripples and beads broke out on the surface of the liquid.

"Thou should'st have followed me," said a voice.

"Me," said another.

And a steam from the sangaree rose high over Napoleon's head, and from it shaped themselves two beautiful female figures. One was fair and very youthful, with a Phrygian cap on her head, and eager eyes beneath it, and a slender spear in her hand. The other was somewhat older, and graver, and darker, with serious eyes; and she carried a sword, and wore a helmet, from underneath which her rich brown tresses escaped over her vesture of light steel armour.

"I am Liberty," said the first.

"I am Loyalty," said the second.

And Napoleon laid his hand in that of the first spirit, and instantly saw himself as he had been in the days of his youthful victories, only beset with a multitude of people who were offering him a crown, and cheering loudly. But he thrust it aside, and they cheered ten times more, and fell into each other's arms, and wept and kissed each other. And troops of young maidens robed in white danced before him, strewing his way with flowers. And the debts of the debtor were paid, and the prisoners were released from captivity. And the forty Academicians came bringing Napoleon the prize of virtue. And the Abbé Sieyès stood up, and offered Napoleon his choice of seventeen constitutions; and Napoleon chose the worst. And he came to sit with five hundred other men, mostly advocates. And when he said "Yea," they said "Nay"; and when he said "white," they said "black." And they suffered him to do neither good nor evil, and when he went to war they commanded his army for him, until he was smitten with a great slaughter. And the enemy entered the country, and bread was scarce and wine dear; and the people cursed Napoleon, and Liberty vanished from before him. But he roamed on, ever looking for her, and at length he found her lying dead in the public way, all gashed and bleeding, and trampled with the feet of men and horses, and the wheel of a tumbril was over her neck. And Napoleon, under compulsion of the mob, ascended the tumbril; and Abbé Sieyès and Bishop Talleyrand rode at his side, administering spiritual consolation. Thus they came within sight of the guillotine, whereon stood M. de Robespierre in his sky-blue coat, and his jaw bound up in a bloody cloth, bowing and smiling, nevertheless, and beckoning Napoleon to ascend to him. Napoleon had never feared the face of man; but when he saw M. de Robespierre great dread fell upon him, and he leapt out of the tumbril, and fled amain, passing amid the people as it were mid withered leaves, until he came where Loyalty stood awaiting him.

She took his hand in hers, and, lo! another great host of people proffering him a crown, save one little old man, who alone of them all wore his hair in a queue with powder.

"See," said the little old man, "that thou takest not what doth not belong to thee."

"To whom belongeth it then?" asked Napoleon, "for I am a plain soldier, and have no skill in politics."

"To Louis the Disesteemed," said the little old man, "for he is a great-great-nephew of the Princess of Schwoffingen, whose ancestors reigned here at the flood."

"Where dwells Louis the Disesteemed?" asked Napoleon.

"In England," said the little old man.

Napoleon therefore repaired to England, and sought for Louis the Disesteemed. But none could direct him, save that it behoved him to seek in the obscurest places. And one day, as he was passing through a mean street, he heard a voice of lamentation, and perceived a man whose coat and shirt were rent and dirty; but not so his pantaloons, for he had none.

"Who art thou, thou pantaloonless one?" asked he, "and wherefore makest thou this lamentation?"

"I am Louis the Esteemed, King of France and Navarre," replied the dis-trousered personage, "and I lament for my pantaloons, which I have been enforced to pawn, inasmuch as the broker would advance nothing upon my coat or my shirt."

And Napoleon went upon his knees and divested himself of his own nether garments, and arrayed the king therein, to the great diversion of those who stood about.

"Thou hast done wickedly," said the king when he heard who Napoleon was, "in that thou hast presumed to fight battles and win victories without any commission from me. Go, nevertheless, and lose an arm, a leg, and an eye in my service, then shall thy offence be forgiven thee."

And Napoleon raised a great army, and gained a great battle for the king, and lost an arm. And he gained another greater battle, and lost a leg. And he gained the greatest battle of all; and the king sat on the throne of his ances-tors, and was called Louis the Victorious: but Napoleon had lost an eye. And he came into the king's presence, bearing his eye, his arm, and his leg.

"Thou art pardoned," said the king, "and I will even confer a singular honour upon thee. Thou shalt defray the expense of my coronation, which shall be the most splendid ever seen in France."

So Napoleon lost all his substance, and no man pitied him. But after cer-tain days the keeper of the royal wardrobe rushed into the king's presence, crying "Treason! treason! O Majesty, whence these republican and revolu-tionary pantaloons?"

"They are those I deigned to receive from the rebel Buonaparte," said the king. "It were meet to return them. Where abides he now?"

"Saving your Majesty's presence," they said, "he lieth upon a certain dunghill."

"If this be so," said the king, "life can be no gratification to him, and it were humane to relieve him of it. Moreover, he is a dangerous man. Go, therefore, and strangle him with his own pantaloons. Yet, let a monument be raised to him, and engrave upon it, 'Here lies Napoleon Buonaparte, whom Louis the Victorious raised from the dunghill.'"

They went accordingly; but behold! Napoleon already lay dead upon the dunghill. And this was told unto the king.

"He hath ever been envious of my glory," said the king, "let him therefore be buried underneath."

And it was so. And after no long space the king also died, and slept with his fathers. But when there was again a revolution in France, the people cast his bones out of the royal sepulchre, and laid Napoleon's there instead. And the dunghill complained grievously that it should be disturbed for so slight a cause.

And Napoleon withdrew his hand from the hand of Loyalty, saying, "Pish!" And his eyes opened, and he heard the booming of the sea, and the buzzing of the flies, and felt the heat of the sun, and saw that the sugar he had dropped into his sangaree had not yet reached the bottom of the tumbler.

### III.—CONCERNING DANIEL DEFOE

DANIEL DEFOE, at the invitation of the judge, came forth from the garret wherein he abode, and rode in a cart unto the Royal Exchange, wherein he ascended the pillory, to the end that his ears might be nailed thereunto. And much people stood before him, some few pelting, some mocking, but the most part cheering or weeping, for they knew him for a friend to the poor, and especially those men who were called Dissenters. And a certain person in black stood by him, invisible to the people, but well seen of Daniel, who knew him for one whose life he had himself written. And the man in black reasoned with Daniel, and said, "Thou seest this multitude of people, but which of them shall deliver thee out of my hand? Nay, but let thy white be black, and thy black white, and I myself will deliver thee, and make thee rich, and heal thy hurts, save the holes in thy ears, that I may know thee for mine own." But Daniel gave no heed to him. So the Devil departed, having great wrath, and entered into a certain smug-faced man standing by.

And now the crowd before Daniel was greatly diminished, and consisted mainly of his enemies, for his friends had gone away to drown their sorrow. And the smug-faced man into whom Satan had entered came forth from among them, and said unto him, "O Daniel, inasmuch as I am a Dissenter I am greatly beholden to thee; but inasmuch as I am an honest tradesman I have somewhat against thee, for thou hast written concerning short weights and measures. And a man's shop is more to him than his country or his religion. Wherefore I must needs be avenged of thee. Yet shalt thou own that the tender mercies of the good man are piteous, and that even in his wrath he thinketh upon compassion."

And he picked up a great stone from the ground, and wrapped it in a piece of paper, saying, "Lest peradventure it hurt him overmuch." And the stone was very rough and sharp, and the paper was very thin. And he hurled it with all his might at the middle of Daniel's forehead, and the blood spouted forth. And Daniel cried aloud, and called upon the name of the Devil. And in an instant the pillory and the people were gone, and he found himself in the Prime Minister's cabinet, healed of all his hurts, except the holes in his ears. And the Minister was so like the Devil that you could not tell the difference. And he said, "Against what wilt thou write first, Daniel?"

"Dissenters," said Daniel.

And he wrote a pamphlet, and such as read it took firebrands, and visited the Dissenters in their habitations. And many Dissenters were put into prison, and others fined and spoiled of their goods. And he wrote other pamphlets, and each was cleverer and wickeder than the last. And whatsoever Daniel had of old declared to be white, lo! it was black; and what he had said was black, behold! it was white. And he throve and prospered exceedingly, and became a commissioner for public-houses and hackney-coaches and the imposing of oaths and the levying of custom, and all other such things as one does by deputy. And he mended the holes in his ears.

But the time came when Daniel must be judged, and he went before the Lord. And all the court was full of Dissenters, and the Devil was there also. And the Dissenters testified many and grievous things against Daniel.

"Daniel," said the Lord, "what answerest thou?"

"Nothing, Lord," said Daniel. "Only I would that the Dissenter who threw that stone at me should receive due and condign punishment, adequate to his misdeed."

"That," said the Devil, "is impossible."

"Thou sayest well, Satan," said the Lord, "and therefore shall Daniel go free. For if anything can excuse the apostasy of the noble, it is the ingratitude of the base."

So the Devil went to his own place, looking very small. And Daniel found himself in the same garret whence he had gone forth to the pillory; and before him were bread and cheese, and a pen and ink and paper. And he dipped the pen into the ink, and wrote *Robinson Crusoe*.

### IV.—CORNELIUS THE FERRYMAN

FOURSCORE years ago there was a good ferryman named Cornelius, who rowed people between New York and Brooklyn. He had neither wife nor child, nor any one to think of except himself. It was, therefore, his custom, when he had earned enough in a day for his own wants, to put the rest aside, and bestow it upon sick or blind or maimed persons, lest they should come to the workhouse. And the sick and the blind and the maimed gathered around him, and waited by the water's edge, until Cornelius's day's work should be over.

This went on until one of the little sooty imps who are always in mischief came to hear of it, and told the principal devil in charge of the United States, whose name is Politicianus.

"Dear me," said the Devil, "this will never do. I will see to it immediately."

And he went off to Cornelius, and caught him in the act of giving two dimes to a blind beggar.

"How foolish you are!" he said; "what waste of money is this! If you saved it up, you would by-and-by be able to build an hospital for all the beggars in New York."

"It would be a long time before there was enough," objected Cornelius.

"Not at all," said the Devil, "if you let me invest your money for you." And he showed Cornelius the plan of a most splendid hospital, and across the front of it was inscribed in letters of gold, *Cornelius Diabolodorus*. And Cornelius was persuaded, and that evening he gave nothing to the poor. And the poor had come to think that Cornelius's money was their own, and abused him as though he had robbed them. And Cornelius drove them away: and his heart was hardened against them from that day forth.

But the Devil kept his promise to Cornelius, and put him up to all the good things in Wall Street, and he soon had enough to build ten hospitals. But the more he had to build with, the less he wanted to build. And by-and-by the Devil called upon him, and found him contemplating two pictures. One of them showed the finest hospital you can imagine, full of neat, clean rooms, in one of which sat Cornelius himself, wearing a dress with a number and badge, and sipping arrowroot. The other showed fine houses, and opera-boxes, and fast-trotting horses, and dry champagne, and ladies who dance in ballets, and paintings by the great masters. Cornelius thrust the pictures away, and the Devil did not ask to see them, nor was it needful that he should, for he had painted them himself.

"O dear Mr. Devil," said Cornelius, "I am so glad that you have called, for I wanted to speak to you. It strikes me that there is a great defect in the plan which you have been so good as to draw for me."

"What is that?" asked the Devil.

"There is no place for black men," said Cornelius. "And you know white men will never let them come into the same hospital."

And the Devil, to do him justice, talked very reasonably to Cornelius, and represented to him that there were very few black men in New York, and that these had very vigorous constitutions. But Cornelius was inflamed with enthusiasm, and frantic with philanthropy, and he vowed that he would not give a cent to an hospital that had not a wing for black men as big as all the rest of the building. And the Devil had to take his plan back, and come again in a year and a day. And when he did come back, Cornelius asked him if he did not think it would be a most excellent thing if all the Irishmen in New York could be shut up in an hospital or elsewhere; and he could not deny it. So he had to take his plan back again. And next year it was the turn of the Chinese, and then of the Red Indians, and then of the dogs and cats. And then Cornelius thought that he ought to provide room for all the people who had been ruined by his speculations, and the Devil thought so too, but doubted whether Cornelius would be able to afford it. And at last Cornelius said:

"Methinks I have been very foolish in wishing to build an hospital at all while I am living. Surely it would be better that I should enjoy my money myself during my life, and leave the residue for the lawyers to divide after my death."

"You are quite right," said the Devil; "that is exactly what I should do if I were you."

So Cornelius put the plans behind a shelf in his counting-house, and the mice ate them. And he went on prospering and growing rich, until the Devil became envious of him, and insisted on changing places with him. So Cornelius went below, and the Devil came and dwelt in New York, where he still is.

# THE POISON MAID[1]

O not for him
Blooms my dark nightshade, nor doth hemlock brew
Murder for cups within her cavernous root.

## I

GRIEVOUS IS THE lot of the child, more especially of the female child, who is doomed from the tenderest infancy to lack the blessing of a mother's care.

Was it from this absence of maternal vigilance that the education of the lovely Mithridata was conducted from her babyhood in such an extraordinary manner? That enormous serpents infested her cradle, licking her face and twining around her limbs? That her tiny fingers patted scorpions? and tied knots in the tails of vipers? That her father, the magician Locuste, ever sedulous and affectionate, fed her with spoonsful of the honeyed froth that gathers under the tongues of asps? That as she grew older and craved a more nutritious diet, she partook, at first in infinitesimal doses, but in ever increasing quantities, of arsenic, strychnine, opium, and prussic acid? That at last having attained the flower of youth, she drank habitually from vessels of gold, for her favourite beverages were so corrosive that no other substance could resist their solvent properties?

Gradually accustomed to this strange regimen, she had thriven on it marvellously, and was without a peer for beauty, sense, and goodness. Her father had watched over her education with care, and had instructed her in all lawful knowledge, save only the knowledge of poisons. As no other human being had entered the house, Mithridata was unaware that her bringing up had differed in so material a respect from that of other young people.

"Father," said she one day, bringing him a book she had been perusing, "what strange follies learned men will pen with gravity! or is it rather that none can set bounds to the licence of romancers? These dear serpents, my

---

1 *The Poison Maid.*—The author wrote this tale in entire forgetfulness of Hawthorne's "Rapaccinip's Daughter," which nevertheless he had certainly read.

friends and playfellows, this henbane and antimony, the nourishment of my
health and vigour—that any one should write of these as pernicious, deadly,
and fatal to existence! Is it error or malignity? or but the wanton freak of an
idle imagination?"

"My child," answered the magician, "it is fit that thou shouldst now learn
what hath hitherto been concealed from thee, and with this object I left
this treatise in thy way. It speaks truth. Thou hast been nurtured from thy
infancy on substances endowed with lethal properties, commonly called
poisons. Thy entire frame is impregnated thereby, and, although thou thyself art in the fullest enjoyment of health, thy kiss would be fatal to any one
not, like thy father, fortified by a course of antidotes. Now hear the reason.
I bear a deadly grudge to the king of this land. He indeed hath not injured
me; but his father slew my father, wherefore it is meet that I should slay
that ancestor's son's son. I have therefore nurtured thee from thy infancy
on the deadliest poisons, until thou art a walking vial of pestilence. The
young prince shall unseal thee, to his destruction and thy unspeakable
advantage. Go to the great city; thou art beautiful as the day; he is young,
handsome, and amorous; he will infallibly fall in love with thee. Do thou
submit to his caresses, he will perish miserably; thou (such is the charm)
ransomed by the kiss of love, wilt become wholesome and innocuous as
thy fellows, preserving only thy knowledge of poisons, always useful, in the
present state of society invaluable. Thou wilt therefore next repair to the city
of Constantinople, bearing recommendatory letters from me to the Empress
Theophano, now happily reigning."

"Father," said Mithridata, "either I shall love this young prince, or I shall
not. If I do not love him, I am nowise minded to suffer him to caress me. If I
do love him, I am as little minded to be the cause of his death."

"Not even in consideration of the benefit which will accrue to thee by this
event?"

"Not even for that consideration."

"O these daughters!" exclaimed the old man. "We bring them up tenderly,
we exhaust all our science for the improvement of their minds and bodies,
we set our choicest hopes upon them, and entrust them with the fulfilment of
our most cherished aspirations; and when all is done, they will not so much
as commit a murder to please us! Miserable ingrate, receive the just requital
of thy selfish disobedience!"

"O father, do not turn me into a tadpole!"

"I will not, but I will turn thee out of doors."

And he did.

## II

THOUGH disinherited, Mithridata was not destitute. She had secured a particle of the philosopher's stone—a slender outfit for a magician's daughter! yet ensuring her a certain portion of wealth. What should she do now? The great object of her life must henceforth be to avoid committing murder, especially murdering any handsome young man. It would have seemed most natural to retire into a convent, but, not to speak of her lack of vocation, she felt that her father would justly consider that she had disgraced her family, and she still looked forward to reconciliation with him. She might have taken a hermitage, but her instinct told her that a fair solitary can only keep young men off by strong measures; and she disliked the character of a hermitess with a bull-dog. She therefore went straight to the great city, took a house, and surrounded herself with attendants. In the choice of these she was particularly careful to select those only whose personal appearance was such as to discourage any approach to familiarity or endearment. Never before or since was youthful beauty surrounded by such moustached duennas, squinting chambermaids, hunchbacked pages, and stumpy maids-of-all-work. This was a real sorrow to her, for she loved beauty; it was a still sadder trial that she could no longer feel it right to indulge herself in the least morsel of arsenic; she sighed for strychnia, and pined for prussic acid. The change of diet was of course at first most trying to her health, and in fact occasioned a serious illness, but youth and a sound constitution pulled her through.

Reader, hast thou known what it is to live with a heart inflamed by love for thy fellow-creatures which thou couldst manifest neither by word nor deed? To pine with fruitless longings for good? and to consume with vain yearnings for usefulness? To be misjudged and haply reviled by thy fellows for failing to do what it is not given thee to do? If so, thou wilt pity poor Mithridata, whose nature was most ardent, expansive, and affectionate, but who, from the necessity under which she laboured of avoiding as much as possible all contact with human beings, saw herself condemned to a life of solitude, and knew that she was regarded as a monster of pride and exclusiveness. She dared bestow no kind look, no encouraging gesture on any one, lest this small beginning should lead to the manifestation of her fatal power. Her own servants, whose minds were generally as deformed as their bodies, hated her, and bitterly resented what they deemed her haughty disdain of them. Her munificence none could deny, but bounty without tenderness receives no more gratitude than it deserves. The young of her own sex secretly rejoiced at her unamiability, regarding it as a providential set-off against her beauty, while they detested and denounced her as a—well, they would say viper in the manger, who spoiled everybody else's lovers and would have none of her own. For with all Mithridata's severity, there was no getting rid of the young men, the giddy moths that flew around her brilliant but baleful candle. Not all the cold water thrown upon them, literally as well as figuratively, could keep them from her door. They filled her house with bouquets and billets doux; they stood before the windows, they sat on the steps, they ran beside her litter when she was carried abroad, they assembled at night to serenade her, fighting desperately among themselves. They sought to gain admission as tradesmen, as errand boys, even as scullions male and female. To such lengths did they proceed, that a particularly audacious youth actually attempted to carry her off one evening, and would have succeeded but for the interposition of another, who flew at him with a drawn sword, and after a fierce contest smote him bleeding to the ground. Mithridata had fainted, of course. What was her horror on reviving to find herself in the arms of a young man of exquisite beauty and princely mien, sucking death from her lips with extraordinary relish! She shrieked, she struggled; if she made any unfeminine use of her hands, let the urgency of the case plead her apology. The youth reproached her bitterly for her ingratitude. She listened in silent misery, unable to defend herself. The shaft of love had penetrated her bosom also, and it cost her almost as much for her own sake to dismiss the young man as it did to see him move away, slowly and languidly staggering to his doom.

For the next few days messages came continually, urging her to haste to a youth dying for her sake, whom her presence would revive effectually. She steadily refused, but how much her refusal cost her! She wept, she wrung her hands, she called for death and execrated her nurture. With that strange appetite for self-torment which almost seems to diminish the pangs of the wretched, she collected books on poisons, studied all the symptoms described, and fancied her hapless lover undergoing them all in turn. At length a message came which admitted of no evasion. The King commanded her presence. Admonished by past experience, she provided herself with a veil and mask, and repaired to the palace.

The old King seemed labouring under deep affliction; under happier circumstances he must have been joyous and debonair. He addressed her with austerity, yet with kindness.

"Maiden," he began, "thy unaccountable cruelty to my son——"

"Thy son!" she exclaimed, "The Prince! O father, thou art avenged for my disobedience!"

"Surpasses what history hath hitherto recorded of the most obdurate monsters. Thou art indebted to him for thy honour, to preserve which he has risked his life. Thou bringest him to the verge of the grave by thy cruelty, and when a smile, a look from thee would restore him, thou wilt not bestow it."

"Alas! great King," she replied, "I know too well what your Majesty's opinion of me must be. I must bear it as I may. Believe me, the sight of me could effect nothing towards the restoration of thy son."

"Of that I shall judge," said the King, "when thou hast divested thyself of that veil and mask."

Mithridata reluctantly complied.

"By Heaven!" exclaimed the King, "such a sight might recall the departing soul from Paradise. Haste to my son, and instantly; it is not yet too late."

"O King," urged Mithridata, "how could this countenance do thy son any good? Is he not suffering from the effects of seventy-two poisons?"

"I am not aware of that," said the King.

"Are not his entrails burned up with fire? Is not his flesh in a state of deliquescence? Has not his skin already peeled off his body? Is he not tormented by incessant gripes and vomitings?"

"Not to my knowledge," said the King. "The symptoms, as I understand, are not unlike those which I remember to have experienced myself, in a milder form, certainly. He lies in bed, eats and drinks nothing, and incessantly calls upon thee."

"This is most incomprehensible," said Mithridata. "There was no drug in my father's laboratory that could have produced such an effect."

"The sum of the matter is," continued the King, "that either thou wilt repair forthwith to my son's chamber, and subsequently to church; or else unto the scaffold."

"If it must be so, I choose the scaffold," said Mithridata resolutely. "Believe me, O King, my appearance in thy son's chamber would but destroy whatever feeble hope of recovery may remain. I love him beyond everything on earth, and not for worlds would I have his blood on my soul."

"Chamberlain," cried the monarch, "bring me a strait waistcoat."

Driven into a corner, Mithridata flung herself at the King's feet, taking care, however, not to touch him, and confided to him all her wretched history.

The venerable monarch burst into a peal of laughter. "À bon chat bon rat!" he exclaimed, as soon as he had recovered himself. "So thou art the daughter of my old friend the magician Locusto! I fathomed his craft, and, as he fed his child upon poisons, I fed mine upon antidotes. Never did any child in the world take an equal quantity of physic: but there is now no poison on earth can harm him. Ye are clearly made for each other; haste to his bedside, and, as the spell requires, rid thyself of thy venefic properties in his arms as expeditiously as possible. Thy father shall be bidden to the wedding, and an honoured guest he shall be, for having taught us that the kiss of Love is the remedy for every poison."

# RICHARD GARNETT: A BIOGRAPHY

## *Early Life and Family Background*

RICHARD GARNETT (1835–1906) was born on February 27, 1835, in Lichfield, Staffordshire, England, into a family with a strong literary and scholarly tradition. His father, also named Richard Garnett, was a noted philologist and Assistant Keeper of Printed Books at the British Museum. This familial environment, steeped in books and intellectual pursuits, profoundly influenced the young Garnett, shaping his lifelong passion for literature, languages, and scholarship.

Garnett's early education took place at a school in Bloomsbury, London. However, his formal schooling was cut short by the death of his father in 1850. At sixteen, Garnett was invited by Anthony Panizzi, a close friend of his father and a prominent figure at the British Museum, to join the institution as an assistant librarian. This marked the beginning of a remarkable career that would span nearly five decades.

## *Career at the British Museum*

Garnett's professional life was inextricably linked to the British Museum, where he began as a junior assistant in 1851. Over the years, he rose steadily through the ranks, demonstrating exceptional dedication, erudition, and organizational skill. In 1875, he was appointed superintendent of the Reading Room, a position that placed him at the heart of the intellectual life of Victorian London. By 1881, he had become editor of the General Catalogue of Printed Books, and in 1890, he succeeded George Bullen as Keeper of Printed Books, the most senior position in the department.

During his tenure, Garnett was instrumental in modernizing the library's operations. He introduced innovations such as the use of photography for copying rare books and the implementation of electric lighting in the Reading Room, making the library more accessible and efficient for scholars. His efforts culminated in the publication of a comprehensive general catalog of the British Museum's holdings in 1905, a monumental achievement that had taken twenty-five years to complete.

Garnett's reputation as a scholar and administrator was matched by his legendary memory and encyclopedic knowledge. He became a fixture in the British Museum, revered by generations of readers and researchers for his willingness to assist and his deep understanding of literature and bibliography.

## Literary Achievements

### POETRY AND TRANSLATIONS

Garnett was a prolific writer, producing works across a range of genres. His early literary output included poetry and verse translations from Greek, German, Italian, Spanish, and Portuguese. His facility with languages and his interest in philology—a discipline combining literary criticism and the history of linguistics—were evident in these translations, which helped introduce European literary traditions to English readers.

### BIOGRAPHIES AND LITERARY CRITICISM

Garnett's biographical works are notable for their depth and insight. He wrote acclaimed biographies of major literary figures such as Thomas Carlyle, John Milton, William Blake, and others. His *History of Italian Literature* and *English Literature: An Illustrated Record* (co-authored with Edmund Gosse) are significant contributions to literary history and criticism. Garnett also contributed numerous articles to the *Dictionary of National Biography* and the *Encyclopædia Britannica*, further cementing his status as a leading Victorian man of letters.

### THE TWILIGHT OF THE GODS AND OTHER TALES

Garnett's most celebrated work of fiction is *The Twilight of the Gods, and Other Tales*, first published in 1888. This collection of short stories, expanded in a 1903 edition, is characterized by its blend of fantasy, irony, and black humor. Drawing inspiration from Greek mythology and the satirical style of Lucian, the stories explore themes of fate, the supernatural, and the follies of gods and men. The title story, which recounts the release of Prometheus from his torment by Zeus, is widely regarded as a classic of the fantasy genre and showcases Garnett's wit and imaginative power.

### OTHER NOTABLE WORKS

Garnett's literary interests were wide-ranging. In 1862, he discovered and published previously unknown poems by Percy Bysshe Shelley in a collection titled *Relics of Shelley*. He also edited the republication of *Original Poetry by Victor and Cazire* in 1898, a collection of poetry by Shelley and his sister. Garnett's own poem, "Where Corals Lie," achieved lasting fame when it was set to music by Sir Edward Elgar as part of the song cycle *Sea Pictures*, first performed in 1899.

### Personal Life and Beliefs

In 1863, Garnett married Olivia Narney Singleton, with whom he had six children. The Garnett family became a literary dynasty in their own right: his son Edward Garnett was a noted critic and editor, his daughter-in-law Constance Garnett was a renowned translator of Russian literature, and his grandson David "Bunny" Garnett was a prominent member of the Bloomsbury Group.

Garnett's intellectual curiosity extended beyond literature. He had a keen interest in astrology, publishing a monograph titled "The Soul and the Stars" in 1880 under the pseudonym A. G. Trent. Although ill health prevented him from pursuing this subject further, it reflected his fascination with the mystical and the unknown. According to contemporary Joseph McCabe, Garnett's religious beliefs were a blend of mysticism and skepticism, combining a genuine spiritual sensibility with a critical attitude toward dogma and priestcraft.

### Honors and Legacy

Garnett's contributions to literature and library science were widely recognized. He was made a Companion of the Order of the Bath (C.B.) and received an honorary doctorate (LL.D.) from the University of Edinburgh. In 1901, he was elected a member of the American Philosophical Society and was a fellow of the Royal Society of Literature.

After retiring from the British Museum in 1899, Garnett continued to write and engage with the literary world until his death from nephritis on April 13, 1906. He was buried on the eastern side of Highgate Cemetery in London.

www.ingramcontent.com/pod-product-compliance
Lightning Source LLC
Chambersburg PA
CBHW050838180626
46814CB00007B/2514